The Diamond of Freedom

The Unaltered Series: Book Three

Lorena Angell

I

Lorena@lorenaangell.com
or

Fantasy Books Publishing, LLC
631 Riverside Dr.
Washougal, WA 98671

ISBN-10: 0-9795248-9-X
ISBN-13: 978-0-9795248-9-9
Library of Congress registration number: 8154573

Cover designed by Lorena Angell and Luna Angell.
Cover photographs by Mike Chiniqua.

II

License Notes

For Rachel and Valerie

Contents

Chapter 1 - Off Grid

He stands by the river, his black leather duster setting him apart . . . as if his mere presence didn't do the trick. Through dark sunglasses, he observes Brand Safferson fight the crowd of boys. As I watch, a tidal wave of evil ripples through my body, causing my skin to prickle. His low voice fills my head, *I can return you to your natural state so you can live your life the way nature intended, not the way Maetha plans for you. You'll be spared from having to watch all your loved ones die, knowing you could save them, but never being allowed to do so. You'll be free to grieve properly, instead of being forced to become cold-hearted, as Maetha would prefer. You can be freed from this terrible future and you'll regain your identity as a human being and be able to live life to its fullest.* He pauses and I can feel the words coming before he speaks them into my head: *Just give me your diamond shard.*

I awake with a jolt as the front tire of the car hits a bump in the road. My body shivers from a cold sweat, and my breath comes in gasps as I try to calm down and remember what has happened. I turn my head to the left and find Chris Harding, both hands on the steering wheel, his prominent facial features illuminated by the tiny lights on the dashboard. His head bobs to the radio music that's playing quietly. He doesn't know I'm awake.

I glance out the rain-splattered windshield between

1

swipes of the blades, seeing headlights of oncoming cars and green road signs which indicate we are traveling on Route 65, ten miles north of Nashville, Tennessee. My heart rate finally slows, and I am able to relax as I contemplate the first dream I've had in two-and-a-half years—since I came to possess the Sanguine Diamond.

Only a few hours ago, not even a full twenty-four, Justin Mcintyre tried to reunite the shards of the Sanguine Diamond. The disaster resulted in his death, along with the deaths of three men: the leaders of the Seers', the Hunters', and the Readers' clans.

Justin had been tricked by another man into believing he could become all powerful, when in fact the other man—who calls himself Freedom—only wanted the diamond pieces for himself. Freedom knew Justin would die in the end.

Freedom is the man from my dream, the one who'd tried to persuade me to give my diamond shard to him. When he walked into the room at Justin's hideout, he carried a new mysterious power-canceling black stone attached inside an old pocket watch. The black stone blocked all the supernatural powers in the room when it was exposed—even Maetha's powers.

My friend Brand narrowed down the cause of our power loss through a series of time-repeats, and with Maetha's help, detained Freedom long enough for Maetha, Chris, and myself to escape with the reunited diamond and the pocket watch. I don't know how we would have gotten away without Brand's sacrifice. Hopefully, we'll be able to rescue him soon.

But there will be no rescue for Charles, Curtis, and Dominic. The clan leaders were shot and killed by Justin's guards and now I am the prime suspect in their kidnappings and murders.

Another major setback is before I picked up the diamond from Justin's lair, Freedom had touched it first, claiming ownership. Because I possess the final piece of the diamond within my heart, the diamond isn't entirely Freedom's—but it can't be mine either. To make the diamond whole and with only one owner, Freedom must reassign his chunk to me, or I must release mine to him. Freedom will never reassign to me. And the only way I can release my shard to him is if I die. As Maetha discovered, my shard is living within me and cannot be removed without killing me.

On the plus side, Maetha and the other Diamond Bearers have voted to end Freedom's life and remove his heart at the first opportunity available. As long as that plan pans out, I'm safe.

Once we reached Indiana following Justin's and the clan leaders' deaths, Maetha closely examined Freedom's pocket watch and found it has two hinges and two doors— common with old watches. Each side of the watch contains a piece of the mysterious black stone, but one stone is significantly smaller. Maetha determined the smaller stone is for personal use only and is probably what Freedom used to remain undetectable for several decades. She found that when the small side of the watch is opened then only the holder loses all powers, including any powers within the Sanguine Diamond. However, the other side of the watch contains the larger stone which removes the powers of everyone in the near vicinity.

I am carrying the pocket watch in a leather pouch in my front jacket pocket along with the incomplete diamond. The watch is open, exposing the large black stone to protect Chris and me from Freedom's ability to locate us through tracking the diamond. As long as Freedom doesn't know where I am, he can't try to recover his diamond, or try to remove my shard. And as he conveniently introduced the mysterious black stone as a weapon of sorts, we'll use the stone's power to hide from him, because the large black stone cancels his powers as well.

Freedom must have other black stones at his disposal because Maetha still cannot detect his whereabouts—something she can do with all the other Diamond Bearers. Likewise, she can't detect my location either while I'm carrying the black stone. Hiding in plain sight is necessary in order for me to survive. Freedom wouldn't hesitate to kill me.

Chris and I are technically "off grid" not only to evade Freedom, but also to avoid being found by Beth Hammond and her team of supernatural vigilantes. They believe, based on fairly convincing evidence, I stole the amulets from the other clan leaders and shot and killed them, while at the same time brutally murdering Justin. All of the clans are up in arms, demanding that their amulets be returned.

Well, that won't ever happen. The amulets were destroyed.

I look over at Chris and admire his profile. I remember the first time I ever saw him in Ms. Winter's office at the Runner's compound and the tingles that raced through my entire being. *Sort of like right now.* Two-and-a-half years have passed since we raced across land as we carried out the task of delivering the Sanguine Diamond to the Death Clan. Chris has only aged slightly. He looks a little older, wiser, and—if at all possible—even better looking than before. To go all that time without seeing him and then to finally find him on the other side of the door in Justin's compound is almost unbelievable, yet here we are, together again.

I reach over and place my hand on top of his.

He turns his head, smiles, and asks, "How do you feel,

Calli?"

"I'm good." I return the smile.

"We have about thirteen more hours of drive time till we reach Miami. Are you hungry?"

I shake my head and place my hand back in my lap. I ask Chris, "Are you tired? Do you want me to drive for a while?"

"No. Just rest."

In truth, I am relieved he doesn't need me to drive yet. I feel exhausted, something else I haven't felt for a long time. I miss my healing powers.

"Calli, what can you tell me about the other people like Maetha?"

I readjust myself in my seat so I face Chris a little better. My gut instinct tells me I can trust him with any and all information, so I launch into Maetha's story head-first.

"Maetha became the first Diamond Bearer back in ancient Egyptian days. The diamond was much larger then, before it was split into twenty-one pieces. No one else but her could touch the magical diamond and live."

Chris interrupts, "Because she's an Unaltered, like you, right?"

"Yes. The Egyptian priests acted the same way the Death Clan did when I carried the stone, causing the stone to shatter and a piece to enter Maetha's heart. A woman named Crimson saved Maetha's life and divided the remaining pieces into twenty other diamonds. She charged Maetha with finding candidates who would do nature's will and to give them diamonds of their own. I don't know how many years Maetha searched to find all twenty candidates, but she finally found the people she wanted, and the group became the protectors of nature.

"Every so often a group of Healers becomes over-balanced like the Death Clan, and nature acts to balance the situation through the use of a diamond. However, once all twenty-one diamonds were inserted into people, one person would have to sacrifice their life and remove their stone so nature could restore the balance. My stone came from a man named Gustave. He was a relative of mine from long ago. In fact, Maetha is related to me as well. She's my many-greats-of-a-grandmother."

Chris asked, "So are you a kind of royalty?"

"No, I don't think so. Maetha said our bloodline always produces an Unaltered human who keeps the line moving forward. My mother is Unaltered too, but she doesn't have an awareness of what that means. Maetha has followed her own line throughout the centuries using one of the Unaltered relatives every now and then when nature needs a balancing act performed. Of course, there are other Unaltered humans not related to Maetha who have been used as Diamond Bearers too."

"So, Calli, when Maetha said you'll receive the whole stone once Agent Alpha, er, Freedom is dead, what she really meant is you'll become an Immortal like her?"

"Not quite. Diamond Bearers aren't immortal, per se."

"Anyone who can live thousands of years is immortal in my book."

"Well, I guess so."

"The question is, how do you kill an Immortal if they can sense you coming and see their own future?" Chris asks.

"I don't know. It's a puzzle."

We both remain quiet for a couple of minutes.

Chris speaks up again. "Calli, what's going to happen to us?"

"I don't know. I can't see the future." I truly don't know. I change the subject. "Chris, what kind of information did you feed to your father when you worked for him?"

He glances at me with a worried look, then settles his eyes back on the road. "Well, clan locations, leaders' names, information about new members, vulnerabilities, magical plants, and crystals used in Ms. Winter's secret concoctions . . . stuff like that."

"Crystals? What do you mean?"

"Well, you know, gemstones and rocks, not unlike the diamond. When we were given the Sanguine Diamond for the delivery it wasn't too difficult for me to believe a stone could hold powers. I've known for some time that different crystals have slight powers. My uncle Don taught me about most of them before my running power ever surfaced. Uncle Don is my father's older brother. I remember my dad talking about what it was like growing up with him. He said Don's pockets were always full of rocks and the shelves in his room were covered with stones of all kinds. My grandparents were frustrated with his obsessive collecting, but understood his passion, so they bought him books about geology. After that, my dad said Don sorted through all his rocks and categorized them as accurately as he could. His whole world was, and still is, centered on rocks, crystals, and minerals. That's why I immediately thought of him as someone who could identify the black stone. Personally, I think it's a black onyx."

"Does black onyx have the ability to take our powers away?"

"I don't know. That's why we're going to my uncle's house." He smiles at me.

"But you said he doesn't know about the world of powers."

"To my knowledge he doesn't. But he believes firmly in crystals containing powers and strengths. If black onyx has any ability to remove powers, he'll know."

Looking out the front windshield, I see a brightly

glowing gas station sign in the distance.

"Chris, can we pull over for a bathroom break?"

"Sure."

Chris brings Maetha's car to a halt in a parking spot by the front doors of the busy fuel station. Several big-rig trucks are positioned off to the side of the building with their engines running, and a few other vehicles are parked at the gas pumps.

Chris checks the Pulse Emitter attached to his jacket to make sure it's turned on to protect him from the dangers waiting for him in the shadows. He reaches in the back and grabs the two backpacks filled with our supplies and the money Maetha gave us. "Here, let's keep these with us at all times."

"Yeah, good idea."

We step out of the car, fling the backpacks over our shoulders, and enter the store.

I spot the restroom sign on the far wall near the postcard display and head in that direction. Even before entering the ladies' room I have an ominous feeling creep over me—the kind that makes your hair stand on end. I look over my shoulder to see if Chris is behind me, only to see him enter the men's room. Shrugging off the all-too-familiar feeling, I hurry and do my business and wash my hands, all the while remembering Maetha had specifically stated that we need to stay "off camera."

As I am about to exit the restroom, I pause when I hear the loud male voices yelling orders outside the door.

Stall doors slam open behind me, and two burly women come out with handguns drawn as if the yelling is their cue to exit. I'm frightened and confused at the same time. Are these ladies simply gun-toting tough chicks who heard some kind of trouble and responded accordingly, or are they actually players in the game?

One points her gun at me and says, "Get out, sister!" My heart begins to race. I pull the door open and see Chris standing nearby, frozen in place with a masked gunman standing close to him. Another masked man has a gun pointed at the cashier, demanding money. The two women exit the bathroom after pulling ski masks over their faces.

Chris looks at me and then focuses his eyes on my front pocket. I know exactly what he's trying to tell me: *close the pocket watch so we can use our powers and run out of here.*

I slowly slide my hand to the zipper and ease it open.

"You two," the nearby thuggish gunman shouts. "Get on the floor!"

We crouch on the floor right away. The two women run by and over to the front doors.

I slip my hand in my pocket and remember I had lodged the diamond inside the watch with an elastic band to keep it open . . . and they are both inside the pouch—which is drawn shut with the strings.

I need both hands to free the watch.

My movement catches the attention of the gunman. "Hey!" He approaches me and pulls me up by my backpack straps.

Chris jumps to his feet and yells at the brute, who then punches Chris in the face, knocking him to the floor.

Before I can react to the violence, one of the women runs over to us. "Come on, Duke, we're out of time!"

"She's got something in her pocket." Duke tells her with a concerned tone in his voice.

The woman looks at my pocket. "Whatcha got in there? You got a phone? Are you calling the cops, sister?"

I don't answer and wait for one of them to reach inside the pocket for the pouch. The man stands behind me and wraps his right arm in front and under my neck while still holding his gun, then pulls my body close to his.

Duke smells like a three-day-old pile of fish guts on a hot summer day. I try not to gag while his left hand comes forward and fumbles to get in my jacket pocket. He pulls out the brown leather pouch and says, "Well, well, well, what do we have here?"

I put on my best act and plead with the man. "Please! It's my grandmother's."

The man tosses the pouch to the woman. She loosens the strings and dumps out the diamond and pocket watch, then whistles to her cronies. "We hit the jackpot!"

The other woman yells to the robber who has the cashier at gunpoint, telling him they have an even better prize.

I choke out my best sob. "Please, don't do this."

The woman holding the dangerous treasure removes the elastic and tosses the pocket watch to her female friend. She raises the diamond to the light. I wait for the inevitable. Her friend closes the watch, and the woman holding the diamond crumples to the ground, dead. The diamond lies on the ground beside her.

My powers return with a force strong enough to take my breath away for a moment. I use my healing power on my own heart, calming it and healing the pain. I catch Chris's eye and ever so slightly shake my head, hoping he'll get the message to stay put. Then I turn my attention back to the ensuing debacle.

"Gina!" the other female shrieks. She bends down and shakes her friend's shoulder.

The man holding me lets go and pushes me toward Chris. I crouch down next to him and notice his bleeding lip, which Duke had split open. Duke joins his co-hort by the lifeless body of their companion, where the woman sobs uncontrollably. "What the hell happened?" he shouts.

"Call an ambulance!" The female shouts through her sobs.

The other man who had collected everything out of the cash register rushes over and says, "No! Pick her up and bring her. We'll get her help somewhere else." Duke leans across the dead woman and reaches for the diamond. As soon as his fingers wrap completely around the stone, he falls forward on top of Gina.

The shrieking woman screams even louder at the sight of a second dead friend.

"What's going on?" the other man yells. He spins around in a 360-degree circle, brandishing the gun at an invisible suspect. The woman's screaming drowns out the approaching sirens.

I glance at the cashier, a frightened, pale-skinned, thin man probably in his forties. A quick mind-read reveals he has alerted the authorities to the robbery by tripping a switch under the counter. I hope the gunman won't shoot him once he realizes they won't be going anywhere.

Once the thug hears the sirens, he grabs the frantic woman by the shoulder, catching her hair and shirt, and yanks her to her feet. "Shut up! You hear me?"

The woman has lost all control. The man's mind reveals he views her as a liability now. He pushes her away forcefully. She falls into a shelving unit and crashes to the floor, hitting her head with a thud. Boxes of cheese crackers tumble on top of her. My healing ability senses she will be all right even though she's been knocked unconscious.

The lone gunman lets off a series of curse words that would make a sailor blush. He's in complete shock and confusion. He raises his gun, points it at the cashier. "You called the cops?"

The cashier doesn't move. He cringes and pinches his

eyes shut, waiting for certain death.

I use my healing powers and cause the gunman's head to hurt by forcing fluid up around his brain. I don't want to kill the guy, just disable him enough for the authorities to get to him, and for us to be able to escape, which with every passing second is becoming more and more difficult. Police cars with flashing lights surround the front of the building.

The man drops his gun, and both his hands fly up to his head in agony.

I leaned over to Chris. "Get his gun. Hurry."

Chris scoots over and grabs the handgun by the barrel, and as he moves back toward me I hear the voice I have feared.

"Calli. There you are." Freedom's low, rumbling voice resonates through my body, sending chills through my entire being. He has bi-located near the end of the aisle, wearing his trademark trench coat.

"Find the watch and open it, Chris," I say.

"Where is it?"

"She dropped it somewhere over by those shelves."

Maetha appears on the opposite side of me. "Calli, what's going on?"

A commanding voice speaking through a bullhorn outside the building announces: "This is the police . . . the place is surrounded . . . come out with your hands up!"

Boy, if there was ever a time for a do-over, this is it. I miss Brand.

Freedom doesn't move. He glances all around the inside of the building, for what I don't know.

Chris locates the pocket watch and holds it up for me to see.

Maetha speaks to him saying, "Not yet, Chris. You two need to escape first, then open the watch." She turns to me. "The camera captured you, Calli. I told you *no cameras*. This is going to put Beth on your trail as well as the authorities—and Freedom. Now go, and make better choices." She motions toward the door.

I pick up the diamond and drop it in the pouch, feeling doubly ashamed for letting Maetha down.

Freedom says, "You won't get far, Calli."

"We'll see about that," I answer him. I take Chris's hand and walk to the front doors. We step by the debilitated robber, who is on his knees, holding his head and groaning in pain.

The cashier stands motionless and pale as a ghost with his back pressed up against the cigarette display.

I use my telepathy to tell Chris, *We'll go out with our hands in the air. On three, we'll run to the left and out into that field and we won't stop for at least five miles.*

He nods.

I add, *You lead the way and lend me your running power because I don't know how this diamond will react.* We walk out of the building with guns aimed at us and our hands raised. I begin counting: one, two . . . I wonder what the surveillance camera will capture. I imagine we'll be in a frame one second, and the next we'll be nothing but a blur.

It wouldn't be the first time a convenience store camera had caught such a picture.

Three!

We run, covering at least five miles of ground before stopping. Chris opens the watch as Freedom's image begins to appear, hot on our trail.

"That was intense." Chris hands me the pocket watch.

"I know. It was a mistake to stop at that place. I should've known better." I insert the watch into the pouch and wedge the diamond inside. I'll need to locate another elastic band to secure everything because the other one was

13

lost at the convenience store.

Chris tenderly grasps both my shoulders. His Pulse Emitter's LED light blinds me. "Stop blaming yourself. There's no way we could have known the place was about to be held up."

"We've been captured on camera, and now our mugs will be plastered all over the media. I just forgot completely."

"So did I, Calli, so did I."

"I guess we're on foot now. Good thing we grabbed the backpacks, right?"

"Right. We have everything we need. Unfortunately, we need a vehicle or some kind of transportation. We can't go back for Maetha's car."

We walk through the fields using the light of the emitter to guide the way. We don't want to get too close to the highway for fear the police might find us.

I think about how Freedom kept looking in different directions when he appeared in the gas station. The only thing I can figure is that he was searching for some kind of clue as to where we were. I don't know if he found what he was looking for. Maybe he will only need to use his connections with the government to pinpoint the location.

We need to keep moving to stay ahead of Freedom, local law enforcement, and Beth. She will be picking up on our location too and heading this way. I can't help but worry about the eventual run-in with her.

I'm comforted when I think about Beth now, compared to the Beth she might have been if she hadn't dumped Justin. She would be in jail right now. I feel better knowing she's doing something productive with her life. Too bad it includes hunting me down.

Up ahead, we approach a small shopping center parking lot. At least twenty Harley Davidson motorcycles are parked in two lines, some with their headlights on, lending light to the rowdy scene. The owners stand nearby, laughing, telling stories, and carrying on. Men and women of all ages and dimensions laugh robustly as each story is outdone by the next.

Chris mutters, "We should probably avoid these guys."

"That's a good idea."

"Hey, what do we have here?" A rather loud, deep voice yells out into the night. "Now, don't be shy little lady . . . wandering around in the dark . . . you must be who the cops are after."

I let out a defeated huff. "I guess we'll go talk with the nice people after all."

"Maybe you should hold the watch in your hand just in case we have to make a quick exit."

I whisper back, "I don't dare expose the diamond." We become surrounded by black leather, beards, spikes, and chains. To say I am intimidated is an understatement, but having seen Freedom dressed in his biker boots, mirrored sunglasses, and leather duster has helped me get used to the overall image.

An idea pops into my head. I say, "Hey guys, yeah, we're on the run. We need to get out of here as quickly as possible."

A particularly stereotypical biker guy steps forward. If a movie was being made and the casting call needed a bad-ass biker dude, this guy would certainly get the part. He has long scraggly hair, an even longer graying beard, and a black bandana with white skulls wrapped around his head. He wears a black leather vest, chaps, and blue jeans, and tattoos covering his arms give him the appearance of wearing sleeves. His low rumble of a voice suggests he just may be the sole reason the cigarette companies are still in business.

15

"Honey, you came to the right parkin' lot. Most all of us is runnin' from the law for sump-thin' or another. What'd ya do?"

Chris takes over the conversation. "Nothin' any worse than any of you. That truck stop is short a bit of cash, and some bodies are scattered around. Feds are after us. Can you help us? We can pay handsomely."

"Son, we don't want your money. Where do you need to git?"

"South, as far as Miami if possible."

"All right," the guy laughs. "Roadtrip!" His companions roar with approval.

Chapter 2 - Uncle Don

Before we can say "Harley Davidson", a few women and men come forward and donate several articles of clothing to help us disguise ourselves from the authorities. We are given helmets and sunglasses to complete our new outfits, and one sweet old man who looks like he would be more comfortable on a horse than a hog asks Chris, "Can you handle one on your own?"

"You bet," Chris replies. The man motions for us to follow him. He leads us to his bike and holds his hand, the keys dangling from his fingers.

Chris takes the keys respectfully. He bends down and admires the shiny chrome and black engine that has been polished to a mirror finish. "You got a sweet ride here."

"You know bikes?" the man asks.

"I do. This is a Harley Dyna Super Glide Custom FXDC. Twin Cam engine with Powerflow III two-into-one pipes that will dump you on your ass if you're not careful . . . and a sissy bar to keep your girl on the back." Chris stands and pats the passenger seat and backrest and smiles at the man.

The man's mouth opens wide, exposing several missing teeth as he grins. "Just keep it upright, and we'll all be doin' fine."

Chris swings his leg over and effortlessly pulls the bike

straight and pops up the kickstand.

I swing my leg over the back seat and wrap my arms around his stomach. The backpack he wears provides an additional barrier between the diamond pouch in my pocket and his back. He starts the bike, and the other riders start theirs as well. The noise and rumbling is something I haven't experienced before. I'm glad my helmet blocks out some of the sound.

Chris lets off the clutch, and we lurch forward with incredible force and control—he has definitely driven a bike before.

Soon we are all on the road heading south, with Chris and me in the middle of the pack. This turn of events is beyond incredible. To think we would somehow end up with a band of bikers . . . well, I would have never guessed. I have never ridden a motorcycle, let alone a Harley. Chris handles the bike as if he's been riding his whole life. Maybe he has—I really don't know. Come to think of it, I don't know much about this guy at all. I don't even know where he grew up or if he has any brothers or sisters.

Holy smokes! I don't know anything about the guy who has become my destiny!

We ride for a couple of hours until we come upon a roadblock. The State Police have the highway blocked as they search for the fugitive suspects of the truck-stop killing. Yet, here we are, amid a group of Hells-Angels-type bikers, hiding in plain sight. The cops aren't about to detain the whole pack. Since we blend right in with the bikers and don't match the description of the robbery suspects, we aren't questioned at all.

We stop at a rest area for a necessary break. I notice a few ordinary-looking families as they usher their kids quickly to their cars before some kind of ruckus breaks out. It's probably better that way—the fewer people to see us, the better.

Chris climbs off the bike and leaves my side. After he walks about twenty feet away from me, he turns around quickly and hurries back. He speaks softly so the people nearby won't hear. "Calli, my powers came back where I turned around over there. Sit still while I experiment a bit."

He walks away from me in a different direction until he's about twenty feet away and turns around again. We quickly establish the larger obsidian piece has a twenty-foot radius power field, except for a small spot where the metal of the watch blocks the power of the stone. If the stone had been sitting out on a table without any metal barriers, it would have been different.

"Open the other door to expose the small stone, Calli."

I pop the other side of the watch open before I close the first door. I don't want to risk having Freedom find me again. I certainly don't want Maetha upset with me either.

"My powers are back," he whispers. He extends his hand out and touches my shoulder. "If I touch you, they go away. I guess I won't be holding your hand and giving you my running power."

Chris fishes a granola bar out of his backpack and gives me a piece for energy.

I observe the other bikers and their behavior while we eat our food. They seem like they don't have a care in the world, no place to be, and no one depending on them to be home at a certain time. Maybe they are so laid back because they have no homes and these fellow bikers *are* their family.

I find myself wishing I could do a mind-read on any one of them. Maybe some other time.

We continue to ride for hours on end, stopping only to gas up or hit a rest stop. Once we reach Miami, Chris and I thank the group, give back the accessories they'd loaned us, and try to offer payment, but they won't take our money.

One of the bikers tells us they'd been listening to the police scanners. "You two best be watchin' your backs. You got multi-state pigs after you. I don't know if you done the things they say you did, but they ain't gonna stop 'til they find you. Stay safe and good luck."

The afternoon drags on by the time we reach the final corner leading to Uncle Don's home. The walk has been invigorating after sitting in the same position atop a rumbling motorbike. My knees still buzz a little.

The neighborhood homes have a dated look of around 1970 with old established yards and landscaping. I feel safe in this area, unlike some of the other areas we passed through to arrive here.

I can tell Chris is nervous. I ask, "Are you okay?"

"Yeah. It's just that my uncle is a bit protective of me. I'm worried about how he'll react to you."

"I'm not concerned. We'll be in good hands, Chris."

"Well, you might not think that when you meet him. He's kind of odd. He uses big words and talks too fast. Uncle Don and my dad had a falling out about the same time my powers emerged, and I haven't seen much of him since. We communicate through email."

We walk along the perfectly laid rock path to his front door. The doorbell is a purple-tinted piece of glass with facets like a gemstone. I lean closer to get a better look and am startled when the door opens abruptly.

Uncle Don stands as tall as the doorway, with tan, weathered skin, several days of beard stubble, and clothing that looks like he's worn it for the better part of the year.

His plaid button-up cotton shirt is ripped in a couple of places and is missing some buttons at the top, exposing a home-strung necklace with different-colored stones around his neck. The blue jeans he wears are two sizes too big and barely cling to his narrow hips. Recognition is slow to meet his eyes, but once he realizes his nephew stands before him, he smiles and stretches out his arms.

"Chris, my boy." He pulls Chris into an embrace and then releases him. "What are you doing here?" Don's eyes travel over my face and then resume their fix on Chris.

"Uncle Don, we need your expertise on something. Can we come in?"

"Of course, of course." He steps aside and allows us to enter. I notice as I walked by him his eyes scan up the street and to the surrounding homes, looking for what, I don't know.

"Uncle Don, this is Calli Courtnae." I extend my hand to him. He grasps mine with his dry, calloused hand.

"Ah, so you're the one he's been going on and on about in his letters." Don smiles at me.

I look over at Chris, who seems flustered and embarrassed. "Well, I certainly hope I'm the one he's writing about."

Chris jumps in with, "Uncle Don, we need to learn what a certain type of rock might be. Calli, show him the pocket watch."

I pull the watch out and extend my hand to him. "Sir, don't close the watch, please." I show him the other side and open it for him. "Do you know what this black stone is?"

Chris asks, "Is it black onyx?"

Uncle Don pulls the watch close to his face. He magically produces a jeweler's loupe from his pocket and holds it to his eye. "No, not onyx. Black onyx is usually artificially colored. This is obsidian." He turns the watch in our direction and points to the stone. "See the curved conchoidal fractures around the edge of the larger stone? Obsidian breaks apart in this way because it's an amorphous solid."

Chris looks at me to see if I have a clue what Uncle Don is talking about. I shrug my shoulders.

Uncle Don continues. "Obsidian is rapidly cooled lava with high silica content and is only found in a handful of locations around the world, always near volcanoes that experienced rhyolitic eruptions and rapid cooling. The inhibition of atomic diffusion through the highly viscous and polymerized lava explains the lack of crystal growth. You see, obsidian isn't a crystal; it's volcanic glass. Come with me. I'll show you my obsidian collection."

He hands the pocket watch back to me and leads us down to the basement. I am blown away by the size of this guy's collection. On the back wall is an assortment of arrowheads mounted on a black background, each labeled with its approximate age and the place where it was recovered. The adjacent wall has shelving units with narrow drawers divided into small compartments. Uncle Don pulls out a couple of drawers and sets them on the table in the center of the room for us to look at.

"Obsidian is unique to its location. Each lava flow contains different levels of iron and magnesium which produce the varying colors and designs of each bed of rock, making it possible for geologists to trace the origins of each piece of obsidian with considerable accuracy."

Chris asks, "Uncle Don, are you saying our stone could be traced to the actual volcano it originated from?"

"Weren't you listening, boy?" Don shakes his head. "Each lava flow that results in the creation of obsidian is an individual, unique occurrence, and yes, your piece of obsidian can be traced to its point of origin through x-ray fluorescence—provided the piece matches a sample that has been registered already."

I ask Uncle Don, "Can you do that here, or do you have to take your samples to a lab?"

"I wish I could. I take my samples to Idaho State University to get them tested."

"Wow, Idaho is a long way from Miami."

"Yes, but always worth the trip, young lady."

I wander around the room with the open pocket watch in my hand, comparing the color of the obsidian in the watch to the arrowheads on the wall and the samples displayed in divided boxes on the table. I wonder if any of these pieces possess the same power-canceling effects as Freedom's watch, but I can't risk closing the watch to tell. Uncle Don has collected so many different varieties of obsidian: clear, striped, and snowflake-speckled specimens, as well as some with a multi-colored sheen, kind of like the rainbow puddles of water at a gas station.

Even more amazing is the detailed cataloguing Uncle Don has done. He's described the individual stones and documented the locations where the artifacts were found. He has many specimens from the western United States— mostly from Oregon and Idaho—and a few from Argentina, Chile, El Salvador, Guatemala, Peru, Greece, Italy, and Iceland.

I glance across the room at Chris and Uncle Don, who are scrutinizing a handful of flint arrowheads. Uncle Don's eyes closely resemble Chris's. The similarity brings a smile to my face.

An idea pops into my head.

"Chris, could I talk to you for a sec?" I ask, interrupting their conversation. He walks over to me, and I whisper, "I want to try something. I'm going to step outside the room for a few minutes to see if your powers come back."

He nods, and I leave the room. I need to get at least twenty feet away from him and it may require leaving the house, so I decide to step outside onto the backyard patio. Uncle Don's well-manicured yard is full of birdbaths and free-standing fountains, all adorned with colorful crystals reflecting in the sunlight. Off to the side of his home is a covered patio with a work station that contains all sorts of jewelry-making supplies and tools, even a diamond-cutting wheel for creating faceted stones. Uncle Don sure loves his rocks.

The weather is beautiful and calm, with crystal-clear blue skies, a perfect Miami day. I think about the fact we now know the black stone is obsidian, and I pull the watch out of my pocket. I study the large stone carefully and look closely at the curved lines where the piece broke away from its larger source.

I already knew obsidian breaks in a different way than other rocks or crystals, creating super sharp edges. I overheard a conversation between my parents a while back where dad told mom that scalpels with obsidian blades leave smaller, less-noticeable scars than steel scalpels because obsidian has such thin smooth edges. Even the sharpest surgical steel scalpels are jagged under a microscope. I doubt the information is relevant to the situation, but knowing more about obsidian adds to my growing knowledge. What I need to find out now is where this piece came from. What is its source, and how did Freedom come to find the obsidian before Maetha or any of the other Diamond Bearers?

"Calli." Chris comes out the patio door and stands next to me. He whispers, "My powers never returned. Uncle Don definitely has some of the same obsidian in that room, but unfortunately he has so many different samples, it will take a long time to figure out which one contains powers."

I think about it for a moment and say, "Let's wait to see if he'll volunteer up any information before we discuss it further. You said he doesn't know about the cosmic powers . . . I think we better keep it that way."

Chris agrees with a nod. We go back inside the house and down to the basement where Uncle Don is busily organizing his rocks.

Uncle Don continues to give us a tour of his displays. He has several other rooms dedicated to the different kinds of rocks, crystals, and gemstones he has collected over the years. He gives us an unsolicited rundown on the perceived powers of each stone.

"Topaz is used to restore the sense of taste, stimulate the appetite, calm emotions, relieve tension, protect against injury or attack, and enhance psychic abilities." He hands me a creamy yellowish crystal. "That's a golden topaz. What I want to get my hands on is an Imperial topaz. It's extremely valuable for a topaz."

I pass the stone to Chris as Don picks up the next stone. "This is quartz. It comes in many colors and is commonly used for healing the body. Amethyst creates a protective energy field around its wearer, assists in transmuting negative energies, and protects the wearer from external negative energies. Onyx helps us to hear and listen to our inner voice. It also assists in maintaining emotional balance, and it's good for self-control and relieving stress." He moves on to more bins, boxes, and drawers.

"There certainly seem to be a lot of healing stones," I say.

"Correct. Bloodstone is another healing stone. It

renews inner strength. The energies of Carnelian are invigorating and uplifting." Uncle Don becomes increasingly excited as he continues the tour of his collection—his pride and joy, his life's passion. I can't help but think how ridiculous it is to think these rocks are able to do what he claims. To me they are all just pretty stones.

Don says, "Would you two like some food? I was about to eat when you arrived."

Chris looks at me. I nod my head and he responds politely to his uncle, "Sure. But we can't stay long."

Don dishes up two plates of barbecued pork and brings them to us on the patio. I enjoy the delicious food and listen to Chris and Don as they talk more about geology.

During a lull in the conversation, I ask Don, "Do you really believe rocks and crystals have special powers?"

"Absolutely." He touches the leather cord around his neck and pulls it out so we can see his home-made necklace of small polished stones: yellow, black, and green. "See here? These are the stones that are lucky for my sign." He touches the yellow stone. "Citrine brightens my mood and brings me wealth." His fingers slide to the pale green stone. "Peridot creates a shield of protection around my body and deflects emotional intensity and the negativity projected by others. Then there's obsidian to keep me grounded and protect me from the energy of others, and onyx to help me hear and listen to my inner voice." He touches the two black stones.

My eyes want to roll at these absurdities, but I remember what Maetha said to Brand at Cedar Point Amusement Park when she demonstrated her Seer ability: *I find it fascinating, Brand, that you are so quick to reject the existence of superpowers when you yourself possess one.* Surely, all those supposed powers or effects associated with crystals and rocks are nothing more than a placebo effect on the mind of the wearer, right? However, Uncle Don said obsidian protected him from others' energies, and the obsidian in the watch certainly has a similar power, so how far off can Uncle Don be? I wonder what I would feel if I closed the pocket watch. Would I be able to detect anything special about these crystals?

I need to use the little girls' room, so I excuse myself and follow Don's directions to the bathroom at the end of the hall. Don has decorated the room with oriental jade carvings of elephants and other creatures. I find the room extremely relaxing and feel like I've walked into another time and place.

When I return, Chris has a perplexed expression on his face.

As I sit down at the table, Uncle Don turns to me and says, "Calli, I've got fresh blackberry cobbler and ice cream. Would you like some?"

"Yes, please. Sounds delicious."

Uncle Don heads into the kitchen, and Chris leans over to me and whispers, "My power didn't return when you left the room. It should have, right? The bathroom is more than twenty feet away and the room downstairs with all the obsidian is more than far enough away. Maybe there's more to this than we understand."

"Yeah, I guess."

A couple of minutes pass and then Uncle Don comes out of the kitchen and sets a bowl of cobbler and ice cream in front of me and one in front of Chris. "Here you go," he says.

As he leans over the table, my eyes are drawn to the necklace dangling out of his shirt. "Uncle Don, may I see your necklace for a moment?"

He removes his necklace and hands it to me.

I point to the black stone. "This stone here is obsidian, correct?" The piece is not quite as large as the large piece in the watch, but close.

He nods in reply.

"You said all obsidian can be traced back to its original location. Where is this one from?"

A smile lights up his face. "That's a special piece of obsidian, Calli. It comes from Obsidian Cliffs in Yellowstone National Park."

"Why is it special?" Chris asks.

"Many years ago, I was at a rock show in Kansas when I saw an arrowhead from the Yellowstone outcropping. The vendor was only displaying his piece and wouldn't even entertain a price for it . . . not even ten-thousand dollars. I was glad he turned me down because at that time I didn't have ten-thousand dollars to back up my offer. His protective stance and unmovable determination to keep the arrowhead raised my curiosity, and I began searching for more samples. I wanted one of my own. What I discovered was there were many samples from the same location, but only some held the power I was looking for.

"Obsidian is an absorber. Energy, both positive and negative, is absorbed into the stone, leaving a person powerless while they are near it. But Yellowstone obsidian is rumored to have even more incredible power-absorbing properties. Based on the hoops I had to jump through to get this piece, I believe it. I had to obtain a special permit to chip off a piece, and Park Rangers and military soldiers watched over my shoulder the whole time. In fact, the original piece I collected was broken down by the authorities to this smaller piece."

I glance over at Chris, wondering if he had picked up on what his uncle said.

Don extends his hand, indicating he wants his

necklace returned. I hand it to him. "Now, Chris and Calli, tell me why you are so interested in my obsidian? Does it have something to do with the obsidian in your pocket watch?"

My stomach clenches. *What should we tell him? How much should he know?* I can see Chris out of the corner of my eye nervously fidgeting in his chair. He's probably waiting for me to say something.

Just as I am about to speak up, Don says, "Chris, do you know why your father and I had a falling out all those years ago? Because I became angry when I learned you were being used as a guinea pig by the military. I know about your special ability, Chris, and I know what kind of tests they performed on you."

Chris chokes and sputters. "What?"

"Yes, you are an amazingly fast runner, so fast, in fact, your father viewed you as a potential threat. That's why he forced you into servitude. He figured if he kept a firm hold on you, he could control your actions. I saw you as finally feeling accepted by your father and embracing what you thought was respect and love. That's what pissed me off so much!" Don slams his fist down on the table, causing the ceramic mugs to clink against the plates.

Chris and I both jump at his sudden display of frustration.

"Why didn't you ever tell me you knew about my ability?" Chris asks.

"I was only following your lead, Chris. I knew you would have been threatened to keep everything secret, so I never pressed you for information."

"I'm sorry, Uncle Don. How much do you understand about powers and abilities?"

"Enough to know I need this piece of obsidian."

I speak up. "Uncle Don, I have powers too, but the

obsidian in the pocket watch and around your neck takes away that power when I'm nearby."

Don smiles. "I know. That's why I wear my necklace day and night. What I don't understand is why you insist on keeping the watch open. Doesn't that cancel out Chris's running ability?"

I answer, "We keep the watch open for the same reason you wear your obsidian 24/7. And, yes, it cancels Chris's ability, but others have abilities, too. Not everyone uses their abilities for good. We've found the stone keeps us from being tracked."

"Tracked? Who's looking for you?" Uncle Don's protective nature visibly engages.

"Uncle Don, the less you know the better." Chris's own protective nature emerges as well.

"Cut the crap, Chris!" Uncle Don raises his voice. "Is it Stanley? I'm not afraid of setting him straight."

"Yes, Uncle Don, Dad is still up to his old games, but now he has the help of a person with powers, someone who has multiple powers and is especially dangerous."

"What do they want with you two?"

Chris looks at me, not knowing what to say. We don't have time to tell him the whole story and we don't even know exactly what he knows. Surely he doesn't know about the Diamond Bearers, or the amulet wearers' murders, or about Freedom. An idea comes to mind. I say, "Don, we don't have enough time to tell you the whole story. What we need is all the protection we can get. Do you own any other fragments of this obsidian?"

"No, that's the only one."

I turn to Chris and say, "That's why your powers didn't return when I left you in the room downstairs, and again when I used the bathroom. He was with you."

Then I face Don and ask, "Uncle Don, do you have

other stones and crystals that would help us? We need to leave soon."

"Certainly, follow me."

We leave the kitchen and go downstairs to his work room. He says, "I'll just need your birthday, Calli."

Chris answers before I can. "August seventh."

I'm surprised he knows my birthday.

"I sneaked a peek in Ms. Winter's files when you arrived," he says with a wink.

"When is your birthday?" I ask.

"August tenth."

"Wow, so close to mine."

"A lot of Runners' birthdays are in August. Apparently it has something to do with the location of the origin of the Running power in the universe and how everything lines up with Earth in that month. August isn't the only time, though."

"Yeah, but I'm not a Runner," I remind him.

Uncle Don rummages through his different collections of beads and polished rocks, trying to locate particular stones.

I spot a loose rubber band on the table. I ask, "Uncle Don, may I have this?" I hold up the band.

"Yes," he smiles. "Your birthdays may be close on the calendar, but they fall in different astrological signs. Chris is Aries and you are Leo."

"I've never actually cared, Uncle Don," I say. "Up until now, I believed all that stuff was just for fun, you know, horoscopes and fortune-telling."

He consults an astrological chart and then checks the polished rocks he's already gathered. He seems to be missing one. He turns and pokes around through his containers and bins again. I become alarmed when he starts to get frustrated over something. He leaves the room and crosses the hallway. Soon he reenters our room, beaming with pride, and begins threading stones onto a thin leather cord.

Chris's necklace has bloodstone, carnelian, and ruby—bloodstone for health and healing; carnelian for mental clarity and focus in high-stress situations; and ruby for high energy and power that promotes healing on all levels.

My necklace includes golden topaz for its ability to store information, as well as energy, thoughts, and love; carnelian for the same reason as Chris's; and sardonyx to prevent misfortune and protect against crime.

Chris smirks and comments on the sardonyx. "We could have used that one a little earlier."

I ask Uncle Don, "Why these particular stones? Why not any of the others?"

Don ties the cords off and hands the newly fashioned necklaces to us. "These stones are specific to your date of birth and will give you the protection you need individually." As I accept my necklace from him, he abruptly grasps my wrist and looks deep into my eyes and says, "Please take care of my favorite nephew."

"Thank you, Uncle Don." I smile and add, "I will."

Chris clears his throat. "She doesn't need to care for me. I'm watching over her."

My mind runs through the new information while Chris and his uncle say goodbye. "Wait." I put my hand up. "What about the obsidian in the pocket watch? Won't it negate all these powers?"

"No, these stones work in tandem with the obsidian. At least that's what I've noticed with my own charm necklace."

"Oh. That's good." I feel a nervousness flood through my body. We have accomplished what we came here to do and it's time to alert Maetha. I don't know how or where, but I know we can't summon Maetha at Uncle Don's house.

"Thank you, Uncle Don, but we have to go now. I hope we can meet again when we're not pressed for time. I'd love to pick your brain." I smile at him and he returns the smile.

"I'm sure you would, Calli. You two better be careful. Now that you're suspects in that gas station robbery, you'll have—"

Chris cut him off. "You know about that?"

"Your faces were on national television this morning. It's not every day a robbery is blundered so badly. Two suspects keel over and die at the scene, one develops an instant case of encephalitis and is now in a coma, another is knocked cold and doesn't remember anything. Two others—that's you two—disappear in a flash, literally, and are nowhere to be found. The clerk claims those who escaped weren't part of the robbery, but the police say that fleeing the scene shows guilt. The whole story is quite fascinating, but don't worry, I know you're innocent."

Chris rubs his brows hard. "Thanks. We stumbled upon the robbery . . . and we did flee the scene."

"I figured as much," Uncle Don replies.

We say our goodbyes to Uncle Don and thank him for his generosity. The time has come to close the pocket watch and summon Maetha. Hopefully she'll arrive before Freedom.

Chapter 3 - Properly Placed Pawns

Chris asks, "Where should we go to contact Maetha?"

"I'm not sure, but it makes sense to go somewhere private or secluded."

"Well, on our way to Uncle Don's, I saw an old warehouse that looked abandoned. We could check it out."

The sun nears the horizon, and I estimate we have about an hour till total darkness. Chris must be thinking the same thing because he turns on the Pulse Emitter attached to his collar.

We hurry to the large deserted building and find an unlocked door. We enter cautiously, look around at the spacious interior, and together decide the abandoned location will be appropriate. The line of windows on the west side of the building allows the final rays of sunlight to illuminate the interior.

I turn to Chris and say, "I don't know what's going to happen, but I assume Maetha will bi-locate here once she senses my diamond, just like at the gas station."

"Well, do you think anything could go wrong?" The light from Chris's emitter casts a glow across his face, revealing stress and concern.

"There's nothing to worry about, Chris. When a Diamond Bearer bi-locates, their powers are limited, and all we have to do is open the watch and they disappear. If

Freedom gets out of hand, we'll just open the watch." I begin to unzip my front pocket.

Chris moves closer, stands in front of me, and takes hold of my elbows. I look up and meet his gorgeous blue eyes and feel my insides melt. My eyes move to his mouth. His split lip from the truck stop robbery is healing nicely, but could still benefit from a get-well kiss. My attention is pulled away as he gently slides his hands down to my wrists and hands, halting them from the task of removing the pocket watch.

He says, "Wait, Calli. I just want a moment alone with you." He pulls my hands to his mouth and softly kisses my palms.

My mind flashes with the realization we haven't been alone much at all since we found each other again, and even that wasn't many days ago. Yet, I feel like I've been with him for a lifetime.

Chris leans closer, still holding my hands to his mouth. His soft gaze lets me know he's about to kiss me. Instinctively, my lips part as my heart races within my chest. I can feel a distinct stab as my heart races with excitement. Even though it hurts, I ignore the pain. Chris lowers our hands, keeping them between us, and moves in for the kiss.

When our lips meet, tingles and electricity shoot through my body, making me weak in the knees. His hot, sweet breath warms my soul. I don't remember closing my eyes. In fact, I forget where we are and why we were here. I know the magic of this moment will linger in my mind forever.

Chris pulls away slightly and rests his forehead on mine. "Calli, I'm never going to leave your side."

I smile and whisper teasingly, "Never say never, Chris."

"Okay. I will stay by your side forever."

"Forever is a long time."

"Not long enough." His lips find mine again, and he kisses me briefly, then pulls back and drops my hands. "Let's get this done, Calli. I have big plans for us once everything calms down."

"Oh, do I have any say in these plans?" I tease, as I pull the pouch out of my pocket and open the drawstrings. The pain in my heart from the over-excitement of the kiss concerns me. I need to heal myself with the diamond's powers.

"Most of them," he says. His tone of voice drops a bit, causing me to glance at him. The expression on his face shoots lightning bolts through my body once again, making my already weak knees nearly buckle. Something is dangerously wrong inside my body. I need to heal myself. *Now.*

I slide the watch and diamond mass out of the pouch and separate the two, then place the diamond back in the pouch and into my pocket. The watch snaps shut as I apply pressure to the cover. My powers race through my body and conflict with Chris's smoldering-gaze-induced enigmatic jolts that have ignited feelings I am still trying to label in my mind. The first thing I do is heal the pain in my heart and restore my loss of strength.

I steal another glance at Chris and enter his mind with ease. I begin to see his future. Right away I can tell this future vision will take place in the near future, not years down the road. He's distressed over something and arguing with me that leaving would be for the best. Through his eyes, I don't have much to say in return. I only look extremely dejected. When he turns his back and walks out the door, his thoughts are that what he's doing is nature's will.

"Calli!" Chris shakes my shoulder to pull me out of my

vision.

My attention is directed to three Diamond Bearers who have bi-located to our position. Their voices enter my mind, announcing their names: Avani, Merlin, and Aernoud. Four more Diamond Bearers appear: Alena, Hasan, Kookju, and Fabian. A loud crashing noise over by the door pulls my attention away from them. I see Maetha, Amenemhet, Neema, and Mary entering through the door. Amenemhet has knocked over a steel barrel.

I say, "Are you bi-located, Maetha?"

"No, dear." She approaches me and wraps her arms around my body in a warm embrace. Maetha seems to fall against my body ever so slightly, as if her powers are gone . . . but that can't be right. The watch is closed.

"You've been following us?" I ask.

"Not exactly." Maetha pulls back. "I arrived in Miami this afternoon and have awaited the appearance of your diamond. I fear Freedom will arrive in person as well. He's been following my position."

I turn back to the group to find eight more Bearers are bi-located to the group: Yeok Choo, Jie Wen, Chuang, Amalgada, Marketa, Rolf, Ruth, and Duncan. My mind automatically recognizes Duncan as the one who was responsible for helping take down the Healer clan referred to as vampires a few hundred years ago. He's my closest, should-be-dead relative.

Maetha says, "Calli, tell us what you've learned about the black stone."

I think for a moment then launch into my explanation. "The black stone is obsidian." A wave of awe echoes around the empty building from the other Bearers, and a few murmurs of confirmation hit my ears. I continue. "This obsidian is different than any other outcropping for some reason. Its origin is from Obsidian Cliffs at

Yellowstone National Park, which is guarded by park rangers and military personnel."

Hasan speaks up in his low baritone voice: "That explains everything, then. Freedom must have found the power-infused stone recently and is using his power within the military to guard the outcropping."

I reply, "Chris's uncle told us obsidian is an absorber and that the Yellowstone variety is rumored to be exceptionally strong. The obsidian cancels powers, but only up to a certain radius—that radius depends on the size of the piece."

Neema asks, "Is there a way to protect us from the power?" Her pitch-black hair with straight-across bangs and beautifully applied makeup reminds me of a Cleopatra movie.

"I don't know. The metal in this watch is able to contain the power when it's closed, but short of traveling in a military tank, I don't think we could feasibly protect ourselves by wearing metal."

Freedom's deep voice echoes through the building. "Maetha, you decided to show up in person, I see."

I, along with everyone else, glance all around, trying to locate him, with no success.

- Maetha speaks in her normal calm voice. "Henry, the time has come for you to surrender your diamond."

"What?" he laughs. "I think what you mean to say is Calli is ready to surrender her shard to me . . . and don't call me by that name!"

Maetha speaks telepathically to me. *Calli, he's here and he has an obsidian stone. I cannot use my mind control on him, nor can I locate him.* Then Maetha says out loud to Freedom, "Henry, the vote is unanimous. You must surrender your diamond."

The disembodied voice answers, "I don't go by that

name any longer. That man died when you chose my fate, Maetha. Calli can remove her shard and merge it with the rest and then hand it over. Her life will be back to normal, and she will be able to live as nature intended."

"No, she can't," Maetha says. "Her shard is living within her, but you can assign her the ownership of the rest of it, *Freedom*." She puts emphasis on his chosen name.

"Or I can kill her and take what's mine."

"Good luck with that," I mutter under my breath.

"It's not luck at all, Calli," Freedom says. "It's properly placed pawns like your boyfriend who will make it possible to get what I want."

"What are you talking about?" I turn and look at Chris, whose eyes are open wide. His face is as white as a ghost.

Freedom chuckles diabolically. "You are naïve, young lady. You have a lot of growing up to do. He and his father work for me!"

Chris lets out a strangled sound, and he quickly grasps his hand around his neck. Maetha's voice enters my mind. *I'm silencing him. Don't be afraid. I saw Chris's true intentions in his mind, and for right now it's better he remains silent.*

True intentions? What?

Freedom adds, "Once a spy, always a spy. He's been acting his part extraordinarily well, wouldn't you agree, Calli?"

He's playing with you, Calli. Maetha's voice tries to calm me. *Don't let him get into your head.*

"Freedom," I address him, "why won't you show yourself? What are you afraid of? Your obsidian will protect you."

Freedom ignores me as well as the fact I know the identity of the black stone. He says, "Where did you get the Grecian Blue, Maetha?"

She doesn't answer.

He continues. "I knew they weren't myths, but where are the others? Are you hiding them from me? Are you hiding Crimson from me as well? You can't hide for much longer, you know. For centuries you've breezed through the world undetected and anonymous. Cameras, video, and satellites hadn't been invented yet. But now, with all the new technology, there's nowhere on earth you can go where I can't find you. There's nothing you can hide from me. Nothing! I will find the Grecian Blue shards and I'll find Crimson as well." A door slams against its frame somewhere in the building.

Chris exhales and coughs repeatedly for a few moments. Maetha must have let go of his voice box. "Sheez, Maetha!" Chris says in a scratchy voice.

Maetha points at me. "Calli, open the large-stone side of the pocket watch." She then orders Neema, Amenemhet, and Mary to do a perimeter search.

I do as she ordered and feel my powers drain away. The bi-located Diamond Bearers disappear, leaving only Maetha, Chris, and myself in the empty warehouse.

Chris coughs again and says, "Calli, I swear, I'm not working with him anymore."

"Anymore? What are you saying?" I can't believe what I'm hearing. I ask in barely more than a whisper, "I thought you said he just works with your father?"

"Well, he does work with my father. Some of the information I gathered was at his request, but that was several years ago."

"You made it sound like he was just another employee. Why didn't you tell me this when you found out he was a Diamond Bearer?"

"I don't know . . . I was more worried about you and your health. I'm sorry, okay?"

Neema, Amenemhet, and Mary enter the building empty-handed, and Maetha interrupts our conversation. "Calli, we must move now. You two can talk this out once we're safe." She turns to the other Bearers. "Go and do what we discussed earlier."

They nod their heads and leave the building ahead of us.

We walk out into the muggy evening air. I have difficulty breathing due to the tightness in my chest. Panic sets in as I remember Chris suggested the deserted industrial building as the place to alert Maetha. Had he prearranged the meeting with Freedom? No, I can't let my brain go down this road. If he's still working with Freedom, then he . . . no! I have to stop thinking this way. Chris wouldn't have set me up like this.

Maetha walks briskly with us for several minutes till we reach a parked vehicle. I admire the silver, slim-line sports car which is dramatically out of place in this run-down neighborhood. Maetha produces a set of keys from her pocket and unlocks the doors with a press of a button. Chris opens the passenger door and hurriedly climbs in the back seat—if it can even be called a back seat—allowing me to sit up front with Maetha.

As we climb in the car, Maetha says, "I was driving around waiting to feel your diamond, and this is where I was when that happened."

She inserts the key and presses a button, starting the car. Maetha flips the car around with ease and merges onto a busy freeway, sliding through the traffic as if she's been driving for years. I wonder how long it took Maetha to learn to drive. I don't mean how many weeks or months to pass the actual test, I mean, how many years passed, after the invention of cars before Maetha decided she could benefit from learning how to drive.

Maetha looks in the rearview mirror. "All right, Chris, tell Calli what she needs to know."

Chris launches in without hesitation. "I resigned being a spy, Calli. I don't feed information to my father or Agent Alpha . . . or um, Freedom. Yes, I've known who he is for a long time, but I swear to you, I didn't know he was working with Justin to gather the shards. I was just as shocked as you were to see him enter the room. I've never experienced a loss of my power until that moment when he had the pocket watch open. I had no idea he was a Diamond Bearer. I don't think my father knows either. In fact, I don't think my father has a clue about the diamonds at all. Please believe me, Calli."

"I believe you." I try not to sound doubtful, but I can't help it. I want to believe Chris.

Chris adds, "Agent Alpha likes to mess with people's heads. That's what he's doing with you, Calli."

Once he finishes speaking, Maetha pulls the car over in a parking lot and orders Chris to switch places with her. She instructs him to drive toward the municipal airport.

With Chris behind the wheel, next to me, I'm comforted. I let my rational thinking reengage.

Maetha pulls a cell phone from her pocket and begins punching in numbers.

"Maetha, I thought you didn't like cell phones," I muse aloud to break the silence between Chris and me.

"I don't, but until I find out how Freedom is getting his information, I don't want to bi-locate and tip him off to our plan. Amenemhet, Neema, and Mary purchased phones as well, so we can communicate in this rudimentary fashion."

"What about the others?"

"Most of them are on different continents and can't help us immediately. There is no point in having them connected in this way." Maetha begins entering numbers into her phone. Her first call is apparently to a pilot because she gives a flight itinerary to be cleared which includes heading to Washington D.C. for the first leg of our journey.

I ask, "Since when is flying a good idea? I thought Homeland Security was an issue."

"I have a private jet that allows me to travel safely and securely wherever I need to go, and we don't have to pass through airport security." Maetha speaks into the phone to whomever she's just reached, relaying the location of the rendezvous. She gives instructions to the individual on the other end of the line to pick up Deus Ex at a specific location and detain her until we arrive.

Chris looks at me and says under his breath, "Why couldn't we take the private plane to Miami?"

Maetha ends her call, she says, "Chris, the plane was in California. I used it to get to California quickly so I could be present for the amulet reuniting. We ran back to Indiana instead of flying because I didn't want to slow our progress by waiting for the plane to be able to fly. Plus it would have exposed the fact I own a private jet." She then turns to me. "Calli, when you closed the watch and I detected your diamond, I sensed you were near death for a moment. What happened?"

Chris shoots a concerned glance in my direction as he maneuvers the car through traffic.

"I don't know what you're talking about. I healed my pain, but I didn't realize I was close to death. What gave you that idea, Maetha?"

"I sensed the diamond shard was close to not having an owner. Were you injured?"

"No, um, I was, well . . . excited." I can tell my cheeks are turning red, and I'm relieved the interior of the car is dark.

"Excited? Over what? Why would that cause you to be near death?" Maetha sounds genuinely confused.

Chris takes over the conversation. "I kissed her."

"You kissed her? That's it? I don't understand." Maetha leans forward so her face is between the front seats. "How does a kiss result in near death?"

Chris answers smugly, "It was a damn good kiss!"

The familiar lightning bolt shoots through my body again at the thought of the "fantastically good kiss," causing a twinge of pain in my heart again. I say to Maetha, "My heart raced when he kissed me. That's when I first noticed the pain. The discomfort intensified the longer we were together until I closed the watch and healed myself."

Maetha becomes angry. "Couldn't you tell you were in danger? Calli, you cannot allow yourself to get into that kind of position again. Are you listening to me? You have a jagged, sharp object in your heart that is like a serrated knife. Normally, you're able to constantly regenerate your damaged tissue, but with the obsidian it appears you are in a constant and precarious state of danger. Didn't you feel weak or lightheaded?"

"Yes," I answer, "but I just thought it was the kiss." I smile and look down at my clasped hands.

Maetha turns to Chris. "You shouldn't touch her intimately again until this issue is resolved. Also, pay attention to her and look for signs of discomfort. Calli, if your heart hurts at all, you need to close the watch and heal it. Think of yourself as an ordinary human with all the implications that go with internal bleeding or blood clots. You're a pre-med major, for goodness sake. Don't ignore your pain."

"But you told me to avoid closing the watch."

"That was before I knew how deadly the diamond

shard in your heart could be."

I don't want to admit that my heart is hurting *this very moment,* but I know better. I could be bleeding out, hemorrhaging, or clotting. "Maetha, I should probably close the watch right now. Does Chris need to pull the car over first?"

Chris automatically lifts his foot from the gas pedal, anticipating a quick maneuver.

"No, keep driving. I don't want Freedom catching up with us. Calli, close the watch, but let me heal you. I want to know the extent of the damage."

I pull the pouch out of my pocket and remove the watch. I can tell Chris is seriously worried and blaming himself for my pain. He keeps turning his head my way, taking his eyes off the road. I say, "Don't worry, Chris. I'll just have to put you out of my mind for a while." I smile to try to reassure him, and lay my head back on the headrest, shut my eyes, and then close the pocket watch.

My powers rush back into my body, but I resist using them. Instead, I feel for Maetha's healing powers. I don't feel anything different at first. Then the pain within my heart subsides, and my body begins to buzz. Maetha's voice enters my mind.

Calli, the sharpest point of the diamond is positioned through your aorta artery, and the bulk of the diamond is in your right ventricle. Your increased heart rate caused the point to move into your artery. Maetha pauses for a second and then gasps aloud: "Open the small side of the watch!"

I open the pocket watch once again and feel my powers drain away. I am hit with a sudden wave of nausea and feel like I am about to vomit. My hand flies up to my mouth in anticipation, with the silly belief I can actually hold in what wants to come out.

"Calli, are you sick?" Chris asks. "Do I need to pull

over?"

I shake my head as the feeling begins to subside.

Maetha explains, "Calli, I infused your body with some of my energy to help you while your body replenishes your blood loss. I apologize for over-doing it. I'm happy to see you have a strong stomach, but what did you do to me at the end?"

"Huh?"

"You used your power on me as I was about to end the connection with you. It felt like you were trying to strangle me from the inside. That's why I ordered you to open the watch."

"I don't—" I lower my hand to my lap, but keep my head against the headrest and my eyes closed to keep from being sick.

Chris asks Maetha, "Is she going to be all right?"

"Yes, for now. I think Freedom's stone is too dangerous to play around with. Chris, I need you to understand that when her heart becomes overactive, damage occurs, and if it's not taken care of quickly, her life is in danger. We need to remove Freedom's diamond from his heart before this dilemma kills us all," she says under her breath, but still loud and clear.

I am in need of topic change to help clear my mind. I ask, "How will we be able to end Freedom's life if he always has the obsidian on hand to prevent us from harming him?"

Chris answers before Maetha does. "Chop his head off! No, wait, blast his heart out with a really big gun. Obsidian won't stop a bullet."

Maetha adds, "A bullet, or should I say a big enough bullet, would do the trick. I think he will need to feel comfortable enough not to use obsidian. I don't think I'll be able to be present when we attempt a take-down."

I ask, "How will we do that?"

Maetha responds, "I don't know. I haven't been able to see the future concerning any of this. This black fog is extremely disconcerting."

"Well, if you can't see the future, then can we assume Freedom can't either?"

"That would make sense if Freedom is in fact only using obsidian to mask his whereabouts. However, he may have something else we aren't aware of yet."

I ask, "Maetha, did you know Chris knew Freedom?"

"No."

"Why not? I mean, you've been in Chris's mind before. I would think Freedom would have stuck out."

"Calli, you know as well as I do, mind reading doesn't work that way. I had no idea he knew Freedom. Why would he? I wasn't aware Freedom was working with the government on this project. Besides, I've learned many times over not to delve into someone's mind just to see what or who they know. Crimson taught me that from the beginning. She warned me to look only for the information pertinent to the task at hand. Delving deeper into someone's mind results in confusion and madness."

"Who is Crimson?" Chris asks.

"Crimson is the one who healed my wounds when the first splintering of the diamond took place many years ago."

"What can you tell us about her?"

"Not much. She doesn't operate like the rest of us. I've seen her only a handful of times in my life. Freedom seems to think her power is something he can obtain, like getting his hands on a Grecian Blue shard. I'm not sure where she derives her power from, but I do know her powers are different than those of the Diamond Bearers. Ours come from a source. She seems to be her own source.

THE DIAMOND OF FREEDOM

Freedom, like any power-hungry human, views her as someone to be found and conquered. I see her as the reason we are all here. I can't quite explain it, and I don't believe I need to. She's separate from our situation. But this is all just my opinion."

Chris asks, "Is she a goddess?"

"No—well, I don't know. I don't think it matters what she is or isn't. Our task is to preserve the Diamond Bearers' lives, end Freedom's, and restore our anonymity, if it's at all possible."

I ask, "Who is Deus Ex? I heard you mention that name on the phone."

"Deus Ex, or Samantha Juarez, is the Repeater who was working for Justin. She calls herself Deus Ex, and we will too to remain in her good graces. We need her on our side. After you and Chris left my place in Indiana, I waited in the tree-line for Freedom to arrive. I knew he would come sooner or later. I just didn't know if he'd bring her along. After all, it was only a guess Freedom and the Repeater were connected. As luck would have it, he brought her. He remained in his car with an obsidian piece and two armed guards, and she went into the building. I used my invisibility to follow her and observe her behavior. She knew exactly where my room was and how to jimmy the lock to enter. She rummaged through my belongings, stealing my gold coins in the process. I understood she was repeating to have everything appear so flawlessly perfect. After having Brand take me with him on a few repeats, I know what that's all about now."

Chris cuts in. "What do you mean 'take you' on a few repeats?"

I explain, "Repeaters can pull people back with them when they repeat."

Maetha says, "Actually, Calli, so far Brand is the only

48

one I've found who can repeat others with him. I was careful to keep that bit of information from Deus Ex. When I watched her steal my gold, I decided I'd seen enough, and I used my mind control to halt her actions. I was still invisible to her, but I spoke to her mind and told her to leave the building from a different door and to then head in the opposite direction of Freedom. Once we were far enough away, I revealed myself to her, but kept her in place with my mind control. She hasn't been taught about the world of the clans and superhuman abilities, so I gave her a crash course. She was still resisting my help and advice, so I told her she could keep the gold she'd stolen from me. I also told her I could teach her how to block her mind from Freedom. I think the reason I won her over was I exposed the fact Freedom had never informed her about the rest of her world. However, even though she's on our side at the moment, she's a mercenary and will go wherever she feels serves her best. She's in a safe location, and Neema will pick her up and meet us in Denver soon."

At the mention of Denver, my mind refocuses on Brand and the fact it's probable he's being held in General Harding's military compound. Brand's sacrifice to save our necks still stirs my emotions. He has grown so much since high school, matured with his power, addressed his issues, and he reconnected with Suz James, his true love. Too bad she ended up being his half-sister. Poor kid. I can't even imagine what that must be like for Brand. I guess it would be like finding out Chris is my half-brother and trying to shut off those feelings. Then again, maybe I should try to view Chris in that way to avoid more damage to my heart.

I half-listen to the two of them debate which route to take to the airport, my mind still on Brand. I wonder if he's had tests done on him and whether or not his ability is detectable in blood work or x-rays. I feel sorry for him, being all alone. I miss him.

Chris's question to Maetha pulls me out of my thoughts. "What makes you think you can trust Deus Ex? And what kind of a name is Deus Ex anyway?"

"I don't know if we can trust her or not. But at the present, I see no other option. As for her name, Chris, I think you already know why she would give herself that name."

Chris lets out a gravelly guffaw. "Because she's a conceited ego-maniac, that's why. She thinks she's God, and she believes only she can save the day." His white-knuckle grip on the steering wheel doesn't go unnoticed.

Maetha says, "The name Deus Ex is derived from the Latin expression *deus ex machina,* literally meaning 'god out of the machine.' It's a plot device used in many plays and books to describe an outside force that unexpectedly comes out of nowhere and solves the seemingly unsolvable problem the characters face in an extremely unlikely or impossible way. Shakespeare used this many times over to resolve a plot. Deus Ex likes to think she's the plot device that solves the problems we mere mortals cannot. I can understand why she would think that, too. Up until a few days ago, she thought she was the only Repeater in the world. She thought she alone held the power to alter outcomes. So, if you think about it, the repeating power creates a sense of invincibility and total control. She feels like a goddess."

My mind brings up the confusing ending to one of my favorite movies where the two lead characters are rescued from their imminent deaths by giant flying eagles that come out of nowhere. That would probably be considered a "deus ex machina" moment.

We arrive at the airport hangar, and Chris parks the car near the door. A middle-aged man comes outside and opens my car door. I climb out and walk with Chris and Maetha to the door of the hangar.

Maetha introduces us. "Chris, Calli, this is my personal pilot, Rodger Rutherfield. Are we cleared for takeoff, Rodger?"

"Yes, Ms. Lightner." Rodger opens the door for us and follows us inside the hangar.

Maetha Lightner. Huh, I never thought to ask about a last name. Something tells me she doesn't normally use one and she probably hand-picked this one. Maetha never does anything without some significance attached.

Chapter 4 - Heartache

Maetha's plane is a custom-designed Gulfstream G550, with seats for at least ten passengers. I flew on a similar airplane with my parents one summer when a pharmaceutical company paid for our trip to the Caribbean. My parents were amused with my behavior, mainly because I was concerned if the plane would have enough fuel to fly over the ocean. The pilot on that plane reassured me the plane could fly over 4,000 miles, which was many more miles than we would be flying that day.

I think I was more comfortable then than Chris is now. He looks uncomfortable and awkward in the posh interior. I figure he must not be used to extravagance—just one more thing I don't know about him and his upbringing.

I've always known I had a good childhood, and I've tried not to rub it in with any of my friends. At least I tried not to let my friends know I was privileged. I think, for the most part, I didn't come across as stuck up, however, as Suz pointed out, I always got everything I asked for. Some things just can't be hidden when you're the only child of two doctors.

At the moment, my being at ease with the situation tells Chris I'm used to this kind of life. I sure wish I could read his mind. Better yet, a bit of telepathy would be great right now. All I can guess is that he's worrying we come from backgrounds that are too different and he won't ever be on my social level. If that's what he's thinking, he's right. I will eventually be a Diamond Bearer. I'm already one, kind of. Someday, probably soon, I will have the full diamond and be an equal to Maetha. I wonder if he's given that much thought yet, or if he's figured out I will outlive him.

I've thought about it a lot.

After the dream I had of Freedom, the subject has been on my mind quite a bit. Freedom was right. Maetha put me on a path that will ultimately lead me to a life of pain and heartache, and then on to numbness and cold-heartedness, not something I would have chosen for myself. "Are you okay, Calli?" Chris asks me.

I redirect my gaze from the window I've been staring out of and smile faintly at him. "Yeah. You?"

"Just dandy."

I watch him try to relax a little. He shifts and wiggles in his seat, attempting to find a comfortable spot.

Maetha brings us a couple of Clara Winter's juice drinks from a mini-fridge and sits down across the aisle. "All right you two. Tell me about those necklaces you're wearing. Did your Uncle Don give those to you?"

Chris answers. "Yeah, he believes in a lot of strange things."

Maetha angles her head to the side and looks at him curiously. "Chris, there are a lot of crazy things in the world of powers, wouldn't you say?"

"Sorry," he says. "My ordinary human side keeps surfacing."

"No problem, Chris. Your time as a regular human was not long ago compared to mine. My human life was several thousand years ago. I do remember how hard it was to break my mind from the programmed thinking of my day. Of course that included believing in Ra and Isis and thinking the king possessed the powers of a god. I've encountered some crazy beliefs in my time, such as: moldy bread can heal an infection, the world is flat like a pancake, and a photograph can steal your soul. Of the three, the moldy bread was not so far off base. Some crazy beliefs are based on superstition, like the photograph example, and others are conclusions based on limited knowledge, like the flat earth concept. Technological advancements are ongoing. The digital age keeps improving, and with it will come more explanations and scientific discoveries. Chris, your mind must always stay rooted in the real world, where mine must solve the mysteries of the esoteric. So, tell me about those necklaces."

The airplane begins to move forward slowly as Chris describes the different effects Uncle Don said were present in the bloodstone, carnelian, and ruby in his necklace and the golden topaz, carnelian, and sardonyx in mine.

Rodger Rutherfield's soothing voice sounds through the cabin. "Seat belts, please. We're cleared for take-off." We fasten our seat belts and continue talking.

Maetha listens intently to Chris's explanation and then says, "I've seen bloodstone used to stop massive hemorrhages. It didn't work every time, but often enough to be considered a remedy. Ruby may be a source for increased energy, or it may just be placebo. It's said sardonyx can protect against crime. I'm unsure about any of these claims, as it's difficult to make a clear judgment when emotions, feelings, and opinions are the main determining factors." Maetha rubs her hand along the smooth leather of the seat and I have to wonder how often she travels this way. My thoughts are drawn back to the subject at hand. "Even so," says Maetha, "there's been some evidence of stones performing in given ways or there wouldn't be claims. The golden topaz is the stone that has me intrigued. I've never heard of that one's power. May I see your necklace, Calli?"

I pull the leather cord over my head and hand it to Maetha. She examines the stones with an intense expression on her face as if she's trying to peer into a soul. She hands my necklace back to me and then takes Chris's and examines it with the same intensity.

I tell Maetha more about Uncle Don and how he had stumbled upon the obsidian when attending a gem and crystal convention.

Maetha asks, "Did he know of any other crystal that could nullify the effects of the obsidian?"

"We didn't ask him. Sorry, didn't think about it," I answer.

Chris interjects, "Oh, but he did say that the obsidian wouldn't affect our lucky stones' powers. He said his were not canceled by his obsidian. Their powers work together somehow."

Maetha's perfectly shaped eyebrows shoot up. "What's your uncle's phone number?"

Chris tells her the number and she enters it into her phone contact list. "I'll call him once we're up in the air. What we need to find is a crystal or rock that will block the effects of the obsidian. I'm not sure if Freedom has figured that out or not. We definitely need to know."

The plane taxis to the end of the tarmac, turns, pauses, and then accelerates down the runway. When the back wheels lift off the ground, my stomach lurches like it always does when any airplane leaves the ground. We climb in altitude quickly and I glance out the window and observe the many ponds and lakes dotting the Florida peninsula like puddles—a mass of green and blue.

Maetha calls Uncle Don once the pilot gives the signal it's okay to do so. I read her lips to follow her side of the conversation. What I gather from Maetha's responses to Don is he's encouraging her to collect a piece of the guarded obsidian from Yellowstone National Park and to then head to the nearest Native American reservation. Once there, she should find the highest ranking tribal elder and ask him about his tribe's past. Perhaps there's a myth or ancient legend with possible links to the obsidian. Maetha then asks Don about the golden topaz. She sits quietly, listening to what he has to say.

What can possibly be so interesting that Maetha hasn't heard about it in all her world travels throughout the ages?

Once Maetha completes her call to Don, she dials up a few more numbers and gives hushed instructions.

Then she asks me, "Calli, would you close the pocket watch? I want to see if Freedom is able to detect you while we're in the air. Before you do, I want both of you to repeat in your minds that we are flying to Washington, D.C. Repeat that a couple of times over. If Freedom is able to connect with us, I want him to know we're heading east."

"You mean, if he tries another thought-extraction, right?"

"That, and he's a trained profiler. He knows what to look and listen for. All right, close the watch, but don't put it away."

I glance over at Chris right before I snap the pocket watch shut. He smiles at me and nods his head. The click of the latch catching and holding the metal together coincides with the return of my powers. This time I am ready for the rush, so my breath isn't taken away. I also observe more closely exactly what I feel. It feels more like my powers are rebounding back into me . . . sort of like an elastic band has stretched tight and then one end has been let go. I promptly use my healing abilities to boost my energy levels. Freedom has not appeared yet.

Chris asks Maetha, "Haven't you bi-located before while in flight? Or hasn't any Diamond Bearer bi-located to you while in flight?"

Maetha's voice enters my mind, and I can tell she's also entered Chris's mind. *Silence. He's attempting to make a connection. Calli, think about Washington, D.C.*

Maetha then says out loud, "Have you ever been to the Smithsonian?"

I answered instinctively, "Yes, with my parents."

Chris answers too. "I've always wanted to go there. Do you think we'll have time to see it?"

"If we don't, we'll make sure we get back to it soon," Maetha adds. She puts her hand up for a moment to pause our speaking, and then she puts it down and smiles. "Very good, you two. He took the bait and left. He might even believe I wasn't aware he was here."

"Should I open the watch, Maetha?"

"Not yet. I want to wait for any others who might try to connect with me.

Chris asks, "Why do you want Freedom to know where we're going? Doesn't that kind of defeat the purpose of hiding?"

Maetha pauses for a moment, closes her eyes, then speaks. "Excuse me, I needed to make sure he isn't listening. I want him to keep his attention trained on us, on Calli, while the others carry out their orders.

"Oh, so we're the decoy,"

"Not exactly, Calli is the target. I saw no reason to place the target with the others who need to accomplish important tasks." She turns her attention to me and says, "Calli, have you spoken with your parents lately?"

"No."

"Why don't you give them a call and reassure them you are okay and your internship with me is going well."

Right. My parents think I am working with Dr. Janice Johnson as an intern. I use Maetha's phone and dial my home number. The term "target" rings in my head. What will I tell my parents? That I'm okay for the moment. No. I'd only make them worry. With each unanswered ring of the phone, I am hit with memories and longing. I can almost smell the coffee percolating in the morning, envision my mother with her evening glass of wine watching the late news, imagine the playful eyebrow wiggle my father always throws my way just to make sure I know he's joking. My call is directed to voice mail, so I leave a brief message to let my parents know I am fine and then leave Maetha's number. I end the call and hand the phone back to Maetha.

Chris puts his hand over mine. "You miss them, don't you?"

I nod, fighting back emotions that are trying to manifest as tears. I haven't been away from them in this way my whole life. Even at college, I was only a short distance away and could go home anytime. That isn't the case anymore, and I honestly don't know when I'll be able to see them next. I also wonder when, if ever, I'll be able to tell them about my powers. When Uncle Don told Chris he'd known all along Chris had powers, I thought about the possibility maybe my parents would say the same thing to me one day. I know they don't know, but it would make things so much easier if they did.

Chris tightens his hold on my hand and says, "They're fine, I'm sure of it."

"Yeah, I'm sure they're okay. I just miss them."

Chris props up the armrests that create a divider between us and puts his arm around my shoulders, pulling me close. My body responds right away. I am in his bubble. Feelings, vibes, and emotions swarm throughout my body, as if I've been given a magic love potion . . . and, yes, I feel the twinges of pain within my heart, but I heal them quickly.

I enter his mind as I inhale his unique scent of cedar and citrus and I find details I haven't seen before, the parts of his past I didn't know. I stop searching, sensing I've crossed a line. I know he wouldn't want me to be aware of some of what I've seen, and other things would just be downright embarrassing for him. I decide to let him tell me what he wants me to know and vow not to dig into his mind again for my own purposes.

"Chris, tell me about your past." I gaze up at his strong jaw line. A small hint of blond stubble indicates he could grow a full beard if he wanted to. My eyes are drawn to his, and I notice the worry lines between his eyes and those across his forehead.

"What do you want to know?"

"Where did you grow up?" I ask, already knowing the answer.

"Kansas."

"Is that where you were born?"

"Yeah."

"So, your powers came out at age twelve?"

"Yep."

Huh. Mr. One-Word Man. I decide to approach this from a different direction. "What's your favorite food, Chris?"

"Pickled asparagus."

"Come on, be serious."

"I am serious, Calli."

"Oh. Sorry." I look away.

"What's your favorite food, Calli?"

"Chinese dumplings," I answer in knee-jerk fashion. I look back up into his mesmerizing eyes and smile.

"Where do you see yourself in ten years?" he asks in a lower voice, almost seductively.

I want to answer, *In your arms!* but not wanting to sound like a love-struck silly girl, I say, "I'm not sure. I'd like to be a doctor. Where do you see yourself in ten years?"

He nearly whispers, "Wherever you are."

Talk about lightning bolts to my pinky toes! I just stare at him with my mouth hanging open.

Maetha's voice cuts into our moment, "When we land, we'll just . . . hey! Chris, what did I tell you about touching her like that? Calli, move over here." Maetha physically removes me from Chris's arms and sets me down across the aisle and opposite Chris.

Chris protests, "But the watch is closed. She can heal herself."

"Yeah, *now* she can, but what about when we open the watch? Did you think of that, Chris?" Maetha is extremely upset. Here's a woman who's been alive for over 4,000 years and has seen everything under the sun and then some, yet this innocent display of intimacy worries her? Now I'm becoming worried. Maetha continues, "Once we open that watch, she will still be excited by you, and the diamond will rip her heart to shreds. Do you really want her to die, Chris?"

"No, but—"

"No buts, Chris. She's not telling you what she's feeling inside. She's in pain just being beside you, but like you said, she's healing herself. Don't be selfish. Think of her for a second!"

"I'm sorry, Calli." Chris apologizes, but Maetha keeps pushing.

"Don't you remember how you felt that day when you picked up her dead body off the altar? She was dead, Chris, but I was able to save her. Now, she holds Freedom's diamond and it clearly acts on Freedom's behalf. Any Diamond Bearer trying to help save her will be assaulted, like I was in the car. Do you understand what I'm saying? She could be dead four minutes from now, and I wouldn't be able to save her. And what if Freedom's diamond turns on her? What if she's not even able to heal herself?"

I stop her. "Enough, Maetha! He's not the only one at fault here. I didn't have to sit beside him, you know, but I did. That was my choice. He and I will make better choices now, won't we Chris?"

He nods his head.

I add, "I guess I didn't understand the danger completely. Now I do." I feel like a teenager being reprimanded for bad behavior. It stings to be called out on inappropriateness, but then I think about the reality of what Maetha is saying. She's trying to get me to realize she may not be able to heal me if my heart is damaged too much. I absolutely need to respect that.

Maetha changes her tone. "Stay separated. Calli, heal your pains and then open the watch to the large stone side. I don't want Freedom tracking us any longer."

I do as she says, and Chris and I remain separated for the rest of the flight to Washington D.C. I think having Maetha upset with me makes me sorrier than anything else. Chris and I were caught up in our hormones and emotions, liking what we were feeling, not thinking about the implications—but honestly, who can blame us?

At one point, my mother returns my call and we speak for about a half hour. Hearing her voice lifts a heavy weight off my chest. I'm relieved to hear everything at home is normal.

Chapter 5 - Business as Usual

We land in Washington D.C. at 11:00 p.m. and are ushered to a waiting car. Maetha takes my left hand with her right and tells me to open the small side of the watch. She orders Chris to sit up front with the driver and— without breaking our hand-to-hand contact—has me get in the car through the back driver-side door. Her skin feels soft, yet her grip is firm, letting me know our situation is serious.

"We're heading to a hotel," Maetha explains. "If there are any people with powers there, I don't want to alert them by waltzing through the lobby with a twenty-foot radius of power-canceling ability. Freedom was able to keep this weapon secret for a century by only using the small side of the watch, and we will do the same."

We drive through the heart of the capital to the classy hotel, where we exit the car with the assistance of the waiting doorman. Maetha still doesn't break contact with me. The doorman's name tag says "Karl," but his six-foot-tall, three-hundred-pound frame says, "Don't mess with me!" However, I notice right away he has kind eyes. His immediate recognition of Maetha tells me she's a regular here.

"Good evening, Ms. Lightner, so good to see you. Here for a much needed vacation, or is this a business stop?" His voice has a southern drawl that's fun to listen to.

"Business, Karl."

"A friend of yours arrived not ten minutes ago with all sorts of boxes and bags. He's in his usual room."

"Thank you. I'll be sure to say hello."

"No luggage for you today, ma'am?"

"Not this time, Karl." I see Maetha hand him a folded bill with her left hand, and we enter the building. I wasn't even aware she had reached in her pocket. She pulls me along with her to the front desk, where she asks for her private room key. The woman behind the desk also recognizes Maetha and promptly gives her the room keycard. We walk to the elevators and enter the first one available. Once inside, Maetha positions Chris on the other side of her. She evidently wants to maintain my health and prevent me from having to close the watch to heal. She flips open her phone, dials a number, and rattles off a set of orders of where to park a car without even addressing the person on the other end. Then she ends the call and calls someone else and does the same thing, but with different orders. I conclude we're not going to be staying here at all.

Maetha puts her phone in her pocket and says, "Follow every move I make, and don't say a word unless it's an emergency. Calli, hold the watch in your hand at the ready in case we need to close it."

I do as she says, and then I glance over at Chris in time to see him shaking out his hands.

The elevator doors open, and Maetha leads the way to her room and uses the key card to open the door, but we don't enter. She stands still for five seconds outside the door and then reaches in, grasps the handle, and pulls the door closed. "Come," she motions Chris to follow us down the hall to the stairway. Along the way she says, "The doors are computerized, cataloguing the date and time they are opened with the keycard. It will look like we entered the room. Hopefully that will buy us just enough time to throw them off our trail so we can slip through their fingers."

The stairway is open to the three levels below and to a flat landing between each level, breaking up the full flight of stairs. Maetha's pace quickens as we descend the stairs. I find it extremely difficult to continue holding her hand and maintain the hold on the pocket watch in my other hand.

We reach the lobby level and hear loud shouting above our heads. I glance up and see four men who have just entered the stairway, coming from Maetha's floor.

One points down and yells, "There they are!"

I guess the attempt to throw them off our trail didn't work.

"Calli, hurry, open the large side of the watch!" Maetha's urgent order reveals her alarm.

With my thumbnail, I pop open the opposite side of the watch. Maetha lets go of my hand and moves in front, leading the way. I have to jog to keep up with her. We turn a few corners and come to a large set of double doors with a sign over the top that says: Laundry.

Maetha says, "They must have picked up on Chris's scent because his power wasn't canceled by the obsidian." She pushes the door open and motions for us to follow.

As Maetha leads the way through the tall stacks of white towels and enormous hampers of sheets and blankets, Chris follows close behind. Laundry workers pause and look our way as we zoom by. We reach the exit and Maetha pushes the door open with gusto. Outside the door we find a dark blue four-door vehicle positioned with the back passenger-side door ajar, waiting for us to enter. Maetha directs Chris to get in first and slide all the way over. Then she climbs in, and I follow. The car is already moving before I can close the door.

"Wait," the male driver says with a British accent. "You brought the weapon with you?" His hand flies up to his rear-view mirror, which he adjusts a little to the right, allowing him to see me while his other hand controls the steering wheel. "How can I track the Hunters if I don't have my abilities, Maetha? I can't sense their location anymore. She needs to put the weapon away." The man wears a plaid jacket and a fedora hat and looks to be about the same age as my dad. Upon closer inspection, I recognize him as Merlin, the Diamond Bearer.

Maetha grabs my hand and says, "Open the small side, Calli."

I am already fumbling with the watch to switch sides before she finishes giving me the order. His close observation of me relaxes, and he readjusts his mirror, removing me from his field of vision. He begins weaving in and out of the heavy traffic with ease. His fluid driving makes me miss my Mini Cooper.

We drive hurriedly for several minutes through downtown Washington D.C. before Merlin says with exasperation, "It's no good, Maetha. I can't shake them. Two cars back, black sedan. Hold on a minute, it's the boy! They're drawn to his scent. We need to get rid of him."

"What?" Chris and I exclaim simultaneously.

Maetha grabs Chris's right hand with her left hand, pulls it in front of her, and places his hand on mine. Chris grasps my hand firmly. Now all three of us are hidden by the small obsidian, allowing Merlin to use his powers and excellent driving skills to evade the black sedan. Chris's touch stirs up feelings I can't control. I look over at him and find his eyes already searching out mine. I look back down at our hands and then turn my head and look out the window in an effort to gain control of my mind and stop the excitement building inside me. I hope I can minimize the damage within my heart long enough for us to escape the clutches of the Hunters.

Merlin makes a series of quick turns and close calls, enough to make Maetha's hair stand on end. I have to remind myself that she can't see her own future with the obsidian affecting her, and it must be extremely difficult to not know what is about to happen.

Chris's warm hand clutches mine anxiously. His thumb moves ever so slightly against my skin, sending goosebumps up my arm and pulsing electricity straight to my hurting heart. I know I should do something, say something, but in the present circumstances with the Hunters so close behind, it won't help us evade them. We would all be visible if I close the watch, and Freedom would know exactly where we are. Then again, if the Hunters know where we are, then Freedom already knows as well, so I make the decision and close the pocket watch.

My powers burst inside my body in a way I haven't experienced before, causing the two hands connected with mine to fly away. Maetha appears to know right away there's a problem, and I feel her trying to heal my heart. I am also trying to stop the blood loss, and perhaps the two of us trying to do the same thing is what had the negative effect. My powers are acting erratically and are actually hurting Maetha.

Maetha speaks firmly: "Stop healing."

I freeze at once, unable to move, think, or even breathe. Chris cries out, "What are you doing to her?"

"Helping her."

I want to move but can't. Maetha is healing my heart. Freedom's diamond heats up in the pouch, and I sense trouble is on the way.

Merlin weaves this way and that, trying to put some distance between our car and theirs, but when he catches a glimpse of what's happening in the back seat, he slams on his brakes, causing a multi-car accident behind us. We are hit from behind, sending us forward in our seats because none of us had fastened our seat belts. The force causes the pocket watch to fly from my hand and into the front seat.

Maetha tries to push herself upright from her crumpled position, managing to clear her head. "Merlin, give me the watch," she orders.

He hands it to her, and she closes the side with the large obsidian and then helps me sit up straight. "Hold it, Calli, if only just to immobilize Freedom's diamond." She closes her eyes, healing herself, and then turns to Chris, who is still crumpled forward in his seat. I watch in horror as she places her hand gently on his back and then throws an anxious look at Merlin. She must have used her telepathy because Merlin hurriedly reaches his hand back and places it on the closest part of Chris's body. Together they focus intently on Chris's injuries, injuries I can't identify because of the small piece of obsidian in my hand.

After what seems like an eternity, Chris begins breathing again, and Maetha helps him sit up. His face is bloody from several cuts and lacerations, but he's alive. I let out the breath I've been holding and close my eyes.

Maetha asks, "Merlin, is this vehicle drivable?"

"We'll find out." The force of the accident stalled the car. He turns the key several times, trying to get the engine to fire up. He puts the car into gear and begins pulling away slowly. Metal rubs against the tires, and something drags on the ground behind us, but the car is operational.

Someone pounds on the outside of my window. I look out and see a panicked woman, desperate for help. I can't hear her, but I read her lips. She needs help for her child . .

. and all we do is drive away. The authorities will be hunting us down. After all, our car caused the pile-up.

Merlin must have deduced the same potential outcome and quickly pulls into the nearest parking lot to commandeer another vehicle. While he looks for a suitable car, the three of us remain in the back seat.

I search Chris's eyes, wishing I could read his mind.

He looks away and says, "All I did was touch you, and look what happened."

I don't know what to say in response.

Maetha interrupts us. "The Hunters' vehicle is incapacitated, and they are off our trail . . . Calli, you're bleeding." She reaches her hand to the right side of my face and touches my hairline. When she pulls her hand back, her fingers are covered in my blood.

Chris turns back to face me. Maetha, sensing danger, orders Chris to get out of the car and go help Merlin. He does exactly what she says, and in an urgent manner. I have to assume she used her mind-control on him.

"Calli," Maetha says as she pulls my hair back and separates it to get a better view of my injury, "I think you're going to be fine. Head wounds always bleed a lot, even if the actual wound is small. You'll just have to deal with this wound for now."

Merlin and Chris drive over to our car in another nondescript, gold-colored, four-door car. Merlin quickly climbs out and opens our trunk. "Let's go, Maetha!"

She and I get out of the car together, holding each other's hand, and climb into the back seat of the new car. Chris and Merlin hurriedly transfer boxes and bags from the trunk to the new vehicle. I try to catch Chris's eye, but he won't look my way. When they finish, Chris sits in the front passenger seat, and we leave the garage.

Merlin says to Maetha, "What happened back there?"

I listen as Maetha explains to Merlin about the dangers of helping me when I'm injured and that Freedom's diamond is a serious threat to the Diamond Bearers. I am only half listening to her when something catches my attention.

She says, "I won't put myself in danger again over this diamond. It's nearly killed me twice."

I can't believe my ears!

Chris doesn't even turn around to give Maetha a nasty glare, like I would expect. Merlin isn't fazed at all. He just listens and continues to drive.

Is no one in this car concerned for my well being?

I feel completely dejected. My own great grandmother isn't going to try to help me anymore and speaks about me as if I'm not even sitting here. Merlin behaves the same way. His indifference is as cold as ice.

We arrive at the small regional airport where our plane sits waiting with the engine idling. Maetha and I board, hand-in-hand, and nod to Rodger Rutherfield as he exits the plane to help load the boxes and bags. With three people transferring the cargo the job goes faster, and soon we are taxiing down the runway. Merlin waves us off, staying with the car, claiming he doesn't want to travel with the obsidian.

Hey, join the club! I want to shout, but restrain myself.

Maetha makes sure Chris and I stay separated on the plane. Chris is seated up near the pilot, and Maetha and I are near the back of the plane . . . sequestered. I feel like I have been placed in time-out.

Maetha says, "Open the large side of the watch, Calli."

I do so and we are finally able to break our physical contact, yet still be protected from Freedom.

After we are up in the air, I close my eyes and try to meditate, only to be pulled out of my trance by Maetha, who brings me warm washcloths to clean up the side of my head. I glance at Chris. He's cleaning his face, too. Once I finish, Maetha leads me to the lavatory, where a couple of bags and boxes wait for me. Merlin had gone shopping on Maetha's orders and purchased new clothes for the three of us. I guess she thought our attire was getting stale. She's right.

"You'll need to change with the door open. The obsidian might not penetrate the door and I won't take that risk."

My modest side kicks in. I look toward Chris.

Maetha must understand my hesitation. She says, "Don't worry about being seen. He's not seeing anything right now."

I enter the small room and change into a fresh outfit consisting of a soft silk top in forest green and black dress slacks that fit me perfectly. When I finish, Chris goes in the bathroom and changes his clothing as well. He comes out looking even more tantalizing in a button-up striped shirt with blue jeans that have a popular worn look. He doesn't acknowledge me.

I know his mind is being controlled, but still.

We land in Chicago as the horizon begins to lighten with the approaching dawn. Maybe today will be a better day.

Maetha says, "Leave the large side of the watch open, Calli. I'll stay close enough to you to benefit from the cancelation."

We step off the plane and climb into a waiting vehicle. Chris sits in the front again, leaving me in the back with Maetha.

Maetha greets the male driver who is obviously not a person of powers because he doesn't balk at the obsidian's effects. "Joe, so good to see you again." She reaches up and squeezes his shoulder.

"How long has it been, Betty?"

Betty?

Maetha answers, "At least two years. Joe, this is my niece and nephew." She then says to Chris and me, "Joe is a good friend of mine. We're going to camp out here in Chicago to pass some time. We can't go any further until the others have finished their assignment."

Joe lives in a suburb northwest of Chicago in an average, comfortable home. When we arrive, Joe ushers us inside, giving us a brief tour that ends in the kitchen at the refrigerator. "Help yourself to anything you want," he says, then heads to the next room with Maetha so they can talk privately.

Chris and I pull out some lunch meats and sandwich fixings. I try to make small talk with him, but he only responds in simple answers as if I am the last person he wants to talk to on the face of the earth. I try not to let my feelings get hurt. I image he's not happy about being around the obsidian.

Maetha joins us after a few minutes, and together we sit around the table, eating our meal in awkward silence. As I hate uncomfortable situations, I ask Maetha, "Is it always this hard for Diamond Bearers to remain hidden? I mean, do you always have Hunters chasing after you?"

"No, Hunters aren't usually a problem for Bearers. The government has sought out different Bearers in the last century—suspecting we were threats to national security—not knowing about our diamonds, of course. So far, they haven't been able to succeed in catching any of us because we keep an eye on our futures . . . or should I say our deaths.

"Diamond Bearers have had to evolve the methods of evasion over the years. As each technological breakthrough surfaced, such as the telegraph, telephone, radio, and television, and as modes of transportation improved like airplanes, faster cars, and trains, the Diamond Bearers have had to stay on our toes to avoid being captured. Computers and satellites have complicated things even further. When you consider the fact that Freedom has aligned himself with the U.S. government and has access to their enormous databases and live feeds, it's becoming increasingly impossible to remain hidden from him. He has an advantage over us with the obsidian, but soon we'll be equal to him when we have our own personal stones . . . well, as long as we stay off the grid."

We finish our meal, clean up our mess, and move into the living room. Chris sits on one end of the sofa and I on the other end. He surfs through the channels on the TV, all the while ignoring my presence.

I lay my head back and try to let the tension relax in my body—not an easy thing to do.

Chris stops his search on a news broadcast discussing the convenience store murders in Tennessee. The female reporter gives an update: "The case of the mysterious gas station robbery in Pigeon Forge continues. The authorities are still searching for four 'persons of interest' who witnessed the robbery and murders."

I bolt upright when I see myself on the television. A picture caught on the security camera shows me and Chris along with Maetha and Freedom. The two dead people on the floor are blurred out.

The reporter continues: "The two younger individuals shown here were seen fleeing the scene, and the other two must have fled as well, although it's not known in which direction they went or how they did so."

The report cuts away to an interview with a male police officer. He says, "The store was surrounded by police, but no one saw the older two leave. It's unclear how they got away." The cameras then shift to the cashier, who stands outside by a vehicle, smoking nervously. A voice-over from the female reporter says, "The cashier reports that the two older witnesses appeared out of thin air and disappeared the same way." The video cuts back to the female reporter, who wraps up by saying, "It's easy to see why the police are calling these people 'persons of interest.' I'd be interested in finding out more about them, too. We'll continue to report on this bizarre story as we learn more. Back to you, Sam."

Chris listens intently to the news report and I half expect him to talk to me about it. He doesn't.

A call comes in at noon indicating we can continue on to Colorado.

Once we are back up in the air, I take a nap until our descent into Denver. The comfortable accommodations inside the airplane make it easy to relax during the two-and-a-half-hour flight. I sit up and stare out the window at the towering Rocky Mountains spotted with autumn colors from the changing Quaking Aspen leaves intermixed with deep-green pine and fir trees. The view is majestic.

We taxi to a stop in front of a private hangar where Neema, Mary, and a young woman stand waiting. I don't recognize her as the girl who brought the Hunter to Justin's lair, but Chris does. The expression on his face as he stares out the window is downright scary.

Maetha says, taking my hand, "Calli, open the small side of the watch." I figure she can't wait to get a small piece of obsidian for herself so she can hide from Freedom the same way he hid from her. I also understand she doesn't want everyone about to board the plane to be affected by the obsidian.

Maetha adds, "We must be careful with Deus Ex. I can't read her mind, or even attempt to the way I can with Brand and the others. Her mind seems blocked. Information needs to be kept close to the chest . . . we don't want to make her more powerful by allowing her to obtain knowledge she doesn't already have."

The three women approach the airplane and board as soon as the pilot opens the door and lowers the steps. I have to admit I'm shocked by Deus Ex's appearance. She's close to Brand's age, with a thin fit body, a flawless complexion, dark brownish-black, shoulder-length hair, and has a beautiful face. She wears a feminine floral blouse, light in color, with gentle ruffles on the short sleeves, and a pair of cream-colored tight jeans. She has a multi-colored stone necklace around her neck that reminds me of the necklace Uncle Don made for me, except hers has many more stones. Deus Ex is strikingly beautiful, and I know that once Brand catches a glimpse of her, he will have to remind himself she's his half-sister. That thought makes me remember the awkward altercation with Suz back in my college dorm room.

Mary and Neema usher Deus Ex inside the plane and sit near us as the pilot secures the door. Maetha catches Rodger's arm as he walks by and whispers something in his ear. He nods and walks to the front of the plane, sits down in his captain's chair, and puts on his headset to communicate with the tower.

Neema makes introductions. "Deus Ex, meet Calli Courtnae. I believe you already know Chris, and of course Maetha."

Before I can say, "Nice to meet you," Deus gives me a cool once-over and then her eyes float over to Chris. An evil grin parts her lips, revealing perfectly straight white teeth . . . and unmistakable dimples.

"How are the legs, Chris?" Her words flow out of her mouth like a melody. Deus Ex has a soft feminine voice, void of the cold calculation I heard at Justin's place. I begin to wonder if this is even the same person. I find myself intrigued—well, until I glance over at Chris and see he looks like he wants to strangle her with his bare hands.

Chris doesn't answer her question with words. Instead he makes a kind of growling sound. My instinctual reaction is to defend him, but Maetha holds me firmly by the hand, indicating I should remain in my place. I obey.

Neema interrupts, changing the subject. "Everything's coming together for surveillance at General Harding's military complex. Amenemhet is installing cameras and has set up a base of operations. He figures he'll be ready in a few days' time."

"Good," Maetha responds, a smile lighting up her face. "We're off to secure our own obsidian."

Chapter 6 - Yellowstone

We arrive at Galatin Field Airport in Bozeman, Montana after a ninety-minute flight. It's nearing dinner time and I swear I'm picking up on the smell of hot charcoal slowly cooking a juicy steak to perfection. I put the idea out of my head, knowing my dinner menu will likely consist of a piece of Clara Winter's amazing granola bars.

Maetha takes my hand and together we lead the group to the two luxury cars waiting for us near the hangars. I'm not exactly shocked to find that everywhere we go someone is waiting for us with bells on, but it's beginning to be almost comical.

A smartly-dressed woman stands nearby, waiting to greet Maetha. The woman hands Maetha two sets of keys after Maetha passes her a sealed envelope.

Maetha throws one set to Mary and points to Chris and Neema. "You three in that car, Deus Ex, Calli, and I will be in the other. We are following you, Mary."

Maetha hands the second set of keys to Deus. Maetha and I climb into the back seat, maintaining the hand-to-hand contact we've had since we de-boarded the plane. Deus sits behind the wheel and starts the car, then follows the other vehicle out onto the road.

"Deus, I want to perform a couple of experiments

with Calli," Maetha says. "Will you repeat back if Agent Alpha finds me?"

"He finds you," Deus confirms calmly.

I can tell she just used her repeating power because of how similar her reaction is to Brand's when he repeats.

I look over at Maetha and ask, "What were you going to do? Er . . . what did you do?"

"I was going to let go of you. Clearly, he's searching for me. Let's try something else. Calli, pull out the watch."

I retrieve the watch from my pocket and hold it in my hand.

Maetha says, "Now, keep the small side open and also open the large side."

As my thumb flips the other side of the pocket watch open, Deus Ex slams on the brakes and pulls the car off the highway onto the steep shoulder. Dust clouds float by the windows. Deus turns to Maetha with an expression that closely resembles the girl I saw at Justin's lair and says, "Maetha, you told me I'd be safe! What's going on? You didn't tell me you had obsidian already!" She opens her door and is on her way to getting out of the car when Maetha tells me to close the large side of the watch. Maetha holds my wrist.

"Deus, I'm sorry. I only wanted to see what would happen. I never meant for you to feel unsafe. Calli has two obsidian stones. One of them is small enough that it doesn't affect your powers. The other, well, does."

I can see Chris's car a few hundred yards ahead of us. They pulled over when they noticed us pull off the road. I wonder why Deus Ex hasn't repeated yet. Why didn't she repeat to the point where I opened the large-stone side of the watch and tell me not to open it? I can only conclude that Deus Ex can't repeat through a small stretch of time where obsidian was used. Yet, Brand repeated after wrestling with Freedom and closing his watch. It doesn't make any sense.

Brand's powers must be significantly stronger than Deus's if he can repeat back into the presence of obsidian. To be sure, I decide to ask Deus a question.

"Deus, I'm just trying to understand your power a little better. I'm curious why you don't just repeat back to before my large stone removed your power?"

Deus Ex lets out a huff of air and says, "As if I have to explain my powers to you. Don't do that again, or you can count me out of the mission."

"We won't," Maetha reassures her. She gives me an expression that lets me know I need to be careful not to offend Deus Ex.

That doesn't stop me from asking Deus, "Who told you the black stone is obsidian?"

Maetha raises an eyebrow and awaits an answer. Deus says, "Mary and Neema told me." Deus Ex pulls back onto the road, and we drive east on Highway 101 to Livingston, then turn south onto Highway 89 and drive toward the small town of Gardiner at the northwest entrance of Yellowstone National Park. The drive is long and tense. Maetha makes numerous phone calls and speaks cryptically. On some phone calls she speaks foreign languages, which I assume is so Deus Ex won't pick up on what she's talking about. The hour-and-twenty-minute drive offers me plenty of time to think about the recent events that have transpired. I unconsciously hold onto the necklace Uncle Don made for me, twisting the little polished rocks between my fingers as I watch the landscape pass by outside the window.

We pay the fee to enter the park and receive a complimentary map. Maetha holds onto my upper arm while I unfold the map and find our position.

Maetha says, "We stay on this road, Deus. We'll pass Mammoth Hot Springs, and then we'll reach Obsidian Cliffs."

I've visited Mammoth Hot Springs before with my parents and we walked the many levels of boardwalks to see the beautiful ponds. The view is truly breathtaking. In fact, the whole Yellowstone caldera is amazing. At this end of the park, however, there aren't as many geysers and hot pools once you get away from Mammoth Hot Springs.

We continue along Highway 89 until we slow to a stop in a pullout across from a meadow that's nestled between a mountain range and some rock cliffs with the shape of long columns that shoot up toward the sky. The map states the cliffs are 7,383 feet above sea level.

Chris, Neema, and Mary get out of their car and come back to the passenger window by Maetha to receive instructions.

Maetha addresses the group: "Chris and Neema will stay here while Mary and Deus Ex run around the edge of these cliffs and check for Park Rangers or military guards of any kind. If you see any, repeat back—"

Maetha is cut off by Deus Ex, who announces, "There are three soldiers with AK-47s guarding a cordoned-off section of obsidian over there." She points toward the cliffs.

Neema and Mary exchange curious glances.

Chris looks in the direction she points. "I don't see anything."

"You wouldn't," Deus says rather snidely. "They are far away."

"Then how do you know?" Chris asks, putting his hands on his hips.

Maetha interjects, "Good, Deus." Without breaking contact with me, Maetha hands Mary a small metal lockbox from her shoulder bag. Mary nods to Maetha and then she and Deus run across the road and toward the cliffs.

I have to assume Maetha and Mary already discussed the order of events and what she expected Mary to do with the metal box. Perhaps that was one of the phone calls she made on our way here.

Chris steps closer to the side of the car and bends over so he can see Maetha better. "Hey, what happened back there? Why did you guys pull over?"

"Deus Ex didn't like losing her power," Maetha mutters.

"None of us do," he responds.

Neema turns to Maetha and says, "Mary needs me." Before Maetha can say anything, Neema runs in the direction of the other two.

Maetha looks at me and then at Chris. I get the impression she wishes she could dare leave us in order to investigate what's going on beyond her line of sight, but I don't think she's willing to risk leaving Chris and me alone together.

I ask her, "Do you think everything's going as planned?"

"I sure hope so. A lot is riding on our acquisition of one of these obsidian stones. We need to perform experiments and find out how to negate the obsidian's effects. If we can't, all Diamond Bearers are doomed. This is the first time in my multi-millennial life that I've ever been afraid of annihilation. I know that's Freedom's intention."

"Well, then we'll just have to work harder at figuring out a solution," I say.

Deus, Neema, and Mary arrive back at our vehicles. Deus Ex tosses the metal box toward Chris, who catches it with ease and then hands it to Maetha.

Deus barks an order: "We need to leave now!" She quickly climbs behind the wheel and shuts her door.

Neema, Mary, and Chris hustle over to their car and jump in. Within seconds we have turned around and are speeding down the road in the direction we came from. Twenty seconds later, a convoy of military vehicles passes us, heading toward Obsidian Cliff. I look over my shoulder to see if any of the vehicles turn to follow us. Nope, not a single one.

Maetha calls ahead to her pilot and orders him to ready the plane to fly to Billings, Montana. I flip the map over to the smaller map on the back that shows the area surrounding Yellowstone National Park. Billings isn't that far from Bozeman. Maetha must have clued in to what I'm thinking, even though she can't read my mind, because she says, "I'm going to speak with the elders on the Crow Indian Reservation south of Billings. They may know a way to defend against the obsidian. We'll fly there instead of driving because it appears Agent Alpha, er, Freedom is already on our trail—which can only mean he'll know where we are headed."

"Why doesn't he just bi-locate to Neema or Mary and see where they are?"

"He probably has already."

Deus Ex asks, "Why do you call him Freedom?"

"It's his requested name," Maetha responds.

"Why did he tell me his name is Agent Alpha?"

"Because he leads a double life. We refer to him as Freedom because that's the name he's indicated he wants us to call him. I think you of all people should respect that." Maetha changes her tone back to all business. "As soon as we're back on the plane, I'll break the obsidian into smaller pieces so we can carry them individually to protect ourselves from Freedom's ability to track us. He always finds us, but we can't always detect him. He's figured out how to negate the obsidian's effects. At least we'll be able to successfully hide from him now."

I turn my attention out the side window to the passing beauty of Yellowstone National Park. My mind swirls with thoughts concerning the known traits of obsidian and why Freedom is able to possess obsidian and still be able to use his powers. I also wonder if there are other outcroppings of obsidian similar to this one.

We arrive at the airport without complication and are soon up in the air, headed to Billings. Maetha maintains her contact with me and sits beside me in the rear of the plane. Chris sits up front, without so much as a glance back at me.

As soon as we're up in the air, Maetha opens the metal box and removes the obsidian. Everyone in the plane groans, especially Deus Ex, at the loss of their powers. Maetha leaves my side, locates a crescent wrench inside the tool box by the plane's door, and then heads to the kitchen area. She takes a hand towel and wraps the obsidian before striking it with the wrench on the hard countertop. After a few attempts, a couple small pieces break free. Deus Ex watches anxiously over Maetha's shoulder. She probably can't wait for Maetha to put the obsidian away. Maetha separates the three small pieces and returns the bundle to the metal box.

Deus leaves Maetha's side and walks in my direction.

Neema and Mary join Maetha, and talk in hushed whispers as Maetha hands them a small piece of the dreaded power-remover. I read Maetha's lips. "Has Freedom bi-located to either of you?"

I can't see Neema's lips, but Mary nods her head and

answers, "While I was running with Deus, I felt his presence, but I don't think he appeared."

Maetha says, "He did the same thing when I was flying. His presence was in my mind, but he hadn't completely bi-located. I think he just connects long enough to pick up on tidbits of information and then he leaves."

Deus Ex moves into my line of vision, obstructing my view of Maetha's conversation. She kneels down onto the seat in front of me with her arms across the top of the seat. In her hands she holds a small package of peanuts.

"Why does Maetha treat you like a little lost kitten?" Deus tears open the nuts and begins crunching on the contents. "What's wrong with you?" Her tone is very matter of fact and neutral, as if she doesn't care either way how I answer. She isn't concerned, only curious.

I wish she'd close her mouth while she eats.

I don't know what Maetha has told her about the diamonds or the world of powers, and I don't want to offer up any information that Maetha doesn't want her to know. I remember my first day at the Runners' compound when Ms. Winter announced to the whole dining room that I hadn't had my orientation yet, implying no one was to talk to me just yet. I adopt this same wisdom and don't respond to Deus.

Deus pours a few more nuts into her cupped hand and tosses them in her mouth. I note that her eyes hold no emotion, even though the corners of her mouth begin to curve up in a smile. All the while she continues to chomp her peanuts without any show of manners.

"So it's going to be like this, is it? Well, I can play this game too." She stands and turns to leave. She says over her shoulder, "I'll figure out a way to get you to talk. I love a challenge."

Did she just use her repeating power on me? How

many times and in how many ways did she try to get me to answer her questions? One could go crazy dwelling on the repeating power.

Ugh, what a headache.

I glance forward at Chris. The high backs of the seats obstruct my view a little, but I can still see his profile when he turns to talk across the aisle. I wonder what's going through his mind, or rather, what isn't going through his mind. How much of Maetha's mind-control power does it require to block his thought processes concerning me? I've never lost any part of my memory, and I have to think it would be extremely frustrating not to be able to remember something you know you should. The question is, does Chris even know he has forgotten to remember me in his Maetha-controlled mind?

After a while, Maetha comes back and says, "We're about to land. Buckle up."

"Maetha, I have a question. How are you able to use your Mind Control ability in the presence of obsidian?"

She smiles gently. "You're a smart cookie, Calli. When I use my mind control power in this manner, the control remains in effect until I use my power again to halt it. Even once obsidian is in my presence, existing controls remain in place and will remain until I release them."

I add, "But you wouldn't be able to use your power to release a control if obsidian was around."

"Correct. Now, buckle up."

"Wait, you said at Justin's building that you couldn't hold everyone much longer."

"You're talking about two different things, Calli. Freezing everyone's actions is not the same as altering perceptions. Buckle up." She leaves my side.

♢ ♢ ♢

The plane lands hard, causing me to clamp down on the armrests with my hands.

Maetha gives orders for Mary to remain onboard with Deus Ex and me. Maetha, Neema, and Chris are going to try to learn more about the obsidian.

The moment Maetha's group leaves, Deus Ex begins to extract information from Mary.

"So, you have more than one power, Mary?"

"Yes, some people have multiple powers."

"Why?"

Deus Ex is probably wondering why she doesn't have multiple powers, I muse to myself. I turn my attention out the window to the beautiful sunset. I don't know why, but I imagine sitting on the back of the Harley with Chris and driving off into the sunset. I look back at Mary and Deus Ex. They could be mistaken as mother and daughter to an unsuspecting passerby, with the exception of Deus's dark hair. Mary's blonde hair and ivory complexion match Deus's, and their fluid voices are delightful to listen to.

Mary's mannerisms are pleasant and polite. It makes me wonder, what is her story?

What is Amenemhet's and Neema's story? When did they become Diamond Bearers and how were they selected to carry a diamond?

I have a lot to learn about my fellow Bearers, that's for sure.

Maetha, Neema, and Chris return after a couple of hours. They board the plane and Maetha walks straight over to Mr. Rutherfield and gives him the flight orders in a hurried, hushed manner. Maetha's lips reveal our destination . . . Alaska.

The airport ground crew, along with Mr. Rutherfield, swiftly attends to a list of regular maintenance and safety checks while another crew refuels the plane.

I've been on an airplane just like this one, in a similar situation, except the ground attendants didn't rush around like these men. I deduce that Maetha has expressed the need to depart as quickly as possible. Deus Ex doesn't act as if any trouble is approaching, the way she did at Obsidian Cliff, so I'm not alarmed either.

We begin the six-hour flight to Anchorage, Alaska after Mr. Rutherfield confirms the plane's safety.

Once in the air, Maetha tells us about the visit with the Crow chief. "He told me the history of the Crow didn't contain an answer to our question concerning a way to defend against obsidian's power. However, he was aware of the powerful obsidian, especially the Yellowstone variety. He relayed a story his grandfather's grandfather told him about a season of great wars a few hundred years ago when the Crows migrated to this area after being pushed out of their Ohio region by better armed tribes. He said some tribes warred with the Crows, pushing them further west, while others aligned with them, bringing valuable strategic solutions in how to fight a fair battle—using arrowheads from Obsidian Cliffs. The natives of the area understood the powerful effects the obsidian had on some warriors. Yet, they also knew of a tribe from the far north that was not affected by the Yellowstone obsidian. It was said the northern tribe had a defensive weapon."

Mary asks, "So, what do you think the secret weapon was?"

"I don't know. The Crow chief recommends we speak with the Alaskan tribes and learn their history."

"What else did he tell you?" Mary persists.

"He spoke of the stories of his ancestors and the

profitable trading and selling of arrowheads and tools fashioned from the obsidian . . . well, until the government restricted the area in 1872 when Yellowstone National Park was created."

Neema scoots forward in her seat and adds, "Oh, and get this, the U.S. Army was used to guard the obsidian from the beginning. They also issued propaganda stating the Native Americans were superstitious and afraid of the Yellowstone region. That wasn't true at all. Stories circulated that trappers would escape the grips of war-parties by entering the Yellowstone Basin because the Indians wouldn't follow them. That wasn't true either. The truth is, humans have been living in and passing through the area for at least 11,000 years."

"Sounds like Freedom might have had a hand in downplaying the truth. By protecting the source, and altering the history of the area, the power-canceling obsidian was successfully hidden from us. It wouldn't be the first time lies and misinformation successfully covered up history and facts," Mary says matter-of-factly, causing me to wonder what other major cover-ups she knows about.

We eat a simple meal and settle into our seats. Some watch movies on the individual flat-screen televisions, while others read books or speak quietly to each other. The view out the window holds nothing but darkness, so I decide to take a nap.

I awake as the plane descends into Anchorage at 4:00 a.m. Maetha walks through the cabin of the plane and advises everyone to keep sleeping because we'll wait till 8:00 a.m. to go exploring.

I roll over and punch my small hard pillow and drift

back to sleep. I dream about Freedom once again. He offers me my own freedom, telling me that if I hand over my shard, I can live a normal life. This time I argue with him, saying he should give himself his own freedom and remove his heart. He is disinclined to jump on that bandwagon. He's had his powers for far too long to just walk away from them.

I awake with a jolt to the sharp clink of a coffee mug falling in the small sink, but I seem to be the only one who is startled. I'm embarrassed to discover I'm the last person to wake up. I sit up and find that someone covered me with a blanket during the night. I rub my eyes and look out the window at the eastern horizon.

The Rocky Mountains in Colorado are nothing compared to the monstrous snow-covered peaks of the Alaska Range. Absolutely breathtaking! I remember my dad telling me Mount McKinley, the highest mountain peak in North America, is situated in these mountains north of Anchorage.

After freshening up in the small bathroom, I step off the plane where everyone else has already assembled. Maetha has a map of a local tribal center that she wants to visit. She issues orders for Neema, Deus Ex, and Chris to go search for local stores or vendors that sell crystals and gemstones. They are to ask vendors if they know of any special or significant stones the natives from the area deemed sacred.

Mary and I are to remain with the airplane. I'm a bit let down. I want to go tour the town and experience the culture. Maetha issues a final order privately to Mary, Neema, and me, ordering us to keep a small piece of obsidian on our person at all times in order to remain hidden from Freedom. That also means we won't be able to use any of our powers.

After everyone leaves, Mary and I climb back on the plane and open up a few snacks to eat. I clean up the food prep area and then sit in my chair and turn on a movie to pass the time since I can't use the Internet.

Mary spends most of the time on her cell phone in the same manner as Maetha did, speaking different languages and talking to many different people.

About an hour later, Maetha returns ahead of Chris's group. She sits and tells us what she learned.

"We've been invited as a group to attend a feast tonight," Maetha says. "It turns out the forefathers of these natives encountered the spears and arrows of death and went in search of a remedy. Their spoken history tells of a woman they called 'Mother of the Earth' who counseled the tribe about how to fight against the obsidian's power. The woman gave the tribe's shaman a yellow stone that would heal anyone injured by the arrows of death. The shaman would wear the stone and lend his power to the stone, then give it to warriors leaving on a hunt. The stone could be used to heal injuries from the arrows of death of neighboring tribes, keeping their tribe alive. The stone has been passed down through the generations and is currently worn by the tribe's shaman."

I ask, "Do you think their Mother of the Earth was Crimson?"

"Yes." Maetha clearly has no doubt.

Mary says, "If Crimson actually delivered a yellow stone to the tribe, will it end up being exclusive to this tribe? Or will it be something found in nature that we can also gather and use?"

"We need to see the stone in action first. I can't imagine it would be something that doesn't exist in our world. Everything we've ever experienced with Crimson is derived from our own resources."

"Except for her powers," Mary contests. "They haven't ever been duplicated, as far as we know, and they are exclusive to her. No Diamond Bearer can fly, or control the natural elements, or control weather. I do agree with you, though. We'll need to see the shaman's stone in action."

I understand how natives would consider a being that could do those things as "Mother of the Earth." I didn't know Crimson has those kinds of powers, either.

All the talk about yellow stones creates a parallel in my mind: The counter-agent to the obsidian, or arrowhead of death, is a yellow stone. Hmmm, Yellowstone National Park. Could it be that the park was actually named after this magic stone of defense instead of the yellow sulfur that smells like rotten boiled eggs?

Chris's group returns a short while later. They gathered information about two different retail shops in Anchorage which sell stones and crystals, but didn't find anything significant about special or sacred stones.

Deus and Neema bicker back and forth in what appears to be an ongoing argument.

Neema says, "You could have given the man your necklace for two seconds. He only wanted to examine the different stones."

"His fingers were dirty."

"They were not."

"He smelled. If he'd touched my necklace, I wouldn't want it touching my skin ever again."

"Well, aren't you prissy?"

"Like you're not?"

Mary raises her hand to Neema to signal her to stop. "Ladies, enough."

Neema ceases arguing and walks away from Deus Ex.

Deus smiles smugly.

In the late afternoon, we travel inland to attend the tribal feast. When we arrive, we find a large fire roaring in a river-rock lined fire pit. Wooden picnic-type tables surround the fire in a wide circle. Food begins to almost magically appear, carried by the women, teen girls, and some of the children. The preparation for this feast must have been going on all day.

Our group mingles with the natives and finds comfortable places to sit. Neema settles herself by my side, giving me the impression she's probably been "assigned" to me.

Neema says, "I don't like this obsidian. I feel vulnerable."

"Yeah," I respond. "I bet you feel strange after having had powers for so long. I didn't like losing my powers when Freedom first exposed the obsidian. I've only had powers for a couple years."

The feast begins and food is piled onto my plate . . . much more food than I could eat in an entire day. My attentions are not on the culinary treat in front of me, but rather on Chris, who sits on the opposite side of the huge fire. Through the flames, I have a partially obscured view of him. I watch, trying to catch his eye, constantly looking in his direction in case he glances my way. He doesn't.

Neema points to a nearby table stacked high with food. "Oh, that looks good. I don't know what it is, but I've got to try some." She takes her plate and walks away.

Several young native girls, maybe ten-years-old, try to carry on a conversation with me. I do my best to be a polite guest, but my eyes keep seeking out Chris's through the fire.

His attentions are being pulled in a different direction.

A particularly beautiful young lady flirts amorously with him. She touches his arm, fluffs her hair, smiles non-stop, and appears overly interested in what he has to say. I read his lips and pick up on his conversation. He's telling her about his childhood and what it was like to grow up as an only child.

I'd wondered about that. I feel upset that this beautiful stranger gets to learn about Chris before I do. I've never been jealous of anyone, but I really feel threatened by this girl.

Chris seems to be enjoying himself, and that doesn't help one bit. He responds by touching her, too.

A small band begins playing hand-carved flutes and drums near the fire, and the girl jumps to her feet and pulls Chris up by the hands, leading him out to the open area by the fire to dance.

He reluctantly allows her to lead him around, or at least I want to believe he's reluctant.

She shows him how to dance a particular way by moving his hands for him. She seductively slides her hands down the length of his arms, moving them left and right, then raising his arms by pushing them up by his elbows and sliding her hands up his forearms to his hands. She clasps his hands and brings her body in close to his . . . intimately close. I wonder why he isn't trying to stop her from seducing him. Maybe this girl has the power of persuasion or the power of hypnotics and Chris is not in control of his own behavior.

I keep shooting my thoughts in his direction, wishing I could get him to look my way, but to no avail. I can't ignore the aching in my gut brought on by watching him gaze at her. The intense look in his eye as he stares deep into the beautiful girl's eyes tells me he has tuned out everyone else except her, and it hurts to watch.

Then Deus Ex saunters over to rub my pain in even further. She nods her head in Chris's direction and says, "Wow, this must be difficult for you to watch." Her sarcastic tone of voice says it all—she loves seeing other people's pain.

"You think?"

"That's what makes it so fascinating for me. I want to repeat this scene over and over again just to relish the look in your eyes, but thirty seconds of the same reaction from you is becoming boring."

"Thirty seconds? Why stop at thirty? Why not go for a full two minutes of relishing in my misery?"

"What I wouldn't do for a longer stretch of time, but I'll take what I can get."

Wait! Is she admitting she can only repeat thirty seconds? Does she know other repeaters, like Brand, can repeat for longer stretches? I certainly am not going to tell her.

"What do you want, Samantha?" I use her given name just to piss her off, and it works.

She looks at me as if I've just sucker-punched her left boob. That expression is quickly replaced with coolness, and she strikes back like a viper. "It hurts you, doesn't it? Who would have thought pretty boy Chris, who was so prepared to die for you not so very long ago, would now be so eager and willing to entertain the chief's daughter just to get Maetha's nugget of information out of her mouth. You see, Kikee over there is studying to be a geologist, and she of all people will know what the yellow stone is called. Of course, Chris will have to coax it out of her. The best part is, he volunteered to do it, or should I say he volunteered to do her . . . and to think that all Maetha had to do was ask *me* what the yellow stone is called."

I can't believe what I am hearing. What is Deus Ex saying?

My attention turns back to Chris, who is being led away from the fire by the chief's daughter. Adrenaline floods my veins, causing my heart to race, bringing about the deadly pain. I want to chase after Chris and interfere. I want to shout out his name and bring him back to his senses, but I worry he will choose to continue his mission. . . basically, choose her over me. Maetha has hold of his mind. I don't want to put him in a position where he has to choose—and where my heart will possibly be hurt further.

Chris and Kikee enter a building and close the door.

I stand, the sweat running down my neck in a river, my throat constricting and my head spinning. I fumble in my pocket for the watch, knowing I am in desperate need of healing.

I hear Maetha's shout from a long distance, as if through a thick fog, "Close it, Calli! Shut the watch!"

I fall to my knees, snapping the watch shut as I fall. The horizon shifts to vertical and my face makes contact with the hard ground. I feel my powers return, yet my heart still hurts. I will my healing powers to repair my heart and wait for the pain to subside.

Maetha is at my side now, along with Mary and Neema. Their mouths are moving and slow drawn-out syllables roll off their tongues. It sounds like Maetha is telling the others to leave me alone: "Don't help her or you'll die," I think she says.

The tribe's shaman kneels by my side, and I sense she is a Healer, but she isn't using her healing power . . . she's using something else.

While she works on my heart, I feel like I can relax, feel like she will fix me, and yet my vision continues to darken and I close my eyes. I waited too long to shut the watch.

Freedom's voice fills my head. *Calli, free yourself from this life. Don't fight it.*

Maetha's voice fights with Freedom's inside my head. *Relinquish the stone to Calli, Freedom. Save her life. Redeem yourself before you die.*

It takes an amazing amount of effort to do so, but I crack my eyelids ever so slightly to see what's going on. Several faces swim before my eyes: Freedom's, Maetha's, Deus Ex's, Neema's, Mary's, and other faces I don't recognize.

Freedom continues to speak telepathically. *I'm not the one about to die, Maetha. Her shard will be mine.*

Neema shoots back at him, *If she dies, I'll be the first to touch her shard, and you know as well as everyone else here that you'll never get the remaining shard from me!*

Neema must have put her obsidian away to be able to speak with her mind. The tribal shaman continues to work on my heart.

Freedom responds calmly. *Neema, let bygones be bygones. That was the past. We should all be looking toward the future now, and the future holds a shift of power. While you antiquated, crusty old fools ignored the advancements of mankind, I embraced them. Now, I have more tricks up my sleeve than you.*

Freedom's thought process is interrupted. He pauses and says out loud, "Deus, I didn't expect to see you here."

Deus Ex says, "I'm beholden to none."

"Evidently," he responds coolly.

A lengthy pause follows before Freedom speaks again. "What are you looking for, Maetha? Do you honestly think I haven't already attempted to accomplish what you are trying to do? The natural supply is already gone, but then again, Deus could have already told you that. Right Deus? You chose the wrong side. It's only a matter of time before you are all wiped out."

Several other Diamond Bearers have bi-located to our location because they felt the presence of Freedom's unguarded diamond in my pocket. My vision isn't stable enough to count, but it doesn't seem like everyone has arrived. Some are still missing.

Mary asks Deus Ex, "What's he talking about?"

"No idea," Deus Ex answers, void of emotion.

"You already know what we're looking for?" Neema presses.

Maetha interrupts, "Leave her be. Freedom is just trying to pit us against each other. It's the only way he knows how to fight."

The pocket watch is pried from my fingers by the shaman. I hear it click open. Freedom's presence disappears and I feel my powers being sucked out of my being. All the frantic voices around me began to fade and tangle together in a mess of unintelligible words. I let go of my senses and fade into blackness.

Chapter 7 - Deus Exed

I awake to a darkened room and the smell of smoked fish. My mind is fuzzy and my memory feels compromised. I try to remember what happened. How did I come to be in this bed? I can't piece it together. I turn my head to the side and find Maetha asleep in a cushy chair. I hear voices outside the closed door, but I can't tell who is speaking. I try to get out of bed by rolling toward Maetha. My movement awakens her, and she jumps up just in time to catch me as I crumble to the floor.

"What's wrong with me, Maetha?"

"You lost a lot of blood," she says as she helps me lie back down.

"Where am I?"

"We're still in Alaska. I didn't want to move you until you were stable. It's time for more medicine, sweetie." Maetha reaches for a syringe and an alcohol wipe and administers the injection into my upper arm before I can protest. I still have questions I want answered.

"Wait, Deus Ex . . . she knows already . . . Chris doesn't nee—"

My growling stomach wakes me, and I become aware I

am not in the same bed as before. I open my eyes and look around. Neema sits on a wooden chair, reading a thick book. I focus intently on the cover and read the title: *Healing Crystals* by Clara Winter. As if on cue, I reach up to my chest and find a mass of hard lumps taped to my skin.

I pull at the tape, realizing I'm not wearing a shirt or bra. "What the heck is this?"

Neema puts her book down and comes over to my bedside. "Calli, we're trying everything we can think of to get your heart to heal without using our diamond powers. Those stones are helping somewhat, so leave them alone."

"Where did my clothes go?"

"They're over here."

"Are we still in Alaska?"

"Yes, but we relocated to a different town because Freedom knew where we were. You need your medicine now."

"No, I don't want to be drugged anymore."

"You have to, Calli. If you don't sleep through this healing process, you'll die."

"Huh?"

"Trust me, you'll undo everything if you don't rest." Neema fills a syringe with a clear liquid and washes my arm. She injects the drug and says, "Very soon we'll have what we need, and you'll be able to heal yourself. See?" She pulls the lucky gemstone necklace that Uncle Don made for me out from under her collar. "I'm charging your topaz. It'll be ready for you to use in a couple of hours. Just rest for now."

"What? Charging what?" My vision blurs and I close my eyes.

I've lost track of time. I don't know if two or three days have passed since the bon fire incident, but Maetha feels I'm strong enough to move so we're headed back to Colorado to break Brand out of imprisonment.

Sitting in my seat with my head cradled in the headrest, I'm able to relax and observe everyone else as they mingle and strategize over things I know nothing about—all because I was knocked out for the last little while.

I reflect back to when I wondered what it might be like to lose one's memory or what it would be like to experience that. Well, now I know.

It stinks.

I'm reminded of the time I had my tonsils removed when I was eight. The anesthesiologist told me to count backward from one hundred. I think I made it to about eighty-nine, and then I blinked my eyes. Suddenly I was back in my hospital room, and my throat hurt really, horribly bad. Some things are better forgotten, I suppose.

Even though I don't like the fact I can't remember much of the last few days, it's probably for the best.

Maetha says my heart sustained considerable damage and I'm lucky to be alive. She talked with me at length about what happened during my unconsciousness in Alaska. The yellow stone was identified as a golden topaz by Kikee and the shaman. The shaman taught the proper way to use the topaz, saying: "It's as useless as a bow without an arrow unless the healing power is mentally infused inside." The topaz I'd been wearing on the lucky necklace from Uncle Don held no power because I had been continually in contact with obsidian, canceling my diamond's powers, leaving nothing to infuse into the stone even if I knew I needed to do so, which I didn't.

Uncle Don had already told Maetha about the properties of topaz and that it can store power. Using what he revealed, coupled with the shaman's knowledge of the stone's capabilities, Maetha altered my necklace to better accommodate my needs. Uncle Don's topaz is now in a gold setting that keeps the stone off my skin to help retain the charged power as long as possible. If I need to access some healing power, I only need to reach up and touch the topaz until I'm healed. I won't have to close Freedom's pocket watch to use the diamond's power unless I drain all the power from the topaz in my necklace.

I asked Maetha how Neema or any Bearer would be able to charge a topaz if they were using obsidian at the same time. Her answer: Bearers have to put away their obsidian during the charging time. Freedom could in theory bi-locate or connect to them in this state but because they have full diamonds, they can block his attempts to extract their minds for information. They only need to be careful about when and where they put away their obsidian so they don't accidentally give Freedom any identifying markers of where they are or where they're heading.

Definitely a different scenario than when he attacked my mind on the airplane in Ohio. I only have a shard of the diamond. I'm hoping once I get the full diamond I'll be able to protect my mind from him as well.

Apparently, Deus Ex has a topaz on her own lucky necklace . . . along with obsidian. The obsidian explains why Maetha wasn't able to read her mind. The topaz must be charged with her repeating power. As Uncle Don said, the gemstones' powers aren't affected by obsidian. Maetha assumes Deus has to remove her obsidian to re-charge her topaz, too. However, no one has noticed her taking off her necklace yet. When Deus was asked why she didn't volunteer the information about the topaz before, she nonchalantly said, "You didn't ask."

Neema walks over and sits down beside me. She hands me a small metal vial with a screw-off lid. She says, "Here's an extra topaz, Calli."

I take the container and open it. Tilting the end up, I capture the rectangular stone as it slides out. It's beautiful. I can feel the healing power emanating from the crystal. Not wanting to drain any of the precious power, I put it back inside the vial and close the lid. "Thank you, Neema."

"Well, you need a backup stone in case you find yourself in a bad situation. Are you doing okay now?"

"Yes, thank you."

"That's good to hear. You sure had us worried for a while. But once I found this stone from a gemstone collector in Anchorage—and after I checked whether or not it would hold powers—we all breathed a little easier."

"It looks expensive."

"Yes. Maetha struck a deal with the store owner, Mr Stoltz, after he explained the history of the stone. He claimed that it was once set in a crown belonging to the Russian royal family. The topaz was, according to Stoltz, 'replaced' with a replica during a regular cleaning of the crown. When the topaz thief fell on hard times, he contacted Mr. Stoltz. Of course, Mr. Stoltz knew topaz of that color and clarity was a rare find, plus, he liked the backstory, so he bought it. He had no idea of the potential power the stone could harness."

"How much did Maetha pay Mr. Stoltz?"

"She didn't. She traded an 1894 matryoshka Russian nesting doll that had been hand-carved by Vasily Zvyozdochkin." Neema name-drops with excitement in her eyes. I get the impression she knew this person. She continues. "However, proving she actually owned the doll and had it in Indiana took a bit of effort, but Mr. Stoltz was more than thrilled to make the trade."

101

Maetha calls for Neema to come to her. Neema excuses herself and heads to the front of the plane.

I think about the major hurdle our team has accomplished. We have obsidian. We have the ability to counter its effects—sort of. At least to the point that I can heal myself without anyone else risking their lives connecting with Freedom's stone. Now, we'll go rescue Brand and find a way to end Freedom's life so I can have the full diamond.

My attention turns to Chris and Maetha who are talking quietly in their seats, then Chris turns his head my direction. When our eyes meet for the first time in what seems like forever, his expression falls. What I wouldn't give to be able to read his mind right now. Too bad one of these topazes isn't charged with that power.

Then again, do I really want to look inside his mind? If Chris and Kikee actually did anything that night, do I really want to know? Would Chris want me to know? Will Maetha be so kind as to wipe it from his memory so Chris won't have to feel guilty for unknowingly cheating on me? If in fact he did.

Then again, maybe he knew full well what he was doing.

Ugh! I squeeze my temples with my fingers. This line of thinking is definitely uncharacteristic for me. It is so petty and stupid—so unlike me.

Deus Ex stands and walks down the aisle toward the restroom, a devious grin spread across her flawless face. She slows down as she passes my seat and says, "I think it's all coming back to him now." She makes a sound of mockery—*tsk, tsk, tsk*—and then continues moving to the back of the plane.

I turn my focus back to the front of the plane and find Chris's eyes on me. The downturned corners of his mouth level out for a second and then fall back down before he looks away. After a couple of minutes, I hear the restroom door open and cringe at the thought of having to deal with Deus Ex again. Thankfully, she continues all the way up to Neema and Mary and begins talking with them.

Chris stands and walks toward me. He stares down at the floor in front of him until he nearly passes me. At the last moment his cloudy blue eyes meet mine. He says quietly, "Hey, Calli," and continues to the back of the plane.

Well, it's a start. Perhaps he missed me. The last thought sends tingles to my toes and a pain straight to my heart. I reach up to my necklace, touch the center stone, and feel the infusion of power rush to my aid. As soon as the pain has healed, I let go to preserve the remaining supply.

Chris is on his way back to his seat when he stops and sits across the aisle from me, just out of reach. He looks over and says, "I can only take just so much of Deus Ex." He lets out an exaggerated exhale and rolls his eyes. I can tell he's trying to strike up conversation to break the ice.

I turn my head to face him. "She's a charmer."

He half-smiles at my sarcastic reply, then his whole face tenses and he becomes serious. Through clenched teeth, he whispers, "She's a sociopathic, abusive— !" He inhales sharply. "She broke my legs just for the fun of it. I wasn't even trying to escape. Justin didn't tell her to do it, either. If I could get my hands on her, I'm pretty sure I'd— except, I wouldn't ever be able to do that because she'd see it coming."

I crack a sly smile and say, "She has to sleep sometime. That's Brand's weakness. Whenever he'd get too full of himself, I'd remind him he should sleep with one eye open."

103

Chris relaxes his facial muscles and smiles in return. "If Deus Ex was any more full of herself, she'd spontaneously combust."

"She's emotionless. That's not normal."

He turns away. "There's nothing normal about her." Chris pushes back into his chair and lets out a huff of air. "That girl is trouble."

"She's Brand's sister. Well, half-sister. All the Repeaters have the same paternal DNA."

He turns his head to look at me. "How do you know that?"

"I learned it from Maetha's scientist, Hans Lindlebauer. He ran tests on blood samples from the known Repeaters and passed along the findings."

He sits up straight and turns his body toward me, obviously intrigued. He says, "I don't know of anyone other than twins who have powers and the same father. The odds of that happening to the same embryo sired by the same man are astronomical. The cosmic powers don't work like that."

"This is a man-made power, Chris. Brand and Deus were conceived in a laboratory that was trying to create people with powers using radiation. At the same time, the lab was creating kids without any powers—Unaltered humans."

Maetha comes back to us and eyes Chris suspiciously.

I say, "I'm fine Maetha. No pain."

Maetha sits beside me and motions Chris to come sit on the other side of her. I pull my knees closer so he can slide past to take his seat. He sits on the edge of his chair and turns toward us. Maetha says in a low voice, "Deus Ex had the answer all along. When I found out her charm necklace has a golden topaz and an obsidian bead, I wanted to— "

Chris cuts her off. "Strangle her?"

Maetha sighs and shakes her head. "How and where she learned about the topaz, I don't know. She won't talk about it. What we need to figure out is why she just played us the way she did."

I say, "She's still playing us. She keeps trying to get into my head and everyone else's."

Maetha gives me a reassuring pat on my forearm. "Calli, she can't use her power on us while we have obsidian present."

"Yes, she can. She's not using her power on you so much as she's using it on herself. The individual small obsidian we use does not affect her ability." I pause, remembering the experience in Yellowstone Park. "Yet, the large obsidian caused her to freak out on our way to Obsidian Cliffs."

Maetha shakes her head. "I don't understand. If she has a topaz charged with her repeating power, then obsidian of any size shouldn't negate the topaz power."

"Maybe her topaz was drained."

Maetha says, "I think you're right, Calli. She's been around the full obsidian since then and she didn't cause a commotion. One thing's for sure, she has a different kind of power than the rest of us. Man-made."

Chris jumps in. "So, how are we supposed to know if she's just played us?"

I answer, "You'll know if she asks you a question pertaining to the world of powers and abilities. She comes across as only asking one question, but what people don't know is she's already asked ten or twenty of them and keeps repeating back to make it seem like it was only one question. My advice is to delay your answers for as long as you can. She can only repeat thirty seconds."

Maetha appears stunned to hear this. "How do you

know that?"

"She told me, well, in a round-a-bout way. The question is, does she know other Repeaters like Brand can go longer?"

"I doubt it," Maetha says. "She hasn't been around the others."

I smile, realizing we have the upper hand on her.

Maetha smiles, too, and gives me a hug. "I'm pleased we were able to solve this problem and find a way for you to heal yourself."

"Would you really have let me die, Maetha?"

Maetha stands to leave. "I wouldn't just sit back and watch my Unaltered line die out. I wanted you to live, but I wasn't going to risk dying to save you, so I did everything in my power to make sure we succeeded." She looks over at Chris, then back at me, before walking to the front of the plane.

Chris sarcastically quips, "Apology accepted, Maetha." He doesn't move back to his seat. Instead, he remains and leans closer, keeping Maetha's empty seat between us. "I'm sorry I hurt you while I was out of my mind, Calli. I didn't know what I was doing."

My knee-jerk reaction is to comfort him. "It's all right, Chris. I understand." But my insecure, jealous side wants to ask if he got friendly with Kikee.

"No, I don't think you do understand. Maetha wiped my emotions for you away. I could see you, but I felt nothing." I think Chris can tell I am grasping to comprehend. He continues, saying "You see the pilot up there?" I nod. "Imagine if I said you and he were lovers."

"That's ridiculous, Chris."

"Why? Is it because there's nothing in your memories to support that claim? Well, that's what I felt when I looked at you. I felt as though you were just another member of our team. I had no attraction to you, just like you have no attraction for the pilot. You *don't* have any attraction for the pilot, do you?"

I laugh. "He's old enough to be my dad, Chris. He has his own attractive traits, I'll have to admit, but no, I'm not attracted to him."

"Well, Calli, I didn't even see anything special or non-special about you when my mind was being controlled. Like a big damper was placed over my feelings and emotions. Because of that lack of feeling, I was pulled in a different direction for a time . . . and . . . I'm sorry."

"Chris, you don't have to explain yourself to me. I know what it's like not to feel emotion for someone you care about. Remember back at Cave Falls when we were transporting the diamond and I saw your future? I didn't want to tell you that I'd watched myself choose you for death. I even watched you die, yet I felt nothing for you. It troubled me so deeply that I set out on a course to make sure it didn't come true. Maetha said it best: she did everything in her power to make sure I didn't die. So, try to think of it as Maetha's fault."

"No. No, it's Deus's fault. She already knew the answer to the problem. She knew the stone we were searching for was golden topaz. You were already wearing one around your neck right where Deus could see it, and yet she said nothing! Now I'll have to live with what I've done. I mean, why couldn't Maetha take *that part* out of my head?" He turns away and looks down at his hands in an angry, regretful way.

His emotions hit me hard, causing my eyes to water at the realization of what he's trying to tell me. I feel his pain from my head to my toes and want to help him, but I am too hung up on the fact that my memory is still completely intact as well. I can still see him staring at Kikee with desire in his eyes, running his hands down her arms as they walk away from the fire to the building. That memory still stings. Like Chris, I wish Maetha could take the memory out of my head.

I reach up and swipe at a runaway tear with the back of my hand.

Chris says quietly, "I understand if you feel you need some space to think about what you want."

"What *I* want?" I ask, my voice squeaking. Tears spill out of the corners of my eyes. "Don't you know?" I whisper.

Deus stands in front of us, materializing out of what seems like thin air. "Trouble in paradise?" she asks in her amazingly innocent-sounding voice.

Chris bounds out of his chair, over my knees, and into her face so quickly that if I had blinked I would have missed it. Just as quickly, though, Neema squeezes her body between them.

"Hey, hey, back down Chris! Sit down!" She pushes his shoulders with force and makes him sit across the aisle from me, then turns to Deus and orders, "Go back to your seat!"

"I won't take orders from the likes of you. You'll have to ask nicely," Deus spits out.

Neema tries to grab Deus's arm but Deus quickly moves beyond her reach.

Deus hisses, "That's the last time you'll ever lay a hand on me, old lady." Deus had obviously repeated after Neema grabbed her.

"You're not as invincible as you think, *young lady*."

"Says who?"

"Go back to your seat, Deus," Neema orders again.

"Why, so everyone can coddle Calli? Why won't anyone tell me why she's so special?"

"You haven't asked," Neema's responds with a quick flash of her eyes. I love how she echoes Deus's own words.

"Not that you'd remember," Deus says as she walks away and back to her seat.

Maetha turns her head and makes eye contact with me. I note her concerned expression. I know she worries about Deus's allegiance.

I wipe my eyes and think back to what we were talking about before Deus interrupted us. Before I can pick our conversation back up, Chris says heavy-heartedly, "I'm going to go sit in the back and sleep. I think we both need some time to ourselves."

I nod in agreement, feeling emptiness fill my gut.

After a couple of hours, I decide to go talk with Chris. I don't want him to feel I hold any of his actions against him when I know he wasn't in control of his mind. He shouldn't be beating himself up over it either. *We're both adults. We can get through this,* I think as I walk back to where Chris is stretched out on a long bench seat. He looks so peaceful that I don't want to disturb his sleep.

I am about to turn and leave when he speaks. "Don't leave." He sits up and rubs his red eyes.

I sit down within touching distance and try to think of a way to say what's on my mind.

Before I can formulate my words, Chris says, "You know, ever since Maetha showed me the vision of you, my life has had purpose and direction. Before that, I felt like I was just my father's guinea pig, a freak trying to live in the normal world. He would remind me of how different I am every time I saw him, telling me how abnormal I am and how the world needs to be protected from those who have dangerous powers. I believed him for a long time, too. I knew being able to run fast wasn't too dangerous in the grand scale of things, compared to angry Healers like the Death Clan. But once I saw you in my vision of Justin's compound and watched you heal my broken legs, I knew my life would have purpose because I would have you. I just didn't know about everything else that would come along the way. Now that the vision has come true, I'm not sure where we go from here. I'm not sure about anything anymore, especially when I started to snap out of Maetha's mind-hold."

"What do you mean?"

He continues, "I had no idea you were near death until two days after Freedom appeared at the bonfire. Maetha kept my mind occupied while you were completely unconscious at a time when I could have been by your side and not causing further injury. I wasn't allowed to feel your pain. Maetha kept us separated, insisting I be with Kikee instead. I've come to realize, Calli, that our time may have passed. I don't know if there's anything more for us. I mean, Maetha showed me a vision of you and that vision came true, but does that mean you and I will be together down the road? I don't know."

I try to wrap my mind around what he's saying. Is he giving up? Is he trying to let me down easy? Is he trying to tell me he has fallen for Kikee? Did Chris snap out of his trance and decide he'd rather be with her than me? My breathing begins to quicken, and my throat clenches with emotion. I couldn't speak if I wanted to. The pain and tightness begin in my chest.

He continues. "Calli, I just don't know anymore. My world is full of confusion. Isn't yours?"

My shaky fingers reach up to my necklace and fumble to locate the topaz. After a few deep breaths I am able to let go and look at Chris with steady resolve. "I also saw the vision of us in Justin's compound, Chris. Maetha gave me the diamond because of the effect we would have on each other. The delivery of the diamond was a success because of my desire to keep you alive . . . because I felt the connection between us as well. Has our time passed? I don't think so. Is there more for us? Absolutely, if you want to pursue it, but if you'd rather pursue Kikee, then I'll just have to get over it."

"What? Kikee? No, that's not what I meant at all." He turns toward me, placing his hands on my shoulders, and looking me deep in my eyes. For a moment he doesn't say anything. Then he leans forward, moving one hand to the back of my head and the other on the side of my face, and kisses me intensely for a few seconds. I am caught off guard, but then caught up with the feel of him and I wrap my arms around his body, weaving my fingers through his hair.

Then the pain sets in.

What a curse! He continues to kiss me even after I stop and my hands fall from his body. When he pulls away, he takes my hand and places it on the necklace at my throat, and then sits back beside me.

"Do you see now, Calli? We can't be together. Fate has it out for us. I don't know if this will ever be resolved, if we'll ever be able to be one."

My strength is restored, and I've gained control of my overly excited heart from his kiss. I let go of the necklace. I do see his point, though. I say, "Chris, the goal of this mission is to find a way to get the diamond out of Freedom's heart—kill him—so he won't have a hold on the rest of my diamond. We first needed protection from the obsidian, now we need Brand so we can attempt to take Freedom down. Once Freedom dies, I'll be able to have the whole diamond inside me, and all of these worries you have will be over. Don't you see?"

"I see very clearly, Calli, but I don't think you do."

I'm caught off guard by his response. I ask, "What happened to the Chris who said he'd never leave my side?"

"That Chris learned, in a really painful way, sometimes things are not in his control. Maetha taught me that my mind is not my own and that once again she has used me and she has used you to get her way. Since my power emerged, I've seen a darker side of life, one full of selfish intentions, and I'm sick of my life being used to further someone else's agenda. I just want to live my own life, enjoy the moments, the pain, the excitement, the struggles, and the joy of living. With Maetha and the Diamond Bearers, my life . . . our life . . . will never be ours. Once you become a Diamond Bearer, your life will be dedicated to saving humanity from itself. You'll be at Maetha's mercy and used at her discretion."

"Only when there's something that requires the help of Diamond Bearers, Chris."

"But you don't understand the ways Maetha operates. I wasn't going to tell you this, but I think maybe it's something you should know about her. She didn't know if Kikee would know the information about the yellow stone or if she'd share the secrets with me. She had me trying to find out. But just in case, she also had a plan B: orchestrating something that would make the shaman come forward and actually use the secret stone. When you nearly died from a broken heart, the shaman used her stones and crystals on you, but it wasn't clear to Maetha which one was the right stone. So Maetha had me continue my efforts with Kikee, figuring she would be able to enlighten us further, which in the end she did. My mind holds the memory of those events, Calli, along with absolute lack of concern for your well-being. Maetha's little game to solve the mystery worked in the end, but at the expense of both our hearts."

I take a slow calming breath. "Chris, I want to do two things here, and then I'm going to go sit up front for the rest of the flight. First, I want to tell you that I don't view this the same way as you do. I see a bigger picture, one that reaches beyond my existence. I see the future of the clans as being in danger, and our efforts here are the only thing that will protect many, many people. If I die trying to help Maetha figure it all out, then so be it. Are you and I doomed? No. I've seen a vision of our grandkids. Secondly, I want you to take my hand."

I extend my right hand toward him, urging him to take hold. Once he takes my hand, I reach up with my left hand and grasp the topaz at my neck. "I want to try to heal your emotions; I want to heal *your* heart. I need you to see this like I do, if it's possible." He tightens his grip and closes his eyes. I'm not sure exactly how to help him feel better about what has happened over the last few days, but I am sure going to try to infuse him with optimism. As it stands, he's ready to high-tail it into seclusion and mope for years to come. No way am I going to sit and watch that happen, not when I saw his name carved so clearly onto a headstone and our grandchildren bounding toward me to visit Grandpa's grave. No, he and I have a future of many years together, and it will be a happy future, unless his father, General Harding, has his way, in which case the world of powers and abilities will cease to exist.

Before long, my heart begins to hurt. causing me to let go of his hand. I must have exhausted the power stored in the stone. Fumbling in my pocket to retrieve the other stone, I quickly pull out the vial and remove the lid, slipping the stone out into my hand. I close my fingers around it and shut my eyes, inhaling deeply until the pain subsides, then I place the topaz back inside the vial for the next time.

I can't tell if my attempts at healing his fears and worries and guilt helped. I stand and smile, then walk toward the front of the plane and sit down by Neema. I reach up and take off my necklace and say, "This needs to be charged again."

Neema takes the necklace from my hand. "What? You drained it in a matter of hours. Do you understand it takes me a full twenty-four hours to charge that thing?"

"I'm sorry. I needed to use it on Chris."

"Why?" she asks, and then pulls my necklace over her head, making sure to reverse its direction so the topaz has skin contact.

"It's personal," I answer. Neema angles her head and stares me down, waiting for a better answer. "He's depressed and feeling self-pity. I wanted to give him hope."

"Did you?"

"I'm not sure, but the attempt drained the stone's power. I still have the other one, though. Plus, I won't be sitting by Chris for the rest of the flight, so things should be fine. Besides, you've been charging that one for a while." I point to the extra topaz she has taped to her chest. Maetha and Mary also have similar crystals attached to their skin, charging them with their power.

Neema's hand reaches up and touches the mass of tape and says, "This isn't a healing stone. It's being charged with Seer ability." She waves a finger at Maetha and Mary and says, "We're charging stones with different powers so, between us all, we're complete."

"Clever." I settle into my seat and recline it back.

"I must say, it takes quite a bit of concentration to direct a power into these little crystals. But once you get the

mental flow going it just kind of continues on its own."
Neema is silent for a few moments before she speaks again.
"Calli," she says in hushed, lower register, "there will be plenty of time for you and Chris after we complete this mission. Don't risk its success on him."

I turn my head and look into her eyes. "Haven't you ever loved someone, Neema?"

She looks taken aback. "Of course. Several times. But, I've learned my lesson."

"Huh?"

"Love only ends in pain. It's been the undoing of many great individuals and civilizations, like when the city of Troy was destroyed because the king's son fell in love with another man's wife, stole her away, and through his actions incited a battle that destroyed the city. Or how about Cleopatra and Mark Antony? She fell in love with a married man, causing the fall of ancient Egypt and that resulted in their suicides. They preferred death to being separated. That kind of love ends in pain, and has the potential to cause destruction."

"Who were you in love with?"

"I had a husband and children before I became a Diamond Bearer."

"You did? Is your line still alive? I mean, are there any—"

Neema interrupts and says, "My line died out in the mid-1300s from the Black Plague. That's when I met Henry—well, Freedom."

"Fr-Freedom?" I almost can't say his name properly, I am so shocked.

"After his wife and children died, but before he became a Diamond Bearer, I took pity on him and became his friend. It was a horrible time to be alive, what with all the death surrounding us from the plague. I felt he would

THE DIAMOND OF FREEDOM

become a Bearer someday, and I wanted him to understand nature's will before that happened. I fell in love with him, felt like I really knew him, and encouraged Maetha to induct him as a Bearer. I truly believed he loved me in return. I hadn't felt that kind of closeness with another person for centuries. Once he became a Bearer, and learned the mission of the Bearers, everything changed. He felt I had betrayed him because I never prepared him for the fact he would outlive his son. He was upset I didn't tell him everything prior to him becoming a Bearer, furious the Bearers didn't save his wife's and daughter's lives the way his life had been preserved. I didn't deceive him on purpose, I just didn't tell him everything because, well . . . you know how the process works. His love for me was replaced with indignation. Since then, I've guarded my heart from love . . . from pain. It's not worth it, not for me."

I feel sorry for Neema. She isn't saying she no longer wants to love and be loved. She just continually guards her heart to keep from falling victim to the pain of loss. I can tell she still loves Freedom on some deep level, but I'm certainly not going to ask her about it. Instead, I say, "I haven't learned the same lessons yet, Neema. Some things in life are easy to learn to avoid without experiencing them, like not touching a burning stick, or keeping your fingers out of the way while slicing bread with a sharp knife. Other life lessons are not so clear. I don't think Chris would set out to hurt me intentionally."

"And I didn't think Freedom would ever hurt me. You know what, Calli? I do believe this is one of those lessons you'll have to learn first-hand . . . unfortunately."

Chapter 8 - Rocky Mountain Madness

The plane slows to a stop in Denver, and we prepare to deplane. I change my clothes once again prior to landing, picking from the options Merlin provided. He has good taste . . . or at least whoever picked out the clothing has good taste. We pile into two SUV-type vehicles, with Maetha directing Chris into a different car than the one I'm in. We began our trip to General Harding's headquarters, which is located in the Rocky Mountains west of Denver, off I-70. Amenemhet's base of operations is a few miles away from the compound.

As we drive through the heart of the city, my thoughts wander back to Chris's concerns. What would it really be like to be a Diamond Bearer? Would I be able to be a mother and raise my own children? Or would I be off saving the world, as Chris supposes? Would I be so busy handling matters of global concern that I'd miss out on the short lives of my loved ones? My heart hurts too much to think about it.

I turn my thoughts to Brand. I hope he's all right and in good condition.

After driving for over an hour, we reach the small, double-wide mobile home where Amenemhet has set up surveillance of Harding's compound. As we slow to a stop on the gravel driveway, Amenemhet walks out of the building, dressed in camouflage and painted up like a Navy Seal. He looks downright terrifying. We get out of our vehicles and walk to the front door.

Amenemhet picks up a box from the ground by the steps and hands it to Chris before turning to speak to Maetha. "We don't have much time. Come." He motions for all of us to follow him inside.

The aroma of simmering herbal tea hits my nose when we enter the open kitchen area. The house doesn't contain much furniture—mainly tables and folding chairs. Several tables line the far wall in the area that would be considered the living room. Monitors and televisions are set up, displaying black and white images of trees and roads. One monitor shows a high fence with razor wire coiled along the top and an entry gate next to a small shack, which I assume houses a security guard. A large building sets further beyond in what looks like grey grass. The building is nothing more than a big box with no windows, only a solid metal door with a security code keypad. As I study the picture, a male guard walks into view with a rifle slung over his shoulder. Another monitor shows movement: a four-door, dark-colored sedan being driven past a camera.

Along the adjacent wall of the mobile home, several shelving units hold all kinds of gadgets: high-powered scopes, cameras, computers, and guns—all sitting ready to aid us in our anticipated break-out of Brand. Next to the shelves, an alcove houses three doors. One is ajar, revealing a bed and dresser. I assumed the other two are most likely a bathroom and another bedroom.

"Chris, bring the box over here," Amenemhet says, standing by the shelving on the wall and pointing to the floor where he wants Chris to place the box. Chris walks over and Maetha follows.

Maetha turns to Amenemhet. "What do you know at this point?"

"A young female employee arrives every night at 11:00. Through a mind-read I was able to confirm that the boy is inside. We have a new problem, though. The building was fortified with additional obsidian stones embedded into the exterior stucco while you were in Alaska. Plus, the guards wear an obsidian pin to protect them from mind-reads and other powers. This is not going to be easy for the girl," —he motions toward Deus Ex— "but Mary tells me she is quite adept at assuming disguises and personalities, and we're hopeful she'll be able to pull this off."

While Amenemhet delivers his report, Deus walks from one monitor to another, studying every detail. Two of the monitors have controllers that can manipulate the camera, allowing it to zoom in close and swivel. Deus Ex seems to know exactly how to operate the controllers as if she had been professionally trained to use them, but the most likely explanation is that she has repeated so she could master the controllers' movements and technical capabilities.

"Any idea if the interior is protected with obsidian as well?" Chris asks.

"The girl's mind didn't show anything, but she's not a person with powers, so she wouldn't notice anything different inside. If I had designed the fortress, I'd have placed obsidian everywhere."

"I agree," Maetha says. "I assume there's at least one obsidian in Brand's cell to prevent him from repeating."

Amenemhet opens the box and pulls out several curious items, including a blonde long-haired wig, black clothing, and small electrical devices. "Deus Ex, these are for your disguise. I gathered a full profile of the night-watch employee for you to go over." He pulls a large three-ring binder from off the shelf and hands it to her.

Deus Ex smiles and says in her sickeningly sweet voice, "I'll just take this in the bedroom while you guys handle the posse."

Amenemhet places his fingertips gently on his forehead and closes his eyes. I find his behavior peculiar, and I watch him closely. He opens his eyes and looks right at me and says, "Calli, you're in danger!"

Maetha peeks through a curtain and turns to me and says, "Calli, Beth is here with her team. Stay here with Amenemhet. Chris and I will go intercept them."

"How did she find us?" Chris asks, his voice reflecting his confusion, as he follows Maetha out the door.

Maetha and Chris hurry out the door, leaving me with Amenemhet, who situates himself between me and the door. Amenemhet wags his finger menacingly at me, trying to indicate without speaking that I need to back up.

I wondered if Maetha ever saw this future outcome when she selected me to carry the Sanguine Diamond. She has said things to me before like: "This has never happened," or "This is the first time anything like this has happened." I guess with the introduction of the obsidian, Maetha has been flying by the seat of her pants for the first time in several thousand years.

I hear Maetha's muffled voice ask, "How did you find this location?"

Beth replies, "We've been tracking Chris. He made a call from Denver."

Maetha sputters, "You're tracing my cell phone?"

"No, his father's phone. Once we had an area to search, it wasn't too hard for our Hunter to locate his scent."

Maetha addresses Chris with a sharp tone that tells me

he's in trouble, "You called your father?"

"Sorry, I had to pass on some personal information for my mother," he answers with a guilty tone.

"I know Calli's in there," Beth says. "You must hand her over. She has to answer for the deaths of our leaders."

"That's not what happened, Beth," Chris answers. "Justin kidnapped everyone, including Calli. He hired a bounty hunter to kidnap me."

Beth retorts back, "The Healers reported that Calli ran the moment she was given the amulet. She stole it, Chris. Now several people are dead and the amulets are missing. You're being investigated also, Chris, as an accomplice."

"What?"

Beth adds, "Apparently you two were involved in a gas station robbery as well. I want to take Calli in before the police find her. Now, bring her out so we can get on our way."

Maetha says, "Beth, your group is seeking the wrong people. The clues were at the scene and you missed them. You're chasing dead-end leads. Go back to the scene and investigate further, and you'll find I was there and witnessed the events unfolding. Calli and Chris are innocent."

Beth stands her ground. "Her innocence is for the council to decide. You're welcome to appear in her defense, if you like, but I'll be taking Calli with me now."

Maetha's voice takes on an authoritative tone, and I suspect she's using her mind-control. "I will turn her over to you when you return with a written report of the scene of the accident and a signed certificate from the council asking for her capture. Now go."

Everything goes quiet for a moment, then Maetha and Chris enter the building. Amenemhet holds the door for them and then resumes his position as guard.

Maetha holds one of the golden topazes in her hand. She drops it on the counter and says, "That was only good for one event. I hope it was strong enough to take hold in Beth's head."

Mary says, "Hopefully your command will last long enough for us to get what we came here for and get out." She tears off a new piece of medical tape and helps Maetha strap the topaz to her chest. "I can hold your obsidian while you recharge that one."

"I don't want to risk having Freedom discover our whereabouts. I'll charge it later." Maetha readjusts her clothing over the tape and whirls around to confront Chris. "I can't believe you called your father from Denver. Why couldn't you have done that from Alaska and lured Beth and her squad up there?"

Chris shrugs his shoulders, embarrassment written all over his face.

Amenemhet keeps Chris busy all evening, which in turn keeps Chris and me apart. I know Maetha is concerned with how quickly I am going through my charged topazes. It makes sense to preserve the power for dire situations.

Around 10:00 p.m. I can hear Deus and Neema in the bedroom, engaging in another verbal battle about Deus's prior knowledge of the topaz and how she has one on her necklace. Their raised voices and clever comebacks make me smile. Across the room, Chris looks at me and returns the smile, sending my heart into a quick pitter-patter. I grasp my topaz and calm myself.

Later, we watch the monitors for the arrival of the night-watch girl. Sure enough, she arrives on schedule at

10:55 p.m. The shift change includes new guards as well. The plan is that in the morning when the girl leaves work, Amenemhet will intercept and subdue her. Then he'll drive her car here so Deus can use it.

After a restless night, one with Deus Ex insisting she sleep outside, which I assume is for her own sense of security, we huddle around the monitors and watch for the morning shift change at the compound.

At 8:02 a.m., the girl leaves the building, waving to the guards and catching a yawn with her other hand. I watch her lips on the silent monitor and find she's telling a guard she'll bring him a plate of her famous peanut-butter cookies when she comes back to work that evening. The male guard smiles in anticipation.

"Uh-oh," I mutter.

"What?" Neema comes over to stand beside me.

"The girl just promised to bring home-made cookies to the guard tonight. If Deus Ex shows up without home-made peanut-butter cookies, well . . . "

"Well, what?" Neema says. "So we go buy some cookies from the bakery."

Deus rudely interrupts. "How do you know that's what she said? There's no sound with the surveillance video."

I shake my head. "No, that won't do. These have to be the real deal, or the guard will look closely at Deus Ex and wonder why she *bought* cookies when she said she'd *make* them. This is a little detail that could blow our whole operation."

"She can read lips," Chris says to Deus.

"No she can't." Deus folds her arms across her chest

and angles her head to the side.

I don't remember telling Chris I can read lips.

"Yes, she can," Chris confirms. "Calli's right. We don't want the guard looking too closely at Deus Ex."

Deus states matter-of-factly, "I'll just take him out if he causes trouble."

"Come on, Deus," I say. "If you start the fireworks' show before you break Brand out of the compound, you'll have a lot less time to work inside."

"Calli's right," Maetha says, joining in. "Mary, take Chris with you and go shopping for ingredients." Maetha looks at me and says, "When they get back, you'll help make the cookies. For now, I want you to go meditate in the bedroom. It's important that you master the practice."

I nod and walk toward the room without turning to look at Chris as he leaves with Mary.

I overhear Maetha give instruction to Deus Ex to study the profile information again so she will look and act exactly like the night employee. Deus answers in an over-confident tone that she has already done so and she doesn't need to waste any more time on the matter.

I enter the bedroom and start to close the door as I hear Maetha respond chillingly, "Young lady, you're not indestructible!"

Inside the room, I sit in a lotus position on the bed, my hands resting on my knees, while I stare at the fake wood paneling on the wall. Deus Ex's excessive confidence could cost Brand his life. Maetha knows it, I know it. Closing my eyes, I tilt my chin up to the ceiling and exhale, letting out my stress. A million thoughts invade my mind. I try to imagine my pinky toenail, try to feel it in my head, try to feel where it connects with my foot. Once I can feel my feet—or what I think are my feet—I exhale and let my mind shed thoughts of everything, of everyone, and focus on my feelings. Thoughts of peace and tranquility flood my body. I feel different parts of my body with my mind, imagining I am infusing energy into them. I'm assuming once I have the whole diamond in my possession, I'll be able to heal myself this way.

Strange, now that I actually have the whole stone, I can't use it all . . . or should I say, I can't use it *at all*. Somehow, we'll figure out how to use Freedom's powers against him. There simply has to be a way to kill him. Many scenarios run through my head of possibilities and probabilities, all of which end in failure. I imagine different locations where we could try to extract his diamond, but nothing stands out in my mind as being the answer. Maetha says there hasn't ever been a reason to forcefully remove another Diamond Bearer's heart. Which doesn't mean it's impossible to do so, only that no one has ever had to do it before.

Diamond Bearers always remove their own hearts.

I clear my mind once again and simply rest my body until Maetha enters the room.

"It's time to bake," she says.

As I help mix up the cookie dough, Amenemhet arrives, driving the pale yellow four-door compact car. I watch him through the kitchen window as he gets out and opens the back door and pulls out the unconscious, restrained, and gagged female. He effortlessly hefts her over his shoulder and carries her into the building and puts her in the other bedroom on the bed.

"Calli," he calls over his shoulder, "come help me remove her lab coat."

I hurry in and assist him as he removes her restraints and eases her arms out of the coat. I catch a glimpse of her identification badge—Sheryl Wong. She certainly doesn't look Asian. Her blonde hair is pulled back in a tight ponytail and her lips are glossed with the trademark hot-pink gloss we'd noted she always wears. The lipstick is smudged from the cloth bandana gag Amenemhet tied around her mouth. He unties the bandana before we leave the room and locks the door behind us.

I finish baking the cookies while everyone else discusses the impending escape plan. After a couple of hours, Sheryl awakes and we can hear her screaming. Amenemhet retrieves a syringe and fills it with clear liquid. As he walks toward the room, I mutter, "Sweet dreams, Sheryl," under my breath.

Deus Ex walks out of the bathroom wearing a black cat suit with a black utility belt strapped around her waist. The blonde wig is slicked back in a tight ponytail, and she has applied a light layer of makeup, including pink lip gloss. I spot one of my Pulse Emitters on her suit up near her neckline. Amenemhet hands her a white lab coat, complete with identification and keycards.

"Where's the girl?" Deus Ex asks, figuring the silence must mean the girl is gone.

"Safe," Amenemhet answers with one word.

"You better just do away with her. She'll only be trouble later."

"Just do your job and I'll do mine." He hands her a headband outfitted with a camera and microphone. Then he pins a second Pulse Emitter to her suit and says, "This one's for the boy."

Deus Ex puts the headband in her lab coat pocket, exits through the door, and starts to walk over to Ms. Wong's car.

Maetha hops out the door faster than lightning and I watch through the screen as she stops Deus Ex and says, "Listen, any information you're able to get will help us understand exactly what's going on inside the building. It's

126

information that will help you in your life as well."

"That's why I'm doing this, Maetha. I'll get everything there is to get." She climbs in the car and peels out in the gravel, spitting tiny rocks into the air.

We all huddle around the monitors, once again, waiting to see her vehicle appear on the screen as she passes the different cameras Amenemhet strategically placed for added security. As Deus Ex's car speeds past each camera, the tension mounts in the room. What if her attitude gets in the way? What if she or Brand are injured or killed in the escape attempt? According to the captured employee's mind, there aren't any black rocks inside the building like there are on the outside. Hopefully, that's the case. We'll find out soon enough.

The final camera shows Deus Ex pulling into the parking lot and turning off the car. She parks in the same spot Sheryl always did and at the same slightly crooked angle. Deus plays the role of Sheryl almost a little too well. We watch her walk toward the gate and swipe her card. She pulls her pink lip gloss out and reapplies more, just like Sheryl always does, and then she enters the gate. The guard appears. He has a big smile on his face when she hands him the cookies and hurries on. She waves to the two guards on either side of her further down the yard and swipes her card again at the door to gain entry. Once the door closes behind her, we wait for her to put on her headband with the camera and microphone.

We wait and wait.

Chris asks the question we are all thinking. "What's taking her so long?"

Finally, the screen begins to come into focus. Deus Ex walks down a dark hallway. She turns into one of the rooms, walks to the time clock and swipes her ID card to clock in.

"That was smart," Mary says. "She won't set off any unnecessary alarms that would indicate Sheryl hasn't checked in yet."

Deus Ex fills a cup of coffee from the carafe and walks down the hallway as if it's just another day at work. She turns the corner and enters a room with several desks and computers. Walking past a few desks, she then stops at one in particular and sits down and accesses the computer. She begins downloading files onto the flash drive she had in one of her utility belt pockets, then rummages through the drawers, pulling out files and papers.

"She's repeating," I inform everyone.

"How do you know?" Amenemhet asks.

"Because everything is too flawless. She seems to know exactly where everything is, but the question is, how many times did she have to repeat until she found exactly what she was after?"

Deus Ex stands, grasps the zipper at her neck, unzips to her cleavage, wriggles her shoulders a bit to loosen the suit, then takes the small pile of files and pushes them down the front of her suit. She zips back up.

Leaving the office, she walks down the hall toward a room with a red light above the door. She swipes her keycard and enters the room. Brand sits on his bed with his back against the wall.

My heart races with excitement when I see Brand on the monitor. He looks a little worn down and tired, but other than that he appears to be just fine.

"Who the hell are you? Where's Sheryl?" Brands voice sounds through the speaker. I'm happy to hear he still has his wits about him.

"I'm her replacement tonight. Come with me."

"Huh? You're letting me out of this room?"

Chris's frustration mounts and he flicks his hand in

front of the screen. "Just do it. Stop asking questions."

Deus extends her hand to Brand. "You and I are both affected by that black rock." She turns her head so the camera is on the large obsidian piece embedded in the wall. "Come out here where there aren't any of those."

"You have powers too?"

"Yes, the same as yours. I'm here to rescue you, so get your butt off the bed and come on!"

Brand jumps up and leaves the room right behind Deus Ex.

"You're a Repeater? You know that makes you my sister, right?"

"What are you talking about?" Deus makes her way down the hallway carefully. She turns her head around to look at Brand.

"We have the same DNA, the same father." He smiles at her and points to his dimples. "Do you have these?"

"Lots of people have dimples." She turns away from him. "Get ready. There are several guards outside."

"No problem. Stand aside. I've got this."

"Don't be arrogant, Brand. You won't be able to repeat once we get outside. So don't go getting yourself into trouble. Here, put this on." She hands him the extra Pulse Emitter.

"Ah, sweet. Thanks. Me, get into trouble? I don't know what you're talking about. Where I come from, I'm a pretty good fighter. Everyone knows to steer clear of me."

We watch them exit the building by way of the outside surveillance cameras. Deus Ex has shed her lab coat and almost blends into the background. Brand, on the other hand, is wearing light-colored scrubs and some kind of slippers on his feet.

The first guard catches sight of them, pulls his gun, and yells out, "Freeze! Stop right there!"

Deus Ex whips out a knife and throws it at the guard so swiftly I almost don't see the movement. The knife pierces the middle of his chest and he drops instantly. The other guard arrives and tries to subdue Brand. The guard doesn't pull his gun. Instead, he acts as if he has been ordered not to shoot. He lands a few good punches on Brand, knocking the wind out of him. Brand's attempt to take down the guard by landing one of his trademark groin kicks fails miserably.

A third guard arrives and begins to fight with Deus Ex. She's able to kick and disable him quickly with a martial-arts-style attack. As soon as the guard is down, she moves to help Brand, who's getting the stuffing kicked out of him. With one precision punch, she knocks out the guard, freeing Brand from further assault. She helps Brand up from the ground and begins yelling at him. "What the fig was that?" She drags him toward the car. "I thought you said you were a good fighter. Did you even land a single punch?"

I can't tell if Brand has caught his breath yet or not. He looks humiliated, but it's clear he knows there's no time to waste. He yanks his arm free from her grasp and hobbles on his own to the passenger side of the car. She has already started the vehicle and backs up before he closes his door.

Deus Ex still has her headband on with the camera and microphone, so we can hear their conversation.

"Who are you working with?" Brand asks.

"Your friends."

"Calli? You mean Calli? Of course you mean Calli. You have her Pulse Emitters."

"Yeah, and some others."

"Where are they?"

"Nearby."

"What's your name?"

"Deus Ex."

"What? That's not a name. What's your real name?"

"That is my name."

"Well, it's a stupid name."

Their conversation pauses. The headband cam only shows the road directly in front of them. We watch on the different monitors as they pass each surveillance camera as they near our headquarters.

Amenemhet clears his throat to bring our attention to the military compound on the other computer monitor. Freedom has arrived, along with many other vehicles. The scramble is underway.

"Amenemhet, can you zoom in on Freedom's face?" I ask.

He maneuvers the mouse and arrow keys and quickly pulls Freedom's face into tighter view. I read his lips. "Set up a ten-mile perimeter ASAP." The soldier he spoke to has his back to me so I can't tell what he says in return. Freedom responds with, "I don't care what the standard perimeters are. I want a five-, ten-, and twenty-mile perimeter! Now!"

I repeat the words out loud that Freedom said so everyone can hear.

Maetha says, "We have to go now or we won't get far."

"Can't we wait for Brand?" I ask.

"He's here now." Chris has the curtain pulled back slightly.

Chapter 9 –
The Things We Don't Know We Said

I run outside to the car and hold the door while Brand climbs out. His beating from the guards has left him sore. He grabs onto my arm for support. I guess I expected him to be a little more excited to see me. Instead, he says, "Why do I lose my powers with you, Calli?"

"I have some of the black obsidian on my body . . . remember, from the pocket watch?"

Chris comes to my side to take over helping Brand walk. Chris says, "You sure took a beating, didn't you?"

Brand turns his head to me and asks, "Think you could use some of your healing power on me? I could really use some about now."

"Sorry, Brand. I'm trying to stay invisible to Freedom."

Brand curses as Chris helps him up the stairs.

Deus Ex is out of the car and already inside, handing over the documents and the loaded flash drive she stole. I hear her say as we walk through the doorway, "This is bad, Maetha. I won't allow this to happen."

"Deus," Maetha says, "I'll have to look over the documents before I'll even know what you're talking about."

"I already looked them over as I downloaded them. The project they're working on puts us all in danger. You thought the obsidian was bad. The vest they're making is going to kill us all. That's the goal. Eliminate all people with powers!"

Maetha looks beyond Deus and says, "We don't have

time to deal with this right now. Our location will be discovered very soon. Take only what's necessary. Everyone leave! Now! Calli, Chris, and Brand will travel together. Calli, keep the small stone open. Brand, repeat when necessary. It may be touch and go for a little while. Again, Brand, repeat as necessary. Chris, take care of her."

"Where are *you* going, Maetha?" I ask.

Deus Ex cuts in with a confused look on her face. "How do you know we're about to be discovered?"

Maetha answers me first. "Somewhere safe, but don't worry. I've asked several Bearers to monitor you." Before I can question, she turns to Deus Ex. I think Maetha's going to admit she can see the future, but instead she points to the video screens and says, "Look."

Amenemhet's voice booms, "Out. Everybody out!"

I take one last look at Maetha, who tosses me a small plastic bag of Pulse Emitters, before I hustle out the door with Chris and Brand. Chris helps Brand get into the back seat of one of the vehicles we arrived in, while I jump into the passenger side in front. Chris climbs in behind the wheel and rips out of the driveway.

"Calli," —Chris points to the GPS device— "turn that on and find out where we are."

I do as he says and wait for the screen to show the map.

Brand says, "Calli, there's a fork in the road two minutes ahead. I think we'll be turning left."

I scroll with my finger, knowing he repeated to give me that information. I find the intersection. He's correct, of course. The road will take us to the main highway, and then on toward Denver.

Chris says, "Where did Maetha want us to go?"

"She didn't say," I answer. "We're just trying to keep from getting captured." I look over my shoulder at Brand

and say, "So far, that won't happen within the next two minutes."

Brand sits forward, sticking his head between the seats, and points to the GPS. "There, Calli. See that little road to the right? We need to turn on *that* one. It's a logging road."

"What about the T in the road?" Chris asks.

"It's no good," Brand says.

We round a corner and to the right is a dirt road that shoots off through the trees. Chris slams on the brakes and swerves onto the road. The washboard surface forces us to slow down dramatically, frustrating Chris. He says, "Where does this road even go?"

I scroll ahead on the map and find that the road eventually dead-ends, with no connecting roads. I look at Brand with concern. "Are we good here?"

"So far."

Chris glances over at the GPS. "What? The road ends? What the hell, Brand?"

I ask Brand, "Did the military catch us?"

"No, your friend Beth did . . . and coming up on our tail was the military. This is our only option. Hopefully the dust will settle before they drive past and they won't follow. The darkness will help us hide."

Chris is getting more and more frustrated. "You mean you don't know yet if this will be good?" Suddenly, and for no apparent reason whatsoever, Chris swerves the wheel to the right, almost driving completely off the road. We narrowly miss hitting a tree head-on before he yanks the wheel back to the left to correct his unexplainable actions. He exclaims, "Whoa! What just happened?"

"I repeated with you so you can see that *I DON'T KNOW* what's going to happen yet!"

Ah, now Chris's driving makes sense. Brand must have

repeated with Chris.

"I don't want to be caught either, dude," Brand says.

The road becomes rougher with deep ruts. Chris has to straddle them with the wheels to avoid bottoming out and high-centering the car. A small animal scampers out of the way when our headlights reflect in its eyes. I think it's a rock chuck. We approach a metal gate secured with a padlock. Chris begins to slow down.

Without warning, Brand yells, "No, ram it open!"

Chris slams his foot down on the gas pedal and tenses his body in anticipation of the impact. I also brace myself. Surprisingly, the gate's chain breaks rather easily with the force of the car, slamming the gate wide open. The gate's momentum bounces it back to the closed position after we blast through. We all breathe a sigh of relief as we continue traveling up the road.

"Sorry for yelling," Brand says. "It's just that I was so frustrated with the lock on the chain. I tried using the crowbar in the trunk to pry it open, and it slipped and knocked me in the head." He rubs his forehead at the memory of the pain.

We come to a stop in a large area that had been cut clear of trees. This is the end of the road. Our headlights illuminate naked stumps and torn-up ground in front of us. The full moon overhead casts a dim glow on everything. The Shadow Demons begin to cluster near our vehicle.

"What now?" Chris asks.

Brand answers, "We have to wait and see."

"Really?" Chris exclaims. "We're sitting ducks!"

Brand says, "Well, only if someone decided to take the road, which we don't know yet if anyone did."

I jump in and say, "Calm down, you two. Brand, what happened while you were held captive? Did you learn anything?"

"Did I learn anything?" He laughs and sits back in his seat. "Yeah, I learned that losing my powers sucks! I learned that his daddy," Brand points to Chris, "is working with the guy I tackled when the diamond necklaces killed that kid. The same guy who offered me a bodyguard job. General Harding called him Agent Alpha. Oh yeah, and I learned that you already knew him, Calli. I just want to know what the crap is going on! Who's on whose side here?"

Interesting that Brand is now accusing me of the same thing I accused Chris of, that I knew Freedom and didn't tell Brand. I answer him, trying to pick through what I know and what he doesn't. "Agent Alpha is like Maetha . . . only he's turned against nature."

"So he's an Unaltered? That would explain how he could pick the diamond out of the dead kid."

Chris says, "He's a Diamond Bearer, like Maetha."

"A what?"

"He has a diamond in his heart, like Maetha."

"Like Calli?" Brand asks as he tries to sort through the information.

"I only have a piece, Brand."

"I know. I saw it during one of the repeats when you were killed and your heart was pulled out."

Chris and I both turn our heads to look at Brand.

"Yeah, on one of the failed attempts that day I watched Agent Alpha rip your heart out and remove the shard. Why do you think I began pulling you along with me on the repeats? The ironic thing was that Agent Alpha ordered the guard to keep me alive, so I was never shot like everyone else, well, except for Calli. Mr. 'AA' wanted to keep me alive . . . and yet, it was because of his order that I was able to tackle him and close his watch and help you guys escape." Brand pauses for a moment and then says,

"Oh yeah, he went on and on about Maetha's 'Blue Diamond power.'"

"Agent Alpha, or Freedom, as we call him . . . " I pause as an idea forms. "Brand, repeat and I'll tell you more, but take me with you so I know what I've already told you."

"Good idea, Calli, but I can't pull you with me. You have that power-canceling rock on you."

I pull out the pouch and remove the watch and diamond. Just before I close the watch, I say, "Freedom will probably show up."

"Yes, and then he'll disappear when I repeat you back to this point."

I snap the watch shut, much to Chris's dismay. My powers flood into my body. I expect the world to spin as Brand repeats with me. Instead Brand says, "What kind of power does the Blue Diamond hold?"

"Invisibility and mind control. Those are the only two powers I know of."

"Yeah, well, Agent—er, Freedom definitely wants that power. So what else can Maetha do? And how many others are there like her?"

Freedom appears outside the car, standing in front of the Demons. He turns a full circle, looking for any identifying landmarks or signs to get an idea where we are. Alena, Duncan, Ruth, Chuang, and Fabian appear in various places around the car as well. This must be what Maetha meant when she said others would be monitoring my diamond. My chest begins to hurt, and I can't catch my breath. It's clear Freedom is accessing the power of the diamond. Then my surroundings begin spinning around as Brand repeats back to where I closed the watch.

We repeat the scenario many times over, each session lasting only about thirty seconds. That's all the time it takes for Freedom to mentally seize the shard within my heart, causing pain. I tell Brand about all the many aspects of the Diamond Bearers, the history of the diamond, the duties of the Bearers, and emphasize that the task in front of us is to find a way to kill Freedom. I tell him about our trip to Uncle Don, how being close to Chris causes my heart to bleed, how holding Freedom's rightful stone causes a conflict with other Diamond Bearers when they tried to heal me, and how we had to first obtain our own collection of obsidian, and then travel to Alaska to learn how to offset the effects of the obsidian. I explain how Deus Ex fits into everything and that Maetha doesn't want Deus to know about the Diamond Bearers, that Deus is only aware that some people have multiple powers.

It feels like an hour has passed thirty seconds at a time. My stomach feels uneasy from all the spinning and whirling, and poor Chris doesn't have a clue what we have been doing. He has been joining in on our many conversations, adding tidbits of information that I seem to be forgetting to mention, but whenever we repeat, he has no recollection of our conversation. The last question asked, which ends up being the one Chris will remember, is about Beth and why she's following us.

Chris answers, "She thinks Calli stole the Healers' amulet and possibly those of the other amulet wearers, then murdered them and Justin."

"Can't you just tell her otherwise?" Brand asks.

"I already tried. She insists on taking Calli to the council. I don't even know what she's talking about. What council?"

Brand takes a sharp intake of breath. "Uh oh. I know what she's talking about. It's a trap. Freedom talked about it as a way to capture Maetha so he can get his hands on her Blue Diamond."

Chris asks, "How do you know about Maetha's Blue Diamond?"

It's so easy to forget the fact that Chris isn't privy to all of the information Brand and I have discussed, even though he's been present for the whole conversation. I want to explain to him what just happened, but Brand interrupts us.

"Beth is two minutes away. As far as I can tell, it's just her group, and not the military. Personally, I think you should just explain everything to her, Calli."

"What?" Chris exclaims in frustration.

"Well, we don't really have any other options now, do we?" Brand answers. He opens the back door and grunts in pain as he climbs out of the car in anticipation of Beth's arrival. The Shadow Demons glide out of the way, confused over his scent, accompanied by the sound of my heartbeat emanating from his Pulse Emitter.

I look over at Chris and say, "It's true. We don't have any other options. It's worth a shot. She will certainly be a better ally than an enemy."

"Okay, but I think you should hide and let us try to convince her first. Brand and I both saw what happened to Justin, so two testimonies should be better than one. Go over there behind those bushes." He points to an area near the tree line, not far away.

I nod and carefully pick my way around the sliced stumps and uneven ground to the bushes and crouch down. Yes, two witnesses would be better than one, but before rescuing Brand, Maetha and Chris tried to convince Beth that I am innocent, and that didn't work.

I peek up through the thick foliage and see Chris standing in front of the car with the headlights shining on him. He looks in my direction, raises his hand, and with his first and middle fingers points to his eyes and then to me.

139

Then he mouths, *I can see you.* I sit all the way down and wait for Beth to arrive. I won't be reading any lips this time.

Just my luck, I have sat in an ant hill. Twinges of stinging pain began cropping up all over my body. The little critters are fast, making it all the way up to my neck in short order. Soon I am slapping and scratching my whole body so much that I don't even notice when Beth's car arrives until I hear Beth yelling at Chris.

"I don't believe you!" she shouts. "Hand her over!"

A sharp sting on the top of my head makes me scratch it quickly and tip my head over, fluffing my hair with my fingers to get the menace out. When I flip my hair back, I find a young man standing in front of me, his face illuminated by the vehicles' headlights. I can tell right away he's a Hunter because of his large nose. Another ant bites my ankle, causing me to slap myself. The Hunter takes my arm at the elbow and then quickly releases me and steps back.

"I know, I know, you don't like losing your power when you touch me," I say as I slap my body.

He ushers me out to the group.

Chris looks over in my direction and lets out an exasperated huff of air. I continue to slap myself in odd places, which probably looks like I am having a fit or something, but damn, those ants are kicking my butt.

Brand says directly to me, "Should I repeat so you don't get caught, Calli? Maybe you can hide behind a different bush this time so you don't give away your position."

"Is she hearing this?" I ask.

"Not so far."

Beth's head bobs back and forth between Brand and me as we speak. "I can hear you guys, you know. Calli will come with us now so the council can determine her involvement."

I notice right away that Beth and her team are wearing something similar to my Pulse Emitters. These units are bigger and bulkier, but they still allow them to be out in the dark without the fear of being torn to shreds. This confirms that Freedom was behind the stealing of Brand's original Pulse Emitter. If Beth is working for the "council" that Freedom runs, he must have given the devices to her.

Brand says to Beth, "Your 'council' is just a place where the government will seize Calli and the diamond."

"What diamond?" Beth asks. The three individuals standing behind Beth peer over her shoulder in curiosity. Two male Runners, and a female whose power isn't obvious to me since I don't have any diamond powers, shift nervously on their feet.

I say to Brand, "No, don't repeat yet. I'm going to show her the diamond." I ask Beth for permission to open my pocket, and she nods okay. I unzip my pocket and pull out the leather pouch, releasing the ties that hold it closed. I slide the opened watch and diamond out and remove the elastic band that holds the stone in place inside the watch. The companions behind Beth gasp in awe, and Beth's eyes grow round.

I hold the diamond up and say, "This is the same diamond I carried on the delivery to the Death Clan, Beth. When it exploded, a piece entered my heart, where it remains even now. That's why I retained powers. I just didn't tell you the reason why."

Chris says as he runs a shaky hand through his hair, "Oh, so *Beth knew* you had powers?"

I try to ignore him, but I know he's incredibly frustrated. "Maetha made amulets out of the pieces of this stone, and Justin thought that if he rounded up the amulets he could reassemble the diamond and absorb the powers just like the Death Clan was trying to do. He kidnapped the clans' leaders, with the exception of the Healers', Andrew Stuart. Brand and I were actually there visiting Andrew when Justin arrived to kidnap him. Andrew gave me his amulet to try to use it to foresee the future."

Brand interrupts. "It's true, Beth. I witnessed it."

I continue. "I ran with the amulet, because if I didn't, those people would have been murdered right then by Justin."

Beth, obviously frustrated, says, "Calli, look, my job is to bring you in, not to decide whether you're innocent or not. If that hunk of rock is really all the diamond shards stuck together, the council can decide what to do. Now, come on." She waves her hand in the direction of her car.

My patience runs thin. "Beth, we don't have time to screw around here! Watch this." I close the watch and feel my powers rush into my body. First off, I heal my burning, stinging ant bites.

"What exactly am I supposed to be looking for, Calli?" Beth asks.

"Keep watching. I'll bet your council leader appears in a moment." I continue healing all the ailments inside my body, sending a surge of white blood cells to my lower right abdomen where I detect infection that wasn't there before.

"Calli, this is a bad idea," Chris says, pulling my attention away from healing my body.

Like clockwork, Freedom appears next to me. Audible sounds of the others' shock are heard. Beth addresses him personally, except she calls him General Sabo. A few other Diamond Bearers appear too: Duncan, Merlin, Avani, Alena, and Aernoud. Duncan asks me mind-to-mind what is going on, but I don't respond.

"Well, Calli," Freedom says with a smirk, "you just can't seem to keep that watch open."

"Oh, I missed you, that's all, *General Sabo*." My emphasis on his additional fake name raises his eyebrow.

Beth shouts, "What's going on?"

I look over at Brand. "Repeat with Beth, Brand. Do it over and over until you can convince her that Freedom is the bad guy here."

"Got it, but first I'll repeat with you so you'll know what we're doing."

I understand him all too well. I know that if he doesn't repeat with me, I won't know what or why he's doing what he's doing. He repeats the stretch of time leading up to the point where I am about to shut the watch. Just as I am about to snap it shut, he orders me rather abruptly to stop. It all happens that quickly. Literally in just a couple blinks of the eye. Beth now has a whole different understanding painted on her face.

Brand says in an exhausted tone, "She understands now, Calli."

I look at Beth, and she bows her head in respect, making me wonder how many times Brand had to repeat to get her to accept the situation. Chris is beside himself. Beth's team stands slack-jawed at her defeated stance. Beth motions for the Hunter to come over to her. He does as ordered, causing the other members of her team to verbally object to Beth's giving in.

Beth says to us, "Give me a few minutes with my team."

Beth and the others walk over to their car and out of earshot. An ant bites my forearm. I slap it, forgetting I'd only healed the irritations in the alternate future when I had closed the watch. My whole body resumes itching and stinging, as I recall the fact I'd become the ant pile's dinner.

I jump up and down and brush my arms wildly in a fit of freaked-out craziness.

Brand eyes me peculiarly. "Something wrong, Calli?"

"Ouch! Dang it!" I exclaim as I scratch at my scalp, behind my knees, under my armpits, and on the back of my neck. I grab my lucky necklace and clutch the golden topaz, feeling the healing power flood my body, relieving my miniscule but plentiful irritations. I feel the location of each individual ant—at least there aren't that many remaining on my body—and I am able to pick them off individually. I decide not to use the topaz to heal the infection in my stomach. I'll deal with that later.

Chris comes over by me and says, "What do you think?"

"I think she'll join us, or at least stop chasing us."

Chris points to the girl with the blonde hair. "I know her. Her name is Anika Evanston. She's a Healer. We should recruit her to travel with us to charge your extra topaz."

Brand interrupts us. "She could do that?"

"Yeah, she only needs to wear the topaz against her skin and mentally charge it," I answer.

"What if I wore a topaz? Would it charge up with repeating power?"

"When we find another topaz, you can give it a try, Brand. For now, I better keep mine to use as a healing stone. How many times did you have to repeat with Beth until she understood?"

"Five times. Once Freedom finally admitted he tricked Justin into rounding up the amulets, Beth saw the light."

Chris listens intently, trying to pick through our conversation. "So, you repeated with her and she saw Freedom? Did you close the watch, Calli?"

"Yes, but because Brand is able to repeat back to

before Freedom appeared, Freedom won't ever know he outed himself to Beth."

Chris shakes his head and rubs his temples. "Man, that's crazy. I bet Beth was freaked out the first time you took her with you. I know I was."

"Me too," I add.

Chapter 10 –
Cat Fights and Visions Realized

We decide to stay put till morning. If for some reason we have to be out in the forest, like if the car breaks down or if the military catches up with us, we don't want to risk having the Pulse Emitters give out, exposing everyone to death. We climb in the car and wait. Beth and Anika join us, and the three of us sit in the back seat, while Brand and Chris sit up front.

The rest of Beth's team stays in their vehicle till morning as well.

I catch Beth up on the many names General Sabo uses but that we're using the name Freedom to refer to him.

Around 8:00 a.m. we wave goodbye to Beth's team and begin our drive to Denver. Brand and I have switched places in the car. He can't help but beam ear to ear, having two beautiful girls on either side of him. Every time I look back at him, I have to roll my eyes.

Once we make it back to the main highway, we come across a roadblock.

"Uh oh," Chris says. "What do we do now?"

Brand stops flirting with Anika for a moment and says, "No worries, Chris. It's fine."

I look out the window and see Amenemhet conducting the vehicle searches. He's dressed in his camouflage, with a rifle slung over his shoulder and certainly fits the part. I have to wonder what happened to the actual guards who were posted at the checkpoint.

Our vehicle is next in line. Chris slowly rolls forward and comes to a stop at the barricade.

Amenemhet leans down and says through the open window, "Folks, I'm gonna need you to drive fifteen miles ahead and pull over at Truckers' Trough and proceed to room nineteen. Move along." He stands and waves his arm in a formal military fashion, while a second soldier moves the barricade out of our way.

I muse, "Truckers' Trough, room nineteen. Sounds legit."

"Man, he didn't miss a beat, did he?" Chris chuckles. "That guy is cool!"

By the time we pull into the busy mini-plaza and locate the small motel, we are nearly out of gas. We park near the door with the black number nineteen stenciled on it and cautiously get out of the vehicle, keeping an eye open for anything suspicious.

I knock on the door, and Maetha opens it. She appears surprised to see Beth has joined us. I look in and see Neema sitting in front of a laptop at a table on the other side of the room, but there's no sign of Deus Ex or Mary. Honestly, I am a little worried about how Beth will interact with Deus . . . and the brief, concerned look in Maetha's eye when she looks at Beth makes me think she having similar thoughts.

"Come in, come in," Maetha says in a welcoming tone that reminds me of how my grandma used to greet us when we'd go visit her. She opens the door all the way and gestures into the room with her arm. "The others are picking up some food for us. Beth, good to see you." Maetha pats Beth on the shoulder and then turns to Anika. "I haven't had the pleasure."

Beth makes the introduction. "Maetha, this is Anika Evanston. She's a Healer."

Maetha's eyes travel to Anika's neck. She obviously recognizes my necklace and can see that Anika is charging it for me. "Nice to meet you, Anika." Maetha closes the door and locks it, then turns to face us and assumes her normal serious demeanor. "Find a seat," she says, motioning to all of us as she takes a seat, too. "Tell me Beth, what happened to change your mind?"

Ah, yes, that's the Maetha I know and love. Straight to the point.

Beth is slightly caught off guard, but she regains her composure and explains how Brand repeated with her so she could see what happened when I closed the watch. She said that after witnessing Freedom explain how he used Justin to round up the diamond amulets, she was convinced of Chris's and my innocence. She tells Maetha that she's, however, concerned that Freedom is working with the government and wonders what kind of implications that will have for the clans in general.

Maetha doesn't have an answer for her. Instead, she removes her obsidian piece from her pocket and sets it on the table next to her. Then she turns to Brand and asks him an odd question. "Well, with that in mind, Brand, do you think it would be effective against Freedom?"

"Yes." Brand's one-word answer to Maetha's strange question leads me to believe they have just completed an extensive Q&A without taking up much time. But what does she mean? What would be effective?

Maetha picks up her obsidian and replaces it in her pocket.

Someone raps on the door, and Maetha bolts up from her position. She is extremely jumpy, but then again it must be nerve-wracking for her to be powerless, which I know is the case. Maetha peeks through the small hole and then unlocks the door for Mary and Deus Ex. They enter, carrying multiple paper grocery bags full of food which they dump on the bed. An assortment of fruits, vegetables, nuts and juice containers tumble out and Deus begins tossing odd items at everyone, including Beth and Anika.

I catch a package of roasted peanuts flying my direction. As soon as I tear open the plastic, the salty aroma hits my nose and turns my stomach. I set the package down and breathe deeply to try to avoid throwing up.

"Who are you?" Deus asks Beth rather rudely as she tosses an apple to her.

"I could ask you the same thing." Beth's hackles are raised in a how-dare-you-take-that-tone-with-me kind of way.

Maetha butts in and says, "She's on our side, Deus. She's a Runner, and her name is Beth Hammond. This is Anika Evanston, a Healer."

"No one is on my side," Deus says with an icy tone that makes me wonder if she's actually on our side at all.

Mary jumps into the middle of the crackling energy. "Listen, Deus, the information you recovered affects all of us. We'll need to work as a team if we want to accomplish anything here. This is not a one-man show." Mary is interrupted by another knock at the door.

Maetha looks through the peep hole and identifies Amenemhet, then opens the door. He enters the room and tosses a small object to Maetha, saying, "That was handy, but it's empty now. I rather liked that ability."

Maetha opens her hand, revealing the small golden-orange stone . . . a topaz. Neema comes over to her side with a large band-aid and helps Maetha attach the stone to her chest.

Amenemhet swivels his head in our direction. "Ah, everyone has arrived in one piece. Good."

I like his dominating presence, how he calms everyone

and asserts control over the estrogen-packed "king of the hill" fight between Deus Ex and Beth. I'm not one to feel that it takes a man to bring order to every situation, but in this case it certainly does. Plus, his size and deep voice are a bit on the intimidating side. Not that Chris or Brand are not men, they are. They just don't have the same effect on Deus.

I walk over to Amenemhet and Maetha and quietly ask, "How did you guys get around the roadblocks?"

Maetha points to the freshly attached stone on her chest. "Amenemhet was able to use the mind-control power to help us get past the guards. I had him wait for your vehicle, figuring you'd head this way instead of west. I knew you'd need a little extra help getting past the blockade." She pauses and accepts a bottle of pomegranate juice and a pear from Mary, then addresses everyone. "Eat up while Neema updates us on the recovered data."

Before Neema can speak, Deus Ex says in an overly confident manner, "I'm better qualified to deliver this report. She won't be able to comprehend in a hundred years what I absorbed in the short amount of time I was inside the compound."

Chris huffs in disgust. I walk back over by him and sit on the edge of the mattress.

"Deus, just sit down and zip it," Brand says. "Let the Diamond Bearers do their job."

"Don't tell me what to do! I saved your life! And those aren't diamonds strapped to their chests, they're topaz crystals. Idiot."

Deus Ex and Brand stand and face each other. They just glare at each other in silence with their shoulders tensed as if they are about to launch into battle. I wait for the showdown, but it doesn't happen. They just stare at each other, frozen in place. Then it hits me . . . they are *both* repeating. Brand told me about his time with Maetha when he met other Repeaters, and I guess that's what gives it away.

I pull out the pouch and loosen the drawstring, allowing the watch and diamond to slide out into my hand. The fact that I am able to do this without either of them repeating me back is a mystery. I remove the band that keeps the diamond inside the small obsidian side and slip the diamond back into my pocket, but I don't close the watch. Instead, I open the large-stone side, blocking at least Brand's repeating abilities. I'm not sure if Deus has a fully charged topaz or not. Then the show begins.

Brand's tensed shoulders release as he issues his verbal attack, consistent with a typical brother-sister fight. "You think you're God, but you're not!"

"Shut up, Brand! At least I use my power to gain knowledge instead of just satisfying my hormonal urges!"

"You're just a know-it-all egotistical loser."

"At least I know that I know it all. You don't know sh—!" Deus stops abruptly and begins spinning in a slow circle, searching the room. Her eyes settle on me and my hands. "You better put that away, Calli," she threatens.

Her topaz must be drained, I presume.

Brand steps between us. "Don't talk to her like that!"

Neema steps between Brand and me, facing Deus Ex, and says, "She'll put it away if you'll sit down and be quiet. I'll present what I learned from the material, and then you can fill in any blanks I miss."

Deus narrows her eyes and says, "How about *you* fill in the blanks?"

I glance around the room to see what the others think of this battle of wills. Maetha sits with a disconcerted expression and closed eyes. Amenemhet has his head in his hands, slowly shaking it back and forth. Chris looks at me with round eyes filled with mild humor that seems to say, "Oh boy." Beth and Anika stare slack jawed, and Mary is on the edge of her seat, ready to launch into action if needed.

Neema quiets her voice in an effort to help Deus Ex grasp the severity of the situation. "Deus, you don't like the feeling of having your power taken away any more than I do. If you can't suppress your need to boss everybody around, you'll lose your power for good once they complete the vests and weapons. Then you'll die, just like the rest of us. Like it or not, we have to work together to stop this from happening. If you can't do that, you need to leave so we can take care of business. You're hampering our progress."

Deus Ex doesn't reply for a couple of seconds. Her eyes travel about the room as she stares intently at each of us. I really wish I could read her mind . . . what is she thinking? Her piercing stare stops at me, and she says while pointing to the watch, "Put that away and I'll cooperate."

Brand asks, "Why? So you can control the conversation? I think she should keep it out."

Deus glares at him. "You repeat fifty times more than I do, Brand."

"Yeah, and yet you're the one who wants her to put it away, not me."

Neema looks at me and says, "Calli, it would be better if you would leave the small side open, but close the large side of the watch for now. Keep it at the ready in case things get out of hand again." Her last comment is directed at Deus Ex.

I snap the watch shut. Deus sits down and throws a look in Neema's direction that means, "Well, go on then."

Neema begins. "Okay. The intel gathered by Deus Ex reveals there's some disturbing research being conducted by General Harding's soldiers and propagated by Freedom. Their objective is to develop a hybrid warrior, one who is outfitted with a protective vest, not unlike a bullet-proof vest, that has obsidian and quartz sewn in or attached to the fabric. Obsidian is the primary threat, but the variety of quartz being used is claimed to be able to be charged with healing power, according to the files."

Mary's eyes widen. "If the soldiers can access the healing power, and disable people with powers using the obsidian, then they would be nearly impossible to detect or kill."

Maetha interjects, "We haven't had any success with quartz. What kind of quartz?"

"I don't know. The report didn't say." Neema looks at Deus Ex to see if she wants to add anything. Deus Ex's haughty expression remains unchanged, so Neema continues. "The report provides a detailed list of gemstones and the locations where they are found, along with the powers they are believed to hold. We also have information about the expeditions of Harding's task force to those locations, their encounters with locals, and the histories associated with the stones. One of the stones is red spinel from Afghanistan." Neema directs that last comment to Maetha, who narrows her eyes in brooding contemplation.

"Interestingly enough," Neema continues, "the military once conducted an investigation into this project, but the funding was cut in the late 1990s. That's when Harding took over the files and expanded the operation with Freedom's help. Oh, and Deus Ex discovered a report about Freedom's expedition to Alaska to search for the rare golden topaz that's believed to act as a battery, storing powers." Neema directs her attention to Deus. "Now, Deus, would you like to tell us why you're listed on the report as being present? Didn't Freedom hint at that when we were in Alaska?"

Deus straightens her shoulders and juts her chin forward. "I was there. I knew what Freedom was looking for, and I knew where to find it. At the last second, I decided to withhold the information from him because I saw the potential for him to harm me. So I repeated and led him in a different direction that turned out to be a dead end. He deduced that the stories about the topaz were fables, and he gave up. I learned more about the topaz and acquired my own after we got back from Alaska." She touches her own gemstone necklace.

"Do you have a red spinel on that necklace?" Maetha asks.

"Not yet, but I will. It's the stone of immortality. That's why Freedom wants one, but not just any red spinel. He wants a particular kind."

Maetha angles her head and lowers her voice. "What do you mean?"

"His red spinel must come from a certain person, an Immortal."

I watch Mary, Amenemhet, Neema, and Maetha exchange anxious looks. I know enough to guess what they are concerned about: Freedom wants to find Crimson. He must believe she has a Red Spinel inside her the same way each of us has a diamond inside us. I don't know if it's true, but I make a knee-jerk decision and say to Deus with a slight chuckle, "No one is immortal."

"That's what the general told him, too," Deus Ex says, "but Freedom is determined to find this person."

Mary asks Neema, "Are there any other stones or crystals the government is interested in that we don't already know about?"

"No. And if Deus Ex was successful in keeping

Freedom from learning about the rare topaz, it's possible we have the advantage."

"He doesn't know," Deus Ex says confidently.

Mary says to Deus Ex, "Are there any other stones or crystals that you know about that the government or Freedom is unaware of?"

"Nothing that would interest you."

Chris bolts to his feet, obviously unable to control his temper any longer. "That's not an answer! The golden topaz was around your neck while we were in Alaska, and you could have saved us time if you had volunteered that info."

"But then you wouldn't have had all that fun with Kikee, Chris," Deus says in her super-sweet, condescending voice.

I reach out and catch him by the wrist as he vaults himself in her direction. I pull him back toward me. Maetha is in the process of reprimanding Deus Ex, but I can't focus on what she's saying because of the pain in my heart. Why am I so affected by even the slightest touch from Chris? There isn't anything intimate about our contact, yet my diamond shifted all the same. His proximity is all it takes to bring me to the edge of death.

He watches me closely, aware of the pain I am experiencing.

I tune out the commotion between Deus Ex and Maetha.

Chris asks me in a soft, caring voice, "Calli, where's your other topaz?"

I choke out, "In my pocket, in the vial." I struggle to pull it out, my fingers shaking.

He takes over the task. He quickly opens the vial and dumps the stone into my hand. It's as if I am having a heart attack and he's administering my nitroglycerin pill. Once I hold the stone in my hand, he gently closes my fingers around it, leans in, and kisses me on the cheek. Then he moves away to a safer location.

The room grew deathly quiet as everyone watched our tender moment. As soon as my heart heals, I place the stone in the vial and twist the lid into place. Again, I choose not to waste any of the healing power on the problem in my abdomen. I shouldn't have wasted so much on the pesky ant bites last night. The topaz Anika is wearing may or may not be charging. She might not know how or be able to charge it. I can't take the risk of depleting the rest of my topaz on my stomach issue just yet.

Deus's voice cuts into the silence. "You're all so quick to accuse me of withholding vital information, but none of you will tell me why 'little Calli' is so fragile. What makes *her* so special?"

No one answers.

"And you wonder why I have an attitude," Deus Ex says with hostility.

"If you stay with us long enough," Maetha says, "you'll find out. If you continue with that chip on your shoulder, you won't. It's that simple."

Deus makes a strangled sound in the back of her throat, letting everyone know she's pissed off and frustrated.

Maetha turns her attention to me and says, "Calli, how powerful is that topaz?"

"Strong enough. Anika is charging my other one." I don't mention the stomach pain. I'll wait till we're through with the discussion.

"Good. Let's get back on topic. What about the obsidian weapons?" Maetha asks Neema.

"Well, apparently they're making bullets laced with

obsidian. If we were to get hit by one of those babies, it would be imperative to remove the bullet ASAP. Knowing how effective a small amount of obsidian is in canceling an individual's powers, it's easy to see the purpose behind these bullets. The government plans to swoop in and disable or even kill entire clans."

"How far along are they on developing them?" Amenemhet asks.

"Hard to tell," says Neema. "I don't know if the files we have are updated or not."

"We need more information," Maetha says. "Were there any other reports or computer files you weren't able to gather, Deus?"

"No, I got everything."

"If only we had an insider," Maetha says to herself. "Too bad Freedom knows Deus has turned against him."

Chris says, "Freedom doesn't know *I'm* traveling with your team, Maetha."

"What?" I exclaim. "No!" I know right away what he's thinking.

Maetha contemplates the idea. "He saw you in Miami, Chris."

"Yeah, and he tried to turn Calli against me by claiming I still work for him. We could build on that."

"He was present on the flight to D.C.," Maetha points out.

"I could tell him I left the group at that point."

Maetha sits pondering quietly for a moment before saying, "He didn't see you in Alaska, only Deus Ex. It might work, but he'll test your resolve. He'll give you a task to prove yourself."

"I can handle it. This way I can bleed information in your direction while misdirecting the others. Also, I might be able to get my father to understand that Freedom has his own agenda. Honestly, when it comes down to it, we're going to need a really big gun to blow his heart out of his chest. A gun like the ones the military have. We're going to need their help."

"A close-range shot with a hollow-point bullet would do the trick," Amenemhet says.

I can't process what Chris is saying. He's going to leave and return to his father . . . just like in the vision I saw in Miami. The group continues to discuss options and ideas of how to lure Freedom out into the open, allowing for a clean shot, but my mind is preoccupied with Chris. I glance over at him only to find him staring at me with a somber look on his face.

He mouths the words, *It's the only way, Calli. First we have to stop Freedom, then my father, before we can have a future together.*

I know he's right, but it doesn't help me feel any better.

Maetha stands and walks over to me and says, "Come with me." She looks at Chris and Brand and asks them to follow as well. The four of us leave the room and walk down the sidewalk to another room. Maetha knocks on the door, and I hear a slight rustling on the other side. Then the door opens slightly, revealing a single eyeball.

"It's all right. Let us in," Maetha says.

The door opens wide, but the person who opened the door hides behind it until we have all entered. I turn around to see a dark-haired young man close the door and turn to face us. He looks familiar in an odd sort of way. I feel as if I should know him.

"Calli, Chris," Maetha says, "I believe you know Jonas Fleming."

Jonas smiles a bright smile, and then I recognize the boy I knew from two-and-a-half years before. He has changed so much. He has grown taller and filled out. I want to rush over and hug him, but I know it could be dangerous because of the diamond.

"Calli, how are you?" he asks in a low, mature voice.

"Wow! Jonas, I'm good. You didn't die after all?"

He chuckles, "Well, I'm standing here alive and kicking." He turns his attention to Chris. "Hey, Chris."

I glance at Chris, who has his eyebrows scrunched together. He says, "I saw you leave the clearing after you turned down the opportunity to be healed, Jonas. I remember thinking, 'There goes the bravest boy around.' I'm happy to see you."

Jonas looks a bit embarrassed. He shyly replies, "Well, I didn't exactly turn down the offer completely." He looks beyond Chris to Brand and nods his head.

Brand says, "How's it going, Jonas?"

"Good. Never a dull moment with Maetha."

I look between Brand and Jonas, shocked as all get out. "Do you two know each other?"

"Yeah," Brand says. "While I was with Maetha, Jonas and I were roomies."

What?

Maetha writes something on a notepad while we converse back and forth. She says, "Brand, there's a change of clothing over in the black bag that might fit you, unless you prefer to keep the clothes you're wearing. Please watch over Calli, Brand." She turns to Chris and says, "Follow the instructions I left on the table." Then she looks me in the eyes and says, "Say your goodbyes." She escorts Jonas out of the room, leaving the three of us.

My stomach lurches at the thought of parting with Chris . . . again! Brand walks to the other side of the room to give us some privacy. Chris asks me in a serious tone, "Where's your topaz?"

159

I pull out the vial and look at him quizzically. He takes the vial and opens the lid but doesn't pour the stone into my hand. Instead, he sets the vial down on the nightstand between the beds, and then turns and faces me. I look up into his stormy blue eyes and see want and need.

"Calli," he says, almost in a whisper. "Close the pocket watch." My heart begins to race with anticipation as I snap the watch shut without question. My breath is taken away as my powers rush back into my body. He reaches up with both hands and gently slides his fingers along my jaw line and past my ears. He buries his fingers in my hair and pulls me to his mouth. I close my eyes and let him kiss me softly and gently. Tingles and sensations race through my body, settling in my heart, twisting and burning. A small gasp escapes from my mouth because of the pain, bringing my mind back to the present. His lips pull away from mine, leaving me feeling unfulfilled.

Freedom appears next to us and mutters something under his breath as he looks around the room, searching for information that will identify this location.

Just as I am about to heal my pained heart, Chris says in a slightly raised voice to Brand, "Now, Brand. And take her with you this time."

Before I can say anything, the ground spins wildly, and I find myself at the point where Chris asks where my topaz is. The memory of his kiss lingers on my lips as I hand him the vial and look up into his eyes. He grasps my face with his hands and looks down into my eyes and says, "Do you remember?"

I nod, with my lips parted.

He lets go of my face, places the vial in my hand, and walks away. He says over his shoulder as he takes the paper from Brand, "I'll be in contact with you. Check your email. I'll be easy to spot. Oh, and make sure you get some medicine for that fever. You're hot."

I'm what? Hot? I raise my hand to my face. I can't tell if I have a fever. My eyes burn when I blink, so maybe I do. I empty the topaz into my hand and clutch it while I heal my heart pain. I don't feel I should waste any of the power on a fever when I can take a couple ibuprofen instead. I place the nearly-drained topaz back inside the vial and close the lid.

Chris and Brand speak quietly, their backs to me, and then Chris pats Brand on the back and turns and heads toward the door. He throws a smile my way just before he leaves the room.

I wonder if I'll ever see him again. Sadness settles into my churning stomach. I slide the metal vial into my pocket.

Brand comes over and sits by me. "That was pretty cool, Calli. That guy is a fast learner. Resourceful too."

"Yeah," I say, recalling Chris's kiss, feeling heavyhearted about his departure.

"You should know he and I had a lengthy discussion about you just now concerning the instructions Maetha gave him."

"What does she want him to do? Did you look over the paper she left for him?"

"Yeah, I snooped. Her instructions are more about what she wants *me* to do. I'm to be your protector, Calli, to follow you wherever you go and never be more than a few paces away from you, so if the need calls for it, I can repeat and keep you safe. Chris was a bit threatened by the order, and he gave me the what-for, promising me all kinds of bodily harm if I let anything happen to you—or if I try anything with you."

"Ah, he understands how you could do that, and I wouldn't even know you had."

"Exactly. I reassured him I would take care of you and

keep you in one piece."

"What else did Maetha's orders say?"

"She told him to go to Montana first and have Clara Winter clear everyone out of the compound, and to have Clara spread the word to all clans that they should disperse and hide from the government. She also gave him detailed instructions on how to communicate through email when he gets any information from his father."

I stand and say, "I know you'll protect me, Brand." My stomach suddenly knots up in incredible pain. I hope I will feel better after using the restroom. I excuse myself and enter the small bathroom, trying not to show how much pain I'm in. After using the bathroom, I sit down on the floor with my back against the wall and my knees pulled up to my chest and wait. After five minutes of intense, knife-stabbing pain, I decide to pull out my golden topaz. The location of the pain concerns me. Chris said I have a fever, and yesterday I detected infection in the same area as my pain. This brings me to the conclusion that I might have appendicitis.

Brand knocks on the door. "Calli, are you okay?"

"Not really. My stomach hurts."

"Should I repeat?"

"No, it's been too long, and I don't think repeating will help. Go get Maetha." I hear him leave the room as I slide the topaz out of the vial and into my hand. I grasp it tightly and extract the power, willing my pain to subside. The healing power in the topaz isn't enough to heal much. In fact, if I had needed to heal my heart, I may not have been able.

Brand says through the door, "Calli, Maetha's here."

I reach up and open the door. She enters, holding the necklace Anika had been wearing. She hands it to me, and I press the topaz to my neck. I draw the small amount of power out of the topaz that hadn't had time to fully recharge. Again, the topaz depletes before I am healed. I hand the necklace back to Maetha, who promptly puts it on so she can charge it.

"Calli, this is not good," she says. "Brand has repeated with me several times to get to this point. First, we tried closing the watch so you could use your diamond's healing power, but Freedom bi-located right away and harnessed the diamond's power, preventing you from healing. I don't know how he does it. Second, we kept the watch open so the obsidian could continue to deactivate the diamond's power and we moved them into the other room. The idea was that I could use my healing on you, but your diamond shard activated once the obsidian was away, and again Freedom was able to bi-locate, only this time he was able to control your diamond and cause you more injury." Maetha rubs her temples. "We're just lucky to have Brand to help us along the way."

Brand stands in the doorway and chuckles. "Lucky is right. Lucky for you, Maetha. He killed you three times over."

"Maetha," I say, "I think I have appendicitis. If I had just one more topaz, I think I could completely heal it."

"That's the problem. We don't have another one charged with healing power. This is going to have to be taken care of by a regular physician, and yet I don't exactly know what to do."

I hear Amenemhet say, "Her father could do it." I didn't know he was standing within earshot.

I look at Maetha. "But he's in Ohio."

"Yes, and it's only a couple hours' flight." She gives instructions to Amenemhet. "Make the necessary calls. I want to be wheels-up in fifteen minutes."

"I guess this is the point where my parents find out

163

about my diamond, huh?"

"It would appear so, Calli. With my obsidian, I can't tell how this will turn out."

"Worst case scenario, Maetha, just use your mind-control and help my parents forget like you did with my classmates and teachers."

Maetha smiles at me and says, "That's not an option this time. For now, we'll just get you into an operating room and on the road to recovery."

I touch Maetha's hand and look into her eyes. "Maetha, it might be nature's will that I die. Have you thought about that?"

"It's not *my* will to fail here, Calli." She stands and helps me up from the floor. Her fingertips touch my bare skin, and she stops suddenly, placing her hand on my forehead. "How long have you had a fever?"

"I'm not sure. Maybe a day."

"All right, let's go," she says and moves me with a quickened pace.

Chapter 11 - Parental Consent

I sit in a reclined position in the silky-smooth leather seat of the airplane.

"Calli, I know I've said this before, but this has never happened in all my years as a Diamond Bearer. This journey we're on is full of firsts every time we turn around. The technological advancements that have occurred in the last 150 years have really been incredible when you compare that period with the thousands of years that came before. And for someone like me, who's been at the top of the hill for so long, to be knocked off and done in by a little black rock, well, it's really humbling. I now have to turn to old-fashioned traditional medicine to help you overcome your illness. I feel so powerless."

I smile. "I can relate to your frustrations. The short period of time when I had all my powers was just long enough for me to start taking them for granted. Being without them really does leave me feeling vulnerable."

"Well, we have to get this situation figured out soon, because you're not the only one being affected by natural bodily failures. You have to remember, some of us are several thousand-years old, Calli. We're normally in a continual state of healing, but now we're all susceptible to natural weaknesses and illnesses, just like you. Continuing to remain off Freedom's radar is taking a toll on our health."

Maetha gives me an ice pack for my head to help with my fever, then goes to deal with Brand and Anika. Brand is obviously using his charms on her. He can't seem to help himself. I chuckle and shake my head and close my eyes. I think Maetha would have rather left Anika in Denver, but she decided to bring her with us to Ohio so Anika could charge one of the topazes. Maetha hopes I'll heal faster after surgery if I have two fully-charged healing topaz stones.

Maetha's phone rings. I try to listen as she talks in a hushed voice, but she's too far away and I'm too weak and tired to care.

I drift asleep and dream of Chris kissing me in the motel room. The kiss feels so real, as does the feeling of his strong arms as he holds me close to his body. Tingles and shivers race up my spine. I awake in a panic, grasping for my topaz because of the pain in my chest. I'm not sure where I am, but then the airplane lurches again as it descends to the airport in Ohio.

An ambulance and a private vehicle wait on the tarmac. The paramedics help me onto the stretcher and Maetha insists that Brand accompany me. I know she wants him with me for the purpose of repeating, if necessary. The paramedics balk and try to convince her to have him ride in her vehicle, but she stands her ground. Brand climbs in and sits beside me with a big grin on his face. Anika remains behind on the plane with Rodger Rutherfield.

I worry about what the surgeons will say about the diamond in my heart. If they try to touch it, they could die. I don't want my father to be in danger.

At the hospital, after the initial examination, I am quickly prepped for surgery which requires undressing and slipping into a gown. I worry about being separated from the leather pouch and the pocket watch as does Maetha. She is able to convince the nurse to permit my leather pouch to be placed inside a sterile plastic bag so it can stay by my side throughout surgery. Brand is allowed to come with me to the point of the swinging doors beyond the yellow and black-striped lines across the floor.

My father hasn't arrived yet, but I am told he'll be there soon to attend the operation to remove my appendix. Just as I am wheeled into the operating room, my father enters and I can tell he's "scrubbed in." He has a stressed look on his face. The anesthesiologist begins to comment on my heart rhythm and its irregularity, and my father assures him it's normal for me. Very soon I feel myself giving in to the anesthesia. I awake what seems only a second later to serious pain in my lower right abdomen.

My mother sits near my bed in an uncomfortable-looking chair, looking more worried than I've ever seen her. Maetha's voice filters in from the hallway. She's speaking with my father about my surgery. He tells Maetha that everything went well, with no complications. My mother's chair squeaks as she shifts around. I look over at her, catching her eye. "Calli," she says, grasping my hand. "How do you feel?"

Her question is overheard, bringing my father and Maetha in from the hall. Brand also comes into view. He has been outside the door as well. I answer in a groggy voice, "I've been better."

"Do you know where you are?" she asks.

"Yes." I look over at Maetha, hoping to learn what she said to my parents while I'd been out of it.

"Everything went well in surgery, Calli," my father says. "Your appendix hadn't ruptured yet, and so it was able to be removed without complications. Your heart, on the other hand, gave us some trouble."

I glance at Maetha again, hoping she will intervene for two reasons: I don't know what to say about my heart, and I don't have the strength to say anything anyway. Maetha remains silent.

Brand comes to my rescue. "What kind of trouble?" he asks.

"Well, any ordinary patient with the same heart rhythm and irregularities that you have would not have been operated on in the first place. Technically, your heart shouldn't have made it through the surgery."

"Calli is full of unexplainable surprises, Dr. Courtnae," Brand says. He squeezes my ankle and smiles at me.

"Yes, I'm finding that out." My father eyes Maetha suspiciously.

The nurse enters the room to check my IV and stats and charts them down before leaving the room, closing the door behind her.

"Why don't we all sit down," Maetha suggests.

I close my eyes out of exhaustion and listen as chair legs scrape the linoleum. I hear my mother say in a hushed voice, "Calli needs her rest. Maybe we should have this conversation somewhere else."

"Charlotte," my father responds, "Calli will be just fine. This conversation must take place in privacy, and Calli should hear as much of it as possible."

"Calli's not in any condition to have a conversation about a life-long issue, Allen. We should discuss this down in the cafeteria while she rests."

Brand intervenes. "Maetha, what do you want her to know?"

I open my eyes and look at Maetha and then at my mother, who has confusion written all over her face. Maetha says, "Tell her everything, Brand."

Brand's gaze meets mine, and he smiles in a way that comforts me, letting me know he will make sure my mother understands my "condition" completely. He takes a deep breath and says, "Your daughter is very special. She has the ability to do many things that fall outside the range of normal."

"I've always known my daughter inherited my genetic makeup," my mother replies. "I just didn't realize it came with special powers."

"No, Dr. Courtnae. She wasn't born with these powers. She got them from the chunk of rock that's lodged inside her heart."

"From the accident in Montana?"

He nods his head. "Now Calli has people tracking her down because they want her rock."

"Oh dear. I guess I should have told you that two military men visited the house a few days ago, asking questions about the woman Calli was working with. They had a picture of Maetha, but I thought Calli was working with someone named Janice Johnson. The men insisted that Maetha and Janice are the same person, but I didn't believe them. That's why I didn't call Calli to let her know. Oh, one of them gave me a card . . . here, I have it in my purse." She digs inside her purse and pulls out a standard white business card and hands it to Maetha. Maetha looks at it and passes it to Brand.

Brand stares at the card. "I can assure you this man, Agent Alpha, is the same man who's after Calli. He's the only one who would know that Maetha and Janice are the same person."

My mother laughs and looks in Maetha's direction. "That's not true. Janice was of a different race altogether."

My father says to Maetha, "If this is true, why would you go to such an extreme to deceive us?"

169

Brand looks at me, worry lines creasing on his forehead, and then over to Maetha and says, "Freedom has been to Calli's house. I wish I could repeat with both of them at the same time, so they'd both remember what we've talked about. Oh well. I guess I'll do this twice. Good thing I don't get nauseous with repeating."

My mother suddenly puts her hand to her forehead and grabs onto my bed railing. She says, "Well, I always thought that was just a bedtime story my great-grand-mother told me. I still don't believe it."

My father angles his head to the side. "What are you talking about?"

Brand calmly responds, ignoring my father, "That story, Charlotte, including the part about the magic crystal being used as a bomb to kill the vampire-like people, is the same type of thing that happened to Calli. Her crystal exploded and killed all the Death Clan, and a piece of the crystal went inside of her and became lodged in her heart. She'll eventually have the rest of the stone inside of her also, like Maetha." Brand looks over at me and said, "Sounds like you have a fun family history."

My father's head bobs back and forth between my mother and Brand.

My mother asks, still holding her head, "Are we going to spin again?"

"No," Brand say, then turns to my father. "Your turn."

"My turn for what?" He stares at Brand for a second, then raises his hand to his forehead and shakes his head back and forth. "This will take some time to sink in. Does Charlotte know what you just told me?"

Brand says, "Mostly. You two can share notes. Just don't tell anyone else."

Maetha addresses my parents. "Do you have a safe

170

place you could go to for a few days until this problem is resolved?"

"But, I have clients," my mother begins to argue.

"Charlotte, we both need a vacation. Especially now that we've just had our perception of reality turned upside down. Your clients will still be there when we get back." My father turns to Maetha, "We have a cabin in Maine. We could go there."

"I'm not leaving Calli in her present condition!"

"Mom, I'll be fine."

My mother asks Maetha. "Why can't you just give the rest of the diamond to the military man so he'll leave her alone?"

Brand answers, "Because he won't stop until he has the whole diamond, and he'll kill Calli if we don't kill him first."

"Why does anyone need to be killed?"

"Mom," I say, "It's the only way he'll release his hold on my diamond."

"But you don't need to be part of hunting this man down, do you?"

Maetha answers this time. "He won't come out of hiding unless he thinks he can capture Calli. We have to resolve this, Charlotte. Calli needs to be able to use her diamond to heal herself, but she can't do that until the danger is removed. Her appendicitis could have been healed without surgery if she could have used her diamond. Go to Maine until this is resolved. Try to keep your heads down so the military doesn't know where you are. Tomorrow, after Calli has recovered enough to be able to travel, we'll fly back to Denver."

"May we have some time alone with Calli?" my mother asks.

"Brand has to stay with her, just in case a repeat is

necessary," Maetha says, then leaves the room.

Once the door clicks shut, my mother grasps my hand. "I'm overwhelmed, but happy you are on the road to recovery. Everything else will take a while to process."

My father nods his head.

"Thanks for not freaking out," I say.

My mom looks at my dad. "Oh, I freaked out plenty with the first repeat. I'm glad none of you remember it, but Brand will." She throws a glance in Brand's direction.

My father says, "I did as well, Charlotte. I'd love to study his mind sometime."

Brand says nothing. He only smiles.

My mother squeezes my hand. "Do you remember when I told you about the girl who felt like she'd foreseen the destruction of her Hawaiian town?" I nod. "You asked me what it would take to believe someone could actually see the future. Well, repeating with Brand for the last hour—or what seemed like an hour—and learning about the many powers that exist is enough for me to believe that girl actually saw the future. I don't know how many patients I've had over the years who claimed they could do any of these things, but now my mind reels with names and faces of people I've met who may have these powers."

I say "Remember Sasha? The girl who could see brains, or in my case, couldn't?" My mother's eyes widen with realization. "Her reason for visiting you was because of her fear of the dark. Did Brand tell you about the dangers in the dark for people with powers?"

She and Brand answer simultaneously, "Yes."

I hope he left out the gruesome details.

I point to the Pulse Emitter attached to Brand's clothing. "I designed that device to protect people with powers from the dangers in the dark. It uses my heartbeat which repels Demons."

My father's expression opens up and I have to assume he's realizing I used his ultrasound to record my heartbeat. I continue. "I only wish I could have figured it out sooner. Maybe people like Charles Rhondell could have used the emitter with kids like Sasha. Charles was a Mind Reader, Mom."

"How do you know?"

"I met him in Montana. He died recently from a gunshot wound when the divided pieces of the diamond merged into the large piece I have in my pouch." Her hand flies to her mouth and her eyes mist over. "The military man who gave you the card is responsible for the death of Charles Rhondell and two other people with powers. He would have killed me as well, but Brand saved my life, and I was able to escape with Maetha and a guy named Chris Harding."

Brand interrupts, "Your future son-in-law."

"Wha— ?" My father isn't able to complete his question.

"Don't worry about that right now," I say quickly, trying to redirect the conversation. "The more pressing issue is the fact that Agent Alpha already located you two and probably will again if he feels he can gain by it. That's why you need to go into hiding."

My mother says quietly, almost breathlessly, "I always thought my great-grandmother was a bit off in the head. I figured she was losing her mind in her old age. Of course, I was quite young when I knew her, and I've often wondered if I fabricated those stories in my own head, because everyone knows vampires don't exist. I chose not to repeat those stories to you. I didn't want to fill your head with all that nonsense. Yet, right here in front of me is proof that my great-grandmother wasn't suffering dementia at all. I inherited her journals when she died, but I've never read them. I didn't want to believe her." She rubs her temples.

I remember helping my mother sort through the boxes in the basement over Spring Break and coming across the taped-up box labeled "G. Grandmother's Journals." I also remember my mother quickly taking the box into the next room. I thought her behavior was strange at the time. Now I understand why.

My father puts his arm around her shoulder. "We can talk about it at the cabin."

We exchange tearful goodbyes full of "I love you's" and longer-than-usual hugs. After charging Brand with my safety, my parents leave my room. Outside the door, I overhear Maetha instructing them to travel by car, use cash, no credit cards, no Internet, no cell phone, etc. I can tell my mother is getting even more freaked out. My father speaks soft words to her. I can't tell what he says, but she calms down.

The next morning, Maetha checks me out of the hospital and hands me a new golden topaz crystal.

"When did you pick this up?" I ask, holding it up to the light and examining the straight-line columns and the interesting way the light dances off the stone's flat sides in an iridescent array. This crystal is smaller and darker than the one from the vial, yet I can feel its healing power flood into my body.

"While you were in surgery, Mary called and reported that she had found a local gemstone dealer on the Internet who had this stone in his collection. I bought it from him."

"How much was it?"

"That doesn't matter, Calli. I had Anika hold it all night. How do you feel now?"

"A hundred percent better. Wow, that's a good stone!"

"I now understand that different pieces of topaz possess a range of power-harnessing abilities, and I've also learned that each stone's point of origin is important. Where does a particular stone come from? What is the composition of the stone? As with obsidian, not all stones of the same classification have the same power. There's golden topaz and natural topaz, which are fine, but they're not as good as Imperial topaz, which is the most intense and rare."

I twist the small crystal between my fingers, admiring its natural formation. "So, what kind of topaz is this one?" I ask.

"I believe it's an Imperial topaz. The dealer had it marked as yellow-orange topaz, but when I picked it up, I could tell it was different. I compared it to the topaz on your necklace and found this one charged faster and held power longer."

"Ah, like the difference between battery brands. They all function as batteries, but some are definitely stronger than others."

"Exactly. Have you healed completely now?"

I nod my head and hand her the crystal to recharge.

"Excellent. This will be recharged in a couple of hours, but in the meantime here are your other two." She hands me my necklace and the vial.

We arrive in Denver a few hours later to find that Neema and Deus Ex have been going at it while we were gone. When Neema discovered Deus was using her repeating power against her, she used Deus's only weakness against her: Neema would wait for thirty-one seconds to respond. Deus feels exploited and continually assaults Neema verbally until Maetha steps in and separates them.

She sends Neema with Brand, Jonas, and me to the other room.

Once inside, I sit down with Jonas and ask him a few questions.

"What was it like to have your cancer healed?"

"It was actually pretty painful. The whole healing process took a couple of weeks to complete."

"Wow, I really thought you died because you refused to be healed."

"I did. I have a grave and everything. But Maetha had other plans for me. She told me she was greatly impressed with my understanding of the will of nature and my acceptance of my impending death. She asked me if I'd be willing to donate my body to science, and I agreed. Of course, I thought what she meant was that I'd be donating my *dead* body to science. She didn't tell me she was going to fake my death and heal my cancer."

Neema says, "Well, the healing part wasn't ever a sure thing. Maetha just wanted to try."

"Get this, Calli," Jonas scoots to the edge of his seat. "Now the Shadows aren't interested in me anymore. I can go out after dark."

My eyes dart to Neema. "She healed his DNA?"

Neema nods her head.

Jonas doesn't seem to understand the significance of what happened. My mind reels with possibilities. If Maetha can heal DNA, then the Shadow Demons wouldn't have anyone to attack. There wouldn't be any class divisions and no competition over who is more powerful than everyone else.

I change the subject and ask Jonas, "Have you seen

your family since . . . well, you know. Did your father's death penalty ever get carried out?"

"Not yet. The death penalty isn't performed very often any more, it seems. I'm not allowed to have any contact with my mother. I understood that fully when Maetha asked me if I'd donate my body. I'm on a new mission now, dedicated to helping the clans further the will of nature."

"Do you miss your running power?"

"No. It's been a nice tradeoff to gain increased intellectual ability and inner calmness in exchange for giving up my old power."

"Oh, come on, you were a smart guy already."

"No, it's different, Calli. Really. Since Maetha healed my cancer, my mind has expanded, and I can learn things at an unbelievable rate. I felt as if a block had been placed on my mind and she removed it. Plus, the calmness I feel is like nothing I've ever felt before. I don't even think there are drugs that could make me feel this way. I'm able to see things with greater clarity and from a broader perspective, like an omniscient point of view. When Maetha told me about the diamonds and the Diamond Bearers, I was able to comprehend almost immediately. Before my healing, I would have freaked out, I'm sure."

"Maetha told you about the diamonds? What did she say?"

"Everything, believe me." He smiles at me. "I don't envy you, Calli. You have a huge job ahead of you. Once you get the rest of your diamond, you'll be limitless, boundless, and in a state of total freedom. That's the part I don't envy. I find that I prefer boundaries and rules. I like to know exactly what's expected of me and what I'm not allowed to do, and I think most people are like me. They need to be guided. The total freedom you'll gain from the whole diamond inside of you scares me, personally."

"Wow, Jonas, I never thought about it like that before."

"Why do you think there have been so many evil leaders in the history of the world? When someone with an evil heart gains ultimate power, they go crazy."

"Well, I believe you have a good heart, Jonas. I know Maetha wouldn't have done what she did otherwise. I'm happy for you."

Jonas leaves my side and goes over to talk to Brand, leaving me to ponder our conversation. I have suspected that being an Unaltered offers benefits above and beyond the normal population. I've always felt I have a calmness that others don't have and a maturity that my peers haven't attained, and I wondered why I was different. I think about what might happen if the entire human population was healed. Would humanity be able to advance intellectually? Or would it be detrimental to have a world in which everyone is the same?

Neema interrupts my thoughts. "I know what you're thinking, without reading your mind. You're wondering if the whole world can be healed."

"Yeah, I am."

"Maetha has been trying relentlessly to heal DNA ever since her scientists discovered the difference between Unaltered and altered DNA. It's a little-known fact in the scientific world that Unaltereds have perfect DNA. All other humans have mutated genes. But because most people have been mutated, their mutated genes come across as being normal. To the regular world, Unaltereds are the abnormal subjects, whereas we're actually the perfect specimens of what DNA should look like. It's a matter of perspective, really. With that in mind, whenever a good candidate is about to die, as in Jonas's case, Maetha recruits them for scientific research. First she heals their life-threatening illness and then tries to heal their DNA. But when you try to alter someone's DNA, it usually causes cancer. So basically Maetha has ended up giving her subjects cancer in the effort to heal their DNA. Only in Jonas's case did healing his cancer result in the proper formula for healing his DNA. He's the first one it worked on, and it happened by accident."

"Wow, so what made his cancer different?"

"She doesn't know yet, but you can believe she won't stop until she finds out. I've known Maetha for a very, very long time, Calli, and if I've learned one thing about her along the way, it's that she never gives up. The last few hundred years have been the most interesting, trust me. Once Henry—er, Freedom went off the deep end, Maetha has worked even harder to stay one step ahead of him."

I contemplate her words a moment and then change the subject. "Neema, what do you think it will take to be able to remove Freedom's heart?"

"I think if we could lure him into a situation where he's using his obsidian and unable to detect his future he won't know we are about to gas him. If we can knock him unconscious, we could then cut his diamond out."

Wow, I hadn't thought of that one.

The phone in our room rings, and Neema picks up the receiver. She listens to the voice on the other end and then utters a few words, including, "yes, okay, I will" and replaces the receiver in the cradle. Then she turns to us and says, "We're mixing things up. Maetha and I are leaving in search of more Imperial topaz, and the rest of you are going to be relocating to a different site. She's not comfortable with this motel any longer. Chris should have contacted us by now."

"What?" I ask. "What are you implying?"

"Calm down, Calli," Brand says. "I'm sure he's fine."

Neema exhales and says, "No, Brand, that's not it. Calli thinks Maetha suspects Chris will turn on us."

"Chris would never give up our location!" I say vehemently. "No amount of torture would get him to—"

"Freedom wouldn't force Chris to talk, Calli. He wouldn't have to. Diamond Bearers are able to extract memories in a way that's different than a mind-read."

I interrupt her. "I know what mind extraction is. I used it when I carried the whole diamond before Maetha disabled the power. Why would Freedom risk exposing himself just to extract Chris's memories?"

"We don't know how he's able to appear whenever your diamond is exposed. Because he has the ability to extract memories, he could locate you. You should understand the need to relocate."

"Yes."

"Be ready to leave in ten minutes," Neema says as she leaves the room.

Brand comes over and sits by me. "Sheez, everyone just bosses us around."

He's only trying to lighten the mood, but my mind is preoccupied with the realization that I'd completely forgotten about that power. I try to remember what I told Chris. How much does Chris know about my family? About Brand's? And why did Maetha allow him to return if she thought Freedom might try to extract his memories? Is she using him as bait? Again? Oh, boy. Chris is going to be pissed when he figures it out . . . again!

Chapter 12 - New Discoveries

We move our group across town to a different motel. Amenemhet and Mary are in charge of us now that Neema and Maetha have left, and with Neema gone, Deus Ex has settled down a bit—well, as long as Beth doesn't say anything to her. I figure Deus needs to feel completely in charge of everyone around her. Feeling threatened is something she likes to avoid, and with the kind of power she possesses, she can make sure no one else is a threat to her. I guess she can be considered the ultimate psychopathic control freak.

Mary and Amenemhet spend most of their time talking quietly between themselves. I read their lips as much as I can, but the conversation is difficult to pick up on. They use names and terms I'm not familiar with, so I turn my focus away from them.

Anika, Jonas, and Brand are quietly flipping through TV channels, while Deus sifts through documents and files on her laptop. Beth lies on the bed with her eyes closed, but I can't tell if she's just resting or sleeping.

Deus calls out to Brand. "Hey, Brand, come check this out!"

He walks over and sits next to her. "What is it?"

"Files on our brothers and sisters and father," she says.

"I already know who my father is."

"No, I don't think you do."

"Let me see what you found."

Deus Ex hands him the laptop and stands to stretch and get herself a glass of water. Brand clicks through several pages of information, growing more and more frustrated. He says, "There's nothing here I don't already know. I've already met the other five Repeaters."

Deus Ex drops her chin a fraction of an inch and says, "Our father is named in the file."

"I already told you I know who my bastard father is. He's the guy who ignored me half my life and was disgusted with me the rest of the time."

"The man is a brilliant scientist. He helped create us and our power. Isn't that fascinating to you, Brand?"

"Nope. My dad wasn't a scientist." Brand closes the laptop and hands it to me. "Have you checked your email lately to see if Chris has sent you anything?"

I shake my head. "I'll check it." I open the laptop and begin navigating to my inbox while watching Deus and Brand stare each other down. I wonder if they are repeating. The email page opens to reveal a new message from a person named "easytospot." I click on it and read his words:

Calli, I need to see you. I miss you. You name the time and place and I'll be there.
— Yours, Chris

I look around the room and find Mary staring at me. I motion for her to come over, which she does. As soon as she reads the email, she walks back to Amenemhet and speaks quietly. When I read their lips, I pick up on the words and phrases "trap", "ambush", "can't trust", and "out of his control."

Mary walks back over to me and says, "Calli, come with me, and bring the computer." She also orders Brand to follow. The three of us exit the room and walk to the second room. Once inside, Mary says, "Here's what you need to tell Chris. Tell him Amenemhet will meet him tomorrow at noon in front of the Colorado State Capitol Building by the Civil War statue. He's to come alone. Amenemhet will then bring him to us when it's determined to be safe."

I type the message quickly, just as she dictated, and click the send button. Brand has remained quiet during the whole exchange. I know he must have repeated a few times because he seems to know exactly what is going on.

I ask Mary, "What will happen to Amenemhet if it's a trap?"

"Nothing. He's going to take Brand with him for protection."

Brand sighs. "Happy to be helping, I think."

I ask Mary, "Do you really think this may be a trap?"

"Anything is possible with Freedom. We've learned to think quickly with him. It's best to catch him by surprise and always try to outguess him, if at all possible. Would you power down the laptop now, Calli? The government can track us now that you've responded to his email." I do as she asks. She says, "Hopefully, Chris will have new information for us that will help in the upcoming battle. Once Maetha and Neema locate more Imperial topaz, we'll be better equipped to attempt an attack on Freedom."

"Neema talked about knocking him out with gas or something," I say. "Is that why Maetha wants to collect more topaz? So everyone can heal themselves while Freedom passes out?"

"Basically, yes. He will never put himself in a position

where he's vulnerable. We assume he will always be surrounded by obsidian."

"Well, if I close the pocket watch right now, Freedom would appear, right?"

"Most likely," Mary says.

"How does he do it if he doesn't have a topaz?"

Brand answers, "He has a Diamond Bearer with him."

Mary and I both exclaim together, "What?"

"I just repeated. You close the watch, and Freedom appears, then Mary bi-locates to Freedom's position and sees a man she knows named Rolf."

"Can you show me, Brand?" Mary asks, her voice shaking.

"Yes. You'll need to put your obsidian on the table first, though. Then go into the bathroom, out of sight." As Mary pulls her personal-sized obsidian off her body, Brand turns to me. "Calli, close the watch."

A second after the watch closes, Mary rushes out of the bathroom and almost falls over. She starts rubbing her head. "I have to tell Amenemhet! I'll be right back." She grabs her obsidian and runs out the door, leaving Brand and me alone.

"What happened, Brand?"

"Freedom bi-located to you, and talked about not being fooled by your boyfriend coming back to his father's side. Then he began to hurt you somehow. You were in pain, so I repeated. Who is Rolf anyway?"

"I've met him before, but I don't know anything about him. Apparently, he's a traitor."

Mary and Amenemhet enter the room, and she shuts the door.

As Amenemhet crosses the room, he demands an answer from Brand. "What will he remember?"

"Freedom?" Brand asks.

"No, what will Rolf remember?"

"Nothing. Mary only remembers it because I repeated with her."

"So, if Rolf is at the Capitol tomorrow at noon, he won't know I know he's helping Freedom?"

"Correct . . . and Freedom doesn't know we know either."

Amenemhet laughs a deep belly laugh like a maniacal villain. It's a bit scary at first, but then we all join in because of his contagious joy. Once he calms down, he says, "Here we thought he had some undiscovered mineral or crystal that he was using against us. But all along it was just a simple answer."

Mary says, "Amenemhet, Maetha suspected at one point that he might have a helper, but she couldn't detect any suspicious behavior in any of the Bearers, so she abandoned that idea. The question now is, how do we best use this information to attain the goal at hand?"

"How does it work?" I ask. "How does having Rolf assist Freedom help him locate me?"

Mary answers. "Rolf doesn't use obsidian. He just sits and waits for you to surface. Then he alerts Freedom. Maetha will be pleased to know she was right all along."

The sun has set, all the television channels have been checked for a decent program, but nothing appeals to anyone. Everyone is restless.

I observe a conversation between Deus Ex and Brand that reveals more about Deus than I knew. She brings up the father issue again with Brand, wondering why he doesn't want to know more about the other half of his DNA. Brand spouts a slew of derogative remarks about his father and how he hurt his mother by cheating on her while they were participating in the government experiment. Of course, Deus is intrigued by Brand's anguish and seems like she wants to understand it better. She asks him a couple of questions that raise my interest.

"Why do you automatically suppose your biological father is the one you grew up with?"

"Because he is."

"But you said yourself your father isn't a scientist. The files clearly state the biological sperm-donor is a government scientist named Dr. Awali, who worked for General Harding."

"Deus, what's your point in all this? I don't need a father in my life! I already have one, and I'm just a huge disappointment in his eyes."

"Maybe he knows you aren't his son."

The room silences completely. The first name that floods into my mind is that of Suzanne James. If Brand's biological father is not the man he grew up with, then he and Suz would not be related. I search his eyes for recognition of that fact, but I can't tell if he's figured it out yet or not.

Brand says, "Learning the identity of the bastard who donated his sperm is the last thing on my to-do list."

"What exactly is on your to-do list?" Deus asks. "Or should I ask . . . who is on your list?"

Brand shoots a nasty glare in her direction.

"Why do you waste your talents on such trivial achievements when you could master any discipline on the face of the earth? You have the ability to make time stand still while you learn information that takes humans years to absorb, yet you mope around because your daddy neglected you. Grow a pair and get over it!"

Mary begins to move toward Deus and Brand, but

Amenemhet catches her arm to hold her back. "Let her finish, Mary."

Deus Ex has the attention of everyone in the room, and she doesn't seem to be bothered by it. Normally an inward personality type, she seems to be thriving on everyone being interested in her information. The whole scene reminds me of a police drama television show where at the end of the episode the bad guy always gives a full-out explanation of how and why he did everything.

Deus Ex continues. "I grew up in the ghetto with a constantly strung-out mother, an uncle who kept her in that condition, and a case worker who couldn't seem to get me out of the environment. I figured other kids' home-life must be so much worse than mine because they were pulled from their homes when I was not. Later on, I learned my case worker only came to check on me to score more drugs.

"The neighborhood kids were tough as they come, and I had to learn at a young age how to fight—how to fight and win. At age six, I practiced throwing a knife at my bedroom wall until I mastered the aim and balance. It took me six months. I learned throughout my childhood and into my teenage years how to use my brain to avoid bad situations in the first place. Once my powers emerged at age thirteen, I began mastering all forms of the martial arts. Repeating was the ultimate tool in learning something that normally takes years. Now I don't have to repeat very often because my defense skills are perfect. I acquired a rifle and taught myself marksmanship. I'm the best assassin, with one-hundred-percent accuracy. Throughout my teen years I've been building up my tolerance to different poisons to avoid being knocked unconscious unknowingly. The fact that you were drugged at the Healers' place, Brand, tells me you haven't been using your powers the best way you could. You probably haven't even learned any new languages, have you?"

Brand pops off. "Oh, let me guess. You know dozens of languages?"

"I learn a language as I need to. I'm a mercenary, Brand. If I'm hired to take care of a target in Kenya, and I need to learn Swahili, I learn it."

"What exactly is a mercenary?" Brand asks. "Surely it doesn't mean you have mercy for your victims."

"No, it means I don't take sides. I go where the money is. I do a job, I do it well, and I get out. Then I look for another job."

"You're not being paid for this job are you?"

"I'm protecting myself and my powers. The vests and weapons the government is developing are a threat to my powers. I'll annihilate the threat and then move on."

Beth can't hold her tongue any longer. "So, you're creating your own perfect world, and we're your chess pieces on a one-sided board?"

"You'd do the same thing, Beth," Deus Ex says.

"No, you're wrong."

"Am I?"

Beth points to Brand. "Look at Brand. He doesn't use his power the same way you do."

"Yeah, and he's neglecting his gift."

"How many people have you killed for money, Brand?" Beth asks.

I look over at Amenemhet and Mary and read their lips. Amenemhet says, "It's like Maetha said. The younger generation has to hammer out their differences like we did."

Mary responds, "We never had these kinds of issues to deal with."

Deus Ex interrupts Beth. "You should be grateful I'm

fighting for the same result as you are right now."

"Or what?"

Deus lowers her voice and speaks slowly, "If I'm with you, I'm not against you."

"Are you threatening me?" Beth stands, trying to look more formidable.

Deus Ex laughs. "I'm not the one standing with my chest all puffed up ready to fight." Her laughter stops abruptly, and she says, "I don't fight for sport, but I also don't take kindly to anyone who thinks they can get the better of me. You better watch what you say."

Amenemhet intervenes. "We need to go over the plan for tomorrow."

Beth sits back down, and Deus Ex turns her attention to Amenemhet as if nothing is out of the ordinary. I observe the others as Amenemhet lays out the plan, the strategy, and the desired results. He covers a few possible outcomes and back-up plans, all designed to protect me. I catch Deus Ex throwing a glance my way, and I know what she's thinking: "Why are you so special?"

We separate into our groups, male and female, and go to our rooms for the night. Deus Ex, however, keeps walking past the door. Mary doesn't seem bothered by it, so I ask her, "Where's she going?"

"She sleeps in an unknown location."

"Well, that doesn't make any sense. Who's going to repeat with me if we get raided in the night?"

Mary stops short and looks at me, then closes her eyes and inhales deeply as if she's trying to keep calm. "You're right. Come on." She walks me back to the other room and delivers me to Amenemhet. "She needs protection. Deus won't sleep in our room."

He grunts his frustration—hopefully directed at Deus, not me—and motions for me to come in the room. He pulls the comforter off the bed and spreads it on the floor. "I'll sleep here. You take the bed, Calli."

The next morning begins uneventfully. The clock ticks at a snail's pace, I swear. My anxiousness to see Chris has me fidgeting nervously and I hope no one notices.

Amenemhet prepares to go pick up Chris. "Brand," he says, "you need to escort Calli to Mary's room." Amenemhet turns to me. "Remember to stay out of sight when I return with Chris. Don't come to the room until I call to let you know it's safe." He opens the door and checks for suspicious activity, then motions for Brand to take me outside.

Once we're outside, Brand says comically, "I don't think Amenemhet will ever get used to my power."

"What do you mean?"

"He still thinks he needs to protect you, checking to make sure the coast is clear before he lets you leave the room. If there was going to be a problem, I would have already known and would have told him."

"Oh well, he's just trying to do his job. Plus, it's probably hard for him to grasp your ability, because he doesn't have the repeating power himself. I know I don't fully understand it and I've been with you a lot longer than he has."

We reach Mary's door, which she opens on our approach. Deus is sitting on one of the beds.

"Nice to see you, Deus," I say, trying not to sound sarcastic but failing.

She scoffs at my remark.

Jonas, Beth, and Anika sit around the table, chatting happily. Mary and Brand joins them. I know Amenemhet won't be back for at least an hour, so I lie down on the other bed, close my eyes, and try to relax.

I practice my meditation techniques and slip into a dream about Chris . . . the kind of dream where your heart races with excitement. I wake up, grabbing for the topaz around my neck. It doesn't have much power, so I pull out my vial and use the Imperial topaz Maetha purchased. I only need a small amount of its power to calm my heart and heal. I save the rest for another time. I take my necklace off and sit up. A quick glance at the clock shows I've slept for nearly an hour.

Anika walks in my direction. "Are you all right, Calli?"

"Yeah. Would you charge this again?"

She smiles and takes the topaz, and returns to the group at the table.

I like Anika's disposition. She doesn't make a scene and is certainly not a drama queen. She's humble and mature, which is a good thing. We already have enough drama as a group.

The high-pitched screech of a car coming to a halt pulls my attention to the curtained window. Mary carefully parts the drapes with her finger and announces: "They're here."

I hurry over to her side and peek through the small opening. I can see Chris, blindfolded, being helped out of the back seat. I say to Mary, "Isn't it overkill to have him blind-folded?"

"Not at all. If Freedom extracts Chris's memory when he returns to the compound, he won't be able to determine where we are staying because Chris won't have known. He won't have to wear it while we talk."

The phone rings and Brand says, "It's Amenemhet telling us we can come to the room."

Mary answers the phone anyway, listens for a moment,

and then hangs up. "Let's go," she says.

I overhear Deus Ex chastising Brand. "You know, it's pretty stupid to broadcast your ability to everyone like that."

"What, as if you didn't repeat too? You knew it was Amenemhet on the phone."

"Who else would it have been? I didn't have to repeat. I used my common sense."

"Well, I'm not as perfect as you, I guess," Brand mutters in frustration.

We reach the door. Exhilaration shoots through my body as I enter the room and see Chris sitting at the table, unharmed and healthy. I want to wrap my arms around him and never let go! Especially after the dream I just had. But I know better.

Without delay, Amenemhet turns to Chris. "Tell Calli what your father wants."

Chris looks at me, and I see emotional pain in his eyes. "My father wants me to bring *you* in to prove my allegiance."

I don't know what to say. My legs feel weak, so I sit down on the bed.

Chris continues, "He's acting on Freedom's wishes, and Freedom wants Maetha. Where is she, anyway?"

Mary answers vaguely. "She and Neema are on special assignment."

"Well, Freedom wants Calli so Maetha will come rescue her," Chris says. "Bait." He takes a long drink of water from a bottle and then adds, "My father's just doing whatever Freedom says without knowing what it's all about."

"Do either of them suspect your involvement with us?" Mary asks.

"My dad interrogated me about the events following

Justin's death, asking where I went, who I was with, and so on."

Mary presses him further. "Did Freedom ever scan your mind? Did he extract your memories?"

Amenemhet answers instead. "I already checked him for it. He's clean."

"Checked me for what? Of course I'm clean! Do you think I'd come back and put all of you at risk? I would never—"

"Calm down, son," Amenemhet says.

"No, I won't calm down! They're torturing people with powers in that facility! My father's operating on the false assumption that Maetha is a threat to the safety of the country, and because of Freedom's misinformation, my father's developing a means of wiping out not just people with powers, but Diam—"

I hold up my hand to hush him before he reveals sensitive information. "We know about the vests, Chris."

"Yeah, but you don't know how they make them. I was forced to watch as captured Runners, Hunters, and Healers were strapped down with clear quartz stones and then pushed into the shadows." Chris leans forward, resting his elbows on his knees and his head in his hands. He continues and I see how painful the memory is for him. "The screams and the gore . . . I'll never forget it." He pauses, and the room is quiet. "When they turned the lights on, the only thing that remained was green rocks on the ground, strewn amongst the shredded clothing and blood. The quartz absorbed the healing powers of the Shadow Demons."

Mary interrupts. "Wait, Chris. What do you mean?"

"The pieces of quartz became charged, like the topaz, with the dead Healers' powers. But it takes the sacrifice of a person with powers for the quartz to activate."

"I wasn't aware the Shadow Demons still had the healing power at all."

"It doesn't stop there," he continues. "The green quartz was then attached to the vests. I watched from an observation room as a young boy, maybe twelve and a day, was brought in wearing the vest. He was so scared. They shot him in the leg without warning—a flesh wound, but painful and bloody. My father ordered the boy to take a green stone and place it on the wound, which he did, and the wound healed. The stone was less green after he was done." Chris sits back up, yanks a couple of tissues from a box nearby, and wipes his face. "They shot the kid three more times in different places, and each time he'd heal the injury with his fading green quartz. Then they shot him one time too many. The quartz had lost its power, and the boy died."

Deus Ex breaks the silence and says, "Yeah, that's sad and all, but what about the guns? The ones with obsidian bullets? Have they completed them?"

Chris just stares at her for a moment, making me wonder what he's thinking. He finally says, "They're still in development. Obsidian is too soft to withstand the firing process. They'll figure it out sooner or later though."

"Unless we stop them," Deus Ex says. "Take Calli back with you so we can get in the door."

"Under no circumstances will Calli go with you to your father's base," Mary says.

Deus Ex confidently overrides Mary's comment. "It's the only way. I'm familiar with the place, as is Brand. Together we can disable Freedom long enough for the rest of you to take him down and destroy the research materials and computers."

"No!" Mary exclaims. "We need to wait for Maetha and the Imperial topaz. Killing Freedom will take a group effort."

Deus Ex clearly doesn't understand why Mary feels it will take an entire group to take down a single man. She says with supreme confidence, "I can kill him faster than you can open your little carrying case and take out your precious topaz."

Chris stands, walks over to my side and says to Mary, "I need to speak with Calli alone."

"Brand will remain with you for safety," Mary instructs.

Deus Ex offers, "I can stay with her and keep her safe better than Brand can. No one ever asks me to guard her."

I turn and face her. "Deus, my safety was left in your hands last night, but you chose not to stay with me. I had to sleep in Brand's room."

Deus is dumbstruck. Mary takes the opportunity to escort her out of the room along with the others.

Chris, Brand, and I are left alone as the others head for the other room. Chris gives me a careful hug and a sweet kiss on the lips. Brand walks to the table and sits down where Chris had sat. I fumble for my vial to heal my over-excited heart.

Chris takes a seat on the bed across from me. "Calli, Freedom knows he has a hold over your diamond shard. He knows you can't use it. The worst thing is, I overheard him talking to his guard, Rolf, saying Maetha's line will die with you . . . and then Maetha will die. I tried to tell my father that Freedom seems to be on his own side and that he may turn against him. But simply suggesting Freedom's disloyalty caused my father to order me to bring you in to prove where my loyalties lie. My father doesn't know about the diamonds, or about Maetha's Blue Diamond. Freedom is keeping him in the dark."

"Taking me in may be the only way to finish this job,

Chris," I say. "You'll have to do it to keep your double-agent spot."

"There's got to be another way. I don't want to have to take you to Freedom."

A quiet knock at the door interrupts our conversation. Brand says without getting up from his seat, "It's just Jonas. It's fine."

I open the door and let Jonas in. He stands in front of me and says, "Calli, before Maetha left, she instructed me to put myself between you and Freedom whenever possible. I'm supposed to be dead anyway, right?" He smiles genuinely. "Have Chris take me back to his father, and tell him that you and Maetha are out of the country right now and that once you return and find that I've been taken, you'll come to my rescue . . . at least, that's what we can tell General Harding."

"It could work," I say to Chris. "It would buy us some time until Maetha gets back, and it would show your father that you're trying to demonstrate your allegiance."

"I don't know," Chris says.

I instruct Jonas to go bring the others back to the room.

Once everyone returns, we discuss the idea of sending Jonas with Chris to buy some time until Maetha returns. The fact that Maetha personally asked Jonas to do whatever he could do to protect me is the clincher in deciding to send Jonas with Chris.

With that out of the way, Chris pulls out a silver wrist cuff from his pocket. "This is my father's new way of subduing captives." He points inside the cuff. "See the small piece of obsidian glued in there? If this was removed and replaced with a harmless black stone, then the cuff wouldn't remove anyone's power."

Amenemhet takes the cuff and twists the silver circular

band in the light. He produces a small pocket knife that he uses to pry the obsidian from the inside of the band. The small black chunk flies across the room and bounces off the television screen. Jonas picks it up and hands it to Amenemhet.

Chris adds, "My father has many of these cuffs. If there was a way to replace all the obsidian, then the cuffs wouldn't remove anyone's power."

"Can you give me an hour or so? I think I have the perfect solution." Amenemhet says to Chris.

"Yes."

Amenemhet goes to work, rummaging through his belongings. He pulls out a box with small tools and a rectangular plastic organizer that reminds me of something Uncle Don would own. He begins pulling out black arrowheads from the organizer and chipping off pieces with his tiny hammer and chisel.

Chris sits beside me with Brand nearby. He says to Brand, "Repeat if she reaches for her vial." Brand nods. Chris says to me, "It's vitally important that I stay in my father's good graces for as long as is necessary. I don't know how long it will be, and I don't know if I'll make it out alive. If he finds out what I'm up to, he will kill me. I'm sure of it."

"How are you feeling, Calli?" Brand asks.

"Fine." My heart is good, but my stomach rumbles with nervousness and fear.

Chris continues, pointing at the laptop. "You can't log into your email on that computer anymore, either. They're tracking it."

"We figured they would be."

Chris speaks across the room to Amenemhet. "I learned that following Brand's rescue, the headquarters you set up was cleared out by Freedom and his men. Each of your cameras were located, and then destroyed. However, learning this gave me a good idea of a secure way to communicate with you guys—by lip reading." Chris looks at me admiringly. "Would it be possible for you to install a new camera near the complex focusing on the main door?"

Amenemhet looks up from his concentrated effort. "Yes, I think I could. It would be dangerous, but I love a challenge."

"If the camera could zoom in on my face, I could mouth updates when standing outside. Calli could read my lips and relay the message. Plus, you just might be able to pick up on conversations as well from the guards."

Amenemhet pauses and stares at Chris for a moment. "I could have one installed by tomorrow afternoon . . . probably. But there'd be no way for you to know if it is operational or not."

Brand says to Chris, "Wait a minute. Let me get this straight. You're going to stand outside the main door and talk to yourself? Hoping Calli is watching? With guards watching you speak? Are you nuts? They'll figure that one out really fast."

Anika speaks cautiously, "Not if he's wearing head-phones, listening to music Of course, he wouldn't be really, but they wouldn't know that if his head was bouncing to the imaginary beat."

Brand becomes the voice of reason. "Why do you have to go outside to listen to your music? What's the excuse?"

"Smoking," I say. "Buy a pack of cigarettes and pre-tend to smoke."

"Yeah, right," Brand says. "The guards will be able to tell he's pretending. They're all heavy smokers."

Deus Ex nods in agreement.

"I won't have to pretend," Chris says. "I used to

smoke."

"Huh?" Several voices all sound at the same time. I'm not sure who all registered their surprise, and I'm not even sure if I spoke out loud or just thought it. Chris—a smoking, Harley-riding badass?

Even Brand is tripped up with Chris's revelation. He says, "Um, well then, do you think your father will allow you to go outside whenever you want?"

"No, but, if we establish message times of noon and 6:00 p.m., I should be able to make it work. That way you won't have to constantly stare at the screen either."

"So it's possible that by 6:00 p.m. tomorrow night you'll be able to pass a message along?" I ask.

"Yes," Chris leans closer to my face and whispers in my ear, "and when I wink, you'll know I'm sending you a personal message that I'm doing all of this for you, for us." He kisses the top of my ear through my hair, sending tingles throughout my body. He moves away from me and walks over to Amenemhet. I pay careful attention to what I'm feeling within my body to see if I need to use the topaz. I know Brand is waiting anxiously at the ready to repeat time on my demand, but I decide I don't need to. My heart is fine.

Beth asks, "What if his mind is read and they find out this whole plan?"

Chris responds. "I can always twist the information and spin it whatever direction I need. That's what being a double agent is all about."

Deus chimes in. "Then how do we know you aren't doing that already and we're the ones receiving twisted information?"

Chris answers coolly, "You don't. You'll just have to trust me."

"Yeah, that's probably what you told them, too," Deus

Ex mutters and walks away.

After another half hour or so, Amenemhet has produced around ten stones that match in diameter and thickness. He gives them to Chris in a small cloth pouch with a drawstring. Hopefully, once he's back at the compound, Chris will be able to replace a few cuffs with the faux obsidian in case they're used in the future. Chris says his goodbyes, and Jonas begins issuing hugs to everyone . . . as if he may never see any of us again. Chris is blindfolded once again and led to the car.

After the car pulls out of the parking lot, Deus mutters, "This is ridiculous. Why bother with the blindfold? Jonas knows exactly where we are."

I have to admit, she has a point. I say, "Deus is right. Perhaps we should find a different place to stay."

Mary's eyes widen with realization, then her expression falls as she says, "Maetha and Neema won't know where we are, or Amenemhet. I can't alert them of the change."

Deus says, with an air of satisfaction, "Let's just move to different rooms here. That way we can watch for the others to return, and keep an eye open for any kind of government raid."

Mary nods, picks up the phone and calls the front desk. After securing new rooms, she says, "Lets move everything. I'll keep watch for Amenemhet's return."

Chapter 13 - Freedom's Diamond

Amenemhet returned late last night after dropping off Chris and Jonas and successfully installing a new camera aimed at the main door. He said the task wasn't easy due to the heightened security around the building.

I begin to watch the surveillance camera monitor at 11:00 a.m., waiting to see Chris. Each time the door opens, my stomach clenches, only to then be let down because it's not him. Each minute ticks by painfully slow. As the noon hour passes as we approach 1:00 p.m., Brand says, "Calli, he's not coming out. Maybe he will tonight."

Disappointed, I agree with Brand and try to relax.

Watching the monitor isn't entirely a waste of time. It's interesting to see the guards exiting the building, muttering insulting statements about their boss. I can't tell if they're talking about General Harding or Freedom, but I bet if their indignant statements were overheard by their boss, they'd lose their jobs.

At 6:00 p.m. the door opens and Chris walks out. He puts in his ear buds, lights a cigarette, looks up, and winks. I watch breathlessly, waiting for his lips to move. The door opens and General Harding comes out and stands next to Chris. Everyone watching the screen lets out audible gasps. I translate the movements of their lips out loud for everyone to hear.

"Since when do you smoke?" General Harding asks.

"A while."

"You haven't left my side all day."

We watch as Chris reaches in his jacket and pulls out a half-empty bubble packet of what looks like nicotine gum and waves it for his father to see. The general nods his head in understanding and says, "Your mother will not be pleased."

"Then don't tell her." Chris offers a cigarette to his father, who declines.

His father pauses for a moment and then says, "I want to talk to you about—" he turns his head, preventing me from reading his lips. His head swivels. "—didn't want him overhearing."

Chris says, "I assure you, he's untrustworthy. I've learned enough to know he's not who or what you think he is."

"If he heard you speaking this way he'd—" General Harding turns away from the camera again. "—not quite what I had in mind."

Chris points his finger to his father. "I thought you were the head of this operation."

General Harding's head is turned again when he speaks, which is frustrating because he speaks for a long time.

Chris says, "If you shoot out his heart, you'll see what I mean."

"Chris, I can't just go around killing—" General Harding bends down and picks something up from the ground, but hasn't ceased talking. "—answer for it."

Sheeze, that man can't hold his head still for a second!

Chris asks, "Is Agent Alpha your man? Or is he a lateral?"

"He was assigned to my research."

"You're a four-star general. Who would have assigned him? Have you ever asked him?"

"He knew the protocol, the language, and he had papers assigning him to my research. Why would I question that? Plus, I wasn't a four-star general at *that* time."

"Well, why don't you ask him a couple questions, or start a sentence and let him finish it. I'll bet he can't answer or complete the correct information."

"What are you saying, Chris?" —indistinct words— "mole or spy?"

"I'm saying watch him closely because based on what I've seen and heard, he's not in your corner. He's using you."

"Do you have proof?"

"By the time I have proof, it will be too late."

"What do you propose I do?"

"Shoot him. Shoot his heart out."

"What? Why?"

"Because his heart holds all the answers. You'll just have to see it to believe it."

Chris deposits his cigarette butt in the nearby receptacle, then opens the door and holds it for his father.

Deus Ex breaks the silence in the room. "What the . . . what's he talking about? Is Freedom an alien or something?" She laughs a bit with her last statement, but when no one else joins her, she stops. Then she says, "That was a waste of time. He didn't pass on any information at all."

Brand replies, "It's clear he's trying to get his father to doubt Freedom's intentions. And encouraging him to kill Freedom. Maybe he'll do the job for us?"

"There's nothing to do but wait till tomorrow," Amenemhet says.

Amenemhet passes around a menu from a Greek

restaurant along with a pencil for us to mark what we each want for dinner. I am intrigued by the fact that Amenemhet and Mary both crave Mediterranean food. Maybe it's the kind of food they've eaten most of their lives. I place my order for a spinach feta salad and fresh lemonade and settle into one of Mary's books: an 1847 first edition of *Wuthering Heights*. Mary told me how the author, Emily Brontë, published the first edition under the pseudonym of Ellis Bell, but following Emily's death, her sister Charlotte, who wrote *Jane Eyre*, had a second edition printed under Emily's real name. The book I hold in my hands is signed inside the front cover by Emily Brontë. It's a precious reminder of just how old the book is, how precarious life is, and how much times have changed.

I continue to read the book up until noon the next day. It's wonderful to have something to pull my mind away from the stress and strain of circumstances I can't do anything about.

At noon, I anxiously fidget in the chair directly in front of the computer screen. Chris walks out of the building and lights up another cigarette.

"He's back," I announce to everyone.

Chris looks upward and gives a quick wink, the puts his ear buds in his ears and begins to bob his head while he slowly and repeatedly mouths words to the camera hidden in the trees. I repeat the words for everyone, holding back the repetitive information.

"Bad news. Freedom wants to kill Jonas. I told him Maetha healed Jonas of cancer and that he's important to her, that she will come, just give her more time."

The door behind Chris opens, and two men in lab

coats come out and walk past Chris toward the parking lot. Chris brings his cigarette to his mouth and continues bobbing his head to the imaginary beat until the men are far enough away. He lowers his hand and mouths his message. "We can't wait for Maetha. I don't think Jonas will still be alive when I come outside at 6:00 p.m." He glances around at his surroundings before continuing. "I have a plan. Calli and Brand will come to the compound as Deus Ex's prisoners. Calli should offer herself as a replacement for Jonas. That will get you in the door. Brand and Deus can repeat to fix the details. Brand should beat me up once you have Jonas. That will cause a distraction so everyone can run from the compound and will keep my father believing I'm loyal." Chris tosses his cigarette in the bin and turns to enter the building. He stops suddenly and mouths to the camera, "Oh, and tell Brand and Deus Ex I'll introduce them to their real father." He enters the building.

The group in the motel room remains silent for a moment.

Deus says, "That was my idea from the start."

Brand lets out an exasperated grunt and throws his hands in the air. "I'm not going back there!"

Beth lights into him. "Jonas is going to die! Chris thinks you three can break him out, and you're going to pull away now?"

Amenemhet raises his voice above Beth's. "It would be certain death for all of you to enter the compound. We will wait for Maetha and Neema to return."

Anika pleads with Amenemhet. "We don't know when Maetha and Neema will return. Jonas will be killed if something isn't done today!"

"Calli doesn't need to go," Deus Ex informs us in her snobbish manner. "I spent the equivalent of one hour in that facility when I went in for Brand. I know exactly where the obsidian is located and where it's not. I'll go rescue Jonas—alone—because I'm the only one who can do it effectively."

"What do you mean you're the only one?" Brand shoots back at her. "I'm a Repeater too, or have you forgotten that?"

"Yeah, but you said yourself, you're too chicken to go back." Deus stands and walks over to her belongings and begins to attach her utility belt.

Brand stands in defiance. "I'm not chicken!"

"Prove it," Deus responds without emotion.

Amenemhet intervenes again, "Deus, you're labeled as a traitor. What makes you think they're going to let you into the compound?"

"They'll let me in. I'm not worried."

"No," Mary admits quietly, "I don't think they will. We know Freedom better than you, Deus. Calli and Brand must go with you."

"Mary, what are you—" Amenemhet tries to protest.

"Freedom wants Maetha. He knows Maetha will come to rescue Calli. However, if Calli simply tries to swap herself for Jonas, like Chris suggested, no one will be freed. I propose Deus takes Calli and Brand as her 'prisoners.' With a little luck, maybe Chris will have been able to insert the 'fake obsidian' into the cuffs and Brand won't actually lose his power. Once the three of you are inside the building, Deus can work her magic and the three of you can free Jonas."

No one makes a sound.

Finally, Amenemhet says, "I believe you're right, Mary. Either no one attempts the rescue of Jonas, or these three do it as a team. There are no guarantees that it will work, and it may result in the capture and death of all three of you . . . well, four with Jonas. However, I understand the value of preserving Jonas's life. Maetha invested a lot of time into her study of him. It would be a huge waste of effort if he's killed before she can determine whether his DNA transformation is successful."

Anika stutters, "What about his life? What about him? Doesn't that matter?"

Mary answers, "Yes, Anika, Jonas matters. Amenemhet wasn't implying he doesn't." Mary turns to Beth. "Remove the topazes. Jonas, Deus, and Brand will need the running power at some point."

Beth unzips her jacket, exposing medical tape that holds two topaz stones in place on her upper chest. She pulls them off and hands them to Mary.

Mary turns to me. "Place these in your vial until they are needed."

Brand asks, "Why does Calli need to carry them? Why can't I keep a topaz on my body?"

"Because it's charged with super-speed. If you hold it, the power might be replaced with repeating."

"Yeah, well that wouldn't be so bad, would it?"

"We don't have time to test your power. You can try to charge a repeating stone later, Brand."

Deus opens one of the pockets on her belt and pulls out a set of handcuffs. She dangles them in front of my face. "If you're going to be my prisoner, you better look the part." She snaps the cuffs around my wrists.

"What about me?" Brand asks.

"I'll hold your arm."

"Huh?"

"I'll tell them that Repeaters can't repeat if they are holding onto each other. They don't know."

"I guess that'll work," Brand concedes.

Beth drives us toward the compound and drops us off a quarter mile from the gate. We walk the rest of the way and arrive at the security gate by 2:00 p.m. Deus drags me along and pulls Brand with her. She lets go of me once we reach the gate, but stands close to my body.

The obsidian-covered main building looms in front of us. The guard in the door-less booth on the other side of the gate ignores our presence and continues reading his motorcycle magazine.

"Hey!" Deus shouts.

The guard tilts his magazine enough to make eye contact. "This is a government facility, little girl. You don't have clearance to pass."

Deus grabs my arm and raises my cuffed hands and says, "She's my clearance."

"So."

"So, get off your ass and open the gate!"

The guard slams his magazine down and stands as he glares at Deus. He exits the booth and walks in our direction. "I don't know who you think you are," he rests his hand on the butt of his holstered pistol, "but you've got ten seconds to vacate the premises."

Deus changes her tone to super-sweet. "But sir, if you don't even alert the general to the fact that I've got Calli Courtnae, you'll be unemployed when he finds out you turned us away. I don't think you want to lose your job, do you?"

The guard's eyebrows scrunch together, and he steps back into the security booth and speaks into a hand-held radio. I can't read his lips or hear what he's saying. He sets the radio down and yells, "Someone is on the way." Then he sits down and picks up his motorcycle magazine again.

The door to the compound opens and three guards emerge. They head our way, carrying silver cuffs.

"I hope those are the dummy cuffs," Brand mutters.

"It doesn't matter, Brand. You can still run with the topaz," I remind him.

"Yeah, but I can't repeat."

Deus Ex snobbishly says, "Well, if you hadn't wasted your life trying to get women and instead learned some fighting skills, you wouldn't be worried right now."

Brand grumbles something unintelligible as the guards arrive.

The guard in the middle speaks to Deus. "You can't enter unless you wear these cuffs."

"Well then, you can't have my prisoners."

The guard looks bewildered and casts glances at his fellow guards. "The rules are no one enters the gates without at least one of these on their wrists.

Deus Ex pushes Brand forward. "Give him your wrist."

Brand raises his hand forward and a cuff is snapped into place. Brand lets out a defeated huff of air and shakes his head. I'm guessing Chris didn't alter that particular cuff.

Deus pulls me to the gate. "Give them your hands, darling," she snarls in my ear.

I do as she says, but not without a serious dose of suspicion rushing through my body. Either Deus is a really good actress or something else is going on here. The guard snaps a cuff on my wrist, but I can't tell whether or not the obsidian has been switched with one of Amenemhet's replacements because I already have obsidian removing my powers. Then the guard orders Deus to remove her handcuffs from my wrists. Deus complies.

Lastly, Deus receives her silver cuff. Nothing in her behavior changes when the cuff is snapped shut. Then the three guards usher us into the building. Right away, I spot Chris through a windowed wall in an office-type room as we are led down the hallway. He doesn't smile or acknowledge that he even knows me. The situation reminds me of the horribly empty feeling I'd had in Alaska when Maetha performed her "Egyptian mind-meld" on him. But I know he has to keep up his act around his father.

The guards open another door and take us into a large interrogation room. They position us in the center of the room, facing an observation window which nearly covers the side wall. In the window I see a table with electronic devices, computers, and a microphone, along with empty chairs.

General Harding and Chris enter the room on the other side of the window. A third man follows them, but he remains close to the door. It's Rolf, the Diamond Bearer.

Then Freedom enters our room with another guard and slowly walks all around, coming to a halt near the observation window. His back is to General Harding and Chris. Freedom's guard stands behind us. Freedom isn't wearing his long coat and sunglasses. Instead he's dressed in a simple white button-up shirt and tan Dockers. He doesn't seem as scary without his "costume." He just looks like an employee of the compound. That is his costume.

Freedom's position in front of the window is a perfect arrangement. I will be able to look past him and read Chris's lips as he talks to his father . . . and at the moment Chris is in the process of telling his father to shoot Freedom while he has the chance.

Freedom speaks in his low growl of a voice. "You expect me to believe you've brought these two in as prisoners, Samantha?"

I glance over at Deus. I know how she hates to be called by her given name.

Through gritted teeth, she says, "I want the boy."

"Who?"

"Jonas."

Freedom chuckles. "Why?"

"I'll trade these two for Jonas."

Freedom looks her over. "What do you really want?"

Deus responds. "I know you want Maetha. She won't come for Jonas, but she will for Calli."

"I already know what *I* want. I want to know why *you* want Jonas."

Brand launches a verbal attack at Deus. "You drag us in just to get Jonas? You're stupider than I thought. He's probably already dead."

"He's alive," Freedom reassures Brand.

"Prove it!" Brand hisses to Freedom.

Freedom stares at Brand for a moment. He flicks a finger to the guard by the door and says, "Bring him in."

While we wait, Freedom turns and faces me, but addresses Deus Ex. "I'll gladly accept this trade, if that's what you want to call it."

Deus retorts, "What's that supposed to mean?"

"It means, you'll get what you want, and I'll get what I want." Freedom's body language seems to be relaxed and confident, but I sense he's on edge.

The door opens and Jonas walks in, followed by another guard. I note right away that Jonas isn't wearing a silver cuff, which only makes sense. Obsidian would be ineffective against an Unaltered.

"Come over here, Jonas," Freedom invites him to his left side.

After Jonas takes his place, Freedom violently grabs him by the back of the neck. Freedom's stance and tone of voice changes as his true nature is shown. "Calli, give me the diamond or I will kill him right now!"

"Wait!" my hands instinctually fly up in front of me. "Don't hurt him! Let him go and I'll give you the diamond!"

Jonas cries out, "No Calli, don't give it to him."

Deus yells, "Hey, what are you doing? What are you talking about? What diamond?"

Freedom ignores her and squeezes Jonas's neck harder, causing him to shriek in pain. "I'll kill him with my bare hands if you don't give me the diamond. Now!"

Deus objects firmly, "You kill him and I won't hand over Calli."

General Harding speaks into a microphone, sending his booming, panicked voice echoing against the walls. "Agent Alpha, what are you doing?"

I can see Chris and his father behind Freedom. They're both on their feet, leaning toward the window.

Freedom doesn't turn his head. He maintains his hold on Jonas. He shouts his response to General Harding. "Everything's under control. I'm securing you more power." With his statement, Freedom gives an extra shake to Jonas's neck, reigniting Jonas's pain.

Brand shouts, "Let go! You're hurting him!"

Deus is livid at this point. "Hey! I brought you these two to make a trade!"

"Did you really think this situation would be in your control, Samantha?" Freedom asks. He looks at me again. "I'm done waiting, Calli."

"Wait! All right, I'll give it to you." I begin to slowly move my hand toward my pocket. This wasn't in our original plan. Should I give the diamond to Freedom? It's pretty clear we're all probably going to die because the silver cuffs are obsidian laced. I've arrived at this conclusion because Deus doesn't understand what's going on. If she was able to repeat, she wouldn't be asking so many questions. Based on a feeling in my gut, I make the decision to surrender the diamond. Maetha once told me how she uses her gut instinct to make some decisions. Well, my gut tells me Chris is working hard to convince his father to kill Freedom. The four guards in the room have the capability to carry out the job, too. But they need the order to come from General Harding, and General Harding needs the motivation to issue the order—he needs to see the diamond.

I reach in my pocket, remove the pouch, and pull out the diamond. I toss the chunk of carbon to Freedom. As it arches through the air, the florescent lights above reflect off the surface, casting glimmering bits of color on the walls. Freedom effortlessly catches the diamond with his right hand, not losing his grip on Jonas for a second.

Behind Freedom, General Harding's eyes are still wide from watching the huge diamond fly across the room. Chris turns and says something to his father—I can't tell what—to which his father nods his head and rubs his jaw.

Deus is genuinely confused. "What was that? No way was that a diamond!"

Freedom says, "Give me my pocket watch as well, Calli."

"Let go of Jonas first." I feel confident making my demand. He knows I hold the one thing that could disable him. He won't risk me opening the watch to the large-stone side.

He lets go of Jonas, who stumbles forward a step and rubs the back of his neck.

I throw the watch to Freedom, half-expecting my powers to rush back into my body once the watch is out of my possession. I don't feel any different, which confirms my cuff contains Yellowstone obsidian.

Freedom catches the watch and snaps it closed. A smug smirk touches his lips. He moves forward, pushing Jonas aside, and stands in front of me just out of reach. He holds the diamond out towards me.

Nothing happens.

His expression changes to a sneer. "The cuffs! Guards, remove Calli's handcuffs."

I don't quite understand what's going on, but I know somehow the obsidian must be keeping Freedom from getting the diamond shard in my heart.

I look over to Brand and say, "Touch him if he gets too close to me."

Brand shifts onto the balls of his feet.

Freedom's gaze flickers between us. "Guards, remove all the cuffs and hold onto the prisoners."

General Harding's voice sounds authoritatively through the room again. "Keep your positions. Agent Alpha, you are not authorized to make a command that violates the facilities' rules."

Freedom doesn't take his eyes off me as he says, "General, they've figured out how to use the obsidian cuffs as weapons. It's best if they are removed from the prisoners. Don't worry, no one is going anywhere."

Over Freedom's shoulder, I see Chris say to his father, "It's a lie! He knows the obsidian can hurt him. You should kill him while you still can. Shoot his heart out!"

Freedom nods to his guards and says again, "Remove the cuffs."

General Harding raises his voice, ordering, "I am your commanding officer! You will follow my orders or face punishment!"

Two of the guards obviously fear Freedom more than General Harding. They move to the three of us. My cuff is taken off first, causing my powers to rush back into my body, along with Freedom's projected voice filling my mind.

He says, *Don't take it personally, Calli. I would have killed anyone to finally possess two Sanguine Diamonds.*

Freedom please, don't do this!

He ignores my plea.

Deus's cuff is removed next, then Brand's. I see General Harding raise a small hand-held radio near his mouth and say, "Max, shoot Agent Alpha in the heart when you have a clean shot."

The guard that came in with Freedom must be Max. I can see his reflection in the glass. He puts his hand up to his earpiece and then tightens the hold on his rifle, raising the barrel in line with Freedom.

Freedom ignores Max and lifts his hand with the diamond in front of him. Instantly, my chest seizes with pain as he leans towards me. I instinctively fight back by using the healing power to try to hold onto my diamond shard. His low voice sounds in my head. *I will take the remaining piece now, Calli.*

A new sensation floods through me. His words echo in my head, rebounding against my skull, then seemingly shoot from my mind to his. Amazingly, an explosion of images break free and flow between our minds. I can see his entire past.

I'm pulled in two directions—the physical focus on the pain of my rupturing heart, and the waves of images of Freedom's memories assaulting my mind.

Jonas cries out, "You're hurting her!" Then he moves toward Freedom in a defensive rage.

Freedom knocks Jonas to the ground.

With an inhuman yell, Brand struggles out of the guard's grip and bolts toward Freedom. The look of shock registers for an instant on Freedom's face before Brand hits him. Freedom regains his balance more quickly and shoves Brand to the floor, the watch flying from one hand, the grip on the diamond tightening in the other.

"Idiot!" Freedom screams. He re-thrusts the diamond toward me and my vision hazes, the pain in my heart unbearable.

A deafening gunshot reverberates through the room as Freedom's left shoulder is blown apart by a bullet fired by Max. Freedom crumples to the floor, near Jonas. The whole room is silent for a moment until Freedom moves to his knees and extends the diamond toward me once again.

Agonizing pain erupts in my chest as the diamond shard breaks through my ribs.

The world begins to spin as Brand repeats with me. When the room comes to a halt, I find myself whole again. The guard behind me is in the process of removing my cuff. My heart races with the knowledge of what's about to happen.

While Freedom is speaking to my mind about my death not being personal, Brand whispers, "We need to both rush Freedom this time."

I nod.

The moment Brand's cuff is off he rushes Freedom, who is extending his hand in my direction with the diamond. I take a few steps forward, but the excruciating pain in my chest stops me cold. I can feel the diamond ripping away from the muscle tissue inside my heart. I fight back, determined not to let my diamond shard leave my body. More of Freedom's past becomes available within my mind. I shove it aside, letting it wash through me, leaving the images to be processed another time.

Jonas also attacks Freedom but is knocked to the ground

This time, the gunshot echoes off the walls, missing Freedom all together, but hitting the bullet-proof glass in front of Chris.

Brand says, "Okay, that's not going to work. Stay put this time."

"The gunshot needs to be through his heart," I remind him.

"I'll try," Brand says, the strain evident in his voice.

The world spins again. Sick to my stomach and hands trembling, I hold my ground. I'm terrified about the pain I know is coming, but determined to fight harder to stay alive. Brand runs forward, head low, and grabs Freedom by the waist, hoisting him up. Jonas once again gets knocked to the ground. Deus rushes into the melee just before Freedom is shot. The bullet hits Freedom in the arm, next to his chest.

"Calli, grab Deus's wrist this time," Brand yells. "She's repeating too, and it's screwing everything up."

We spin again. My head takes longer to balance itself once everything comes to a halt. Brand attacks Freedom and I reach out to grab Deus's wrist, but before making contact, she whips her head in my direction with an angry expression and moves away. I assume I must have actually grabbed her wrist, and then she repeated back to avoid allowing me to touch her.

Brand lifts Freedom up, twists, and the bullet hits Freedom again in the arm.

"This doesn't work!" Brand yells. "I need to . . . something else . . ."

We reset again back to the point where Freedom has his arm extended toward me, the diamond calling for my shard. The excruciating pain in my chest is unbearable which causes Jonas to react by trying to stop Freedom. Jonas is knocked to the ground. I expect Brand to break free from his guard's hold, so I reach for Deus Ex, who avoids my contact.

Brand moves differently this time. Instead of ramming into Freedom, He rushes forward and stops next to Freedom, not touching him in the process. Freedom turns slightly to see him.

Freedom obviously doesn't want to drop the diamond, but he also doesn't want Brand attacking him. I can see in Freedom's mind an instantaneous change of thinking. His prior thoughts are replaced with admiration as he realizes Brand just repeated *with him*. He has greatly underestimated Brand's abilities. Freedom smiles, dimples forming on his cheeks. He thinks about how he can use Brand's new-found ability to his advantage.

Brand uses the small moment of confusion and wraps his arms around Freedom's waist, lifting him a few inches. This time Freedom doesn't squirm and the shot flies true, narrowly missing Brand, and ramming straight through Freedom's heart. Brand drops Freedom who topples sideways toward Jonas. As Freedom's body crashes down, his hand with the diamond slams onto Jonas' chest.

A blinding white flash and explosion rocks the room, nearly knocking us off our feet. Everyone, including Chris, General Harding and Rolf, are caught up in a frozen state of awe, with all eyes on the carnage lying on the floor: two people with deadly chest injuries

"Oh my God," Brand says, his voice high with panic, "I can't do this!"

I look at him, not knowing what he's referring to exactly.

He continues, "He's my father! He has dimples. And Jonas! I have to fix this."

"Brand, wait!" I cry out.

Deus screams, "What's happening?"

218

I ask, "Can't we get Jonas out of the way before he's injured?"

"I don't know how!" Hysteria tinges Brand's voice, his eyes bloodshot. "If Freedom lives, you die. But if he dies, so does Jonas!"

"I'll push Jonas out of the way."

"No! You have to grab Deus, remember?"

General Harding's voice rumbles through the chaos, but I don't hear what he says. I respond to Brand, "Okay. I'll grab Deus. You deal with Freedom. I think I can heal Jonas with Freedom's diamond."

Brand looks terrified. "Calli . . ."

"We can do this," I tell him.

He gives a jerk of a nod. The ground whirls around me with Brand's repeat. He takes me back only a few seconds so the others won't know we've spoken. My ears ring from the diamond explosion that has just occurred. I rush forward, ignoring the pain in my own chest, and slide next to Jonas. Freedom's diamond lies nearby against the wall under the observation window, and the other diamond— the one I still possess the remaining shard—has just entered Jonas's chest.

Chris and his father are positioned the same way as what I saw a few moments ago. Their jaws hang open and they're both leaning forward toward the glass to be able to see what lies below.

General Harding's voice thunders over the intercom: "What the hell is going on?"

I know my perception of what transpired in the last four or five seconds is not the same as General Harding's perception, or of anyone else's in the area, for that matter. Not even Brand.

A strange thrumming vibrates through my body, bringing me back to the present. I look over at the heart, feeling strangely ill at ease that I can no longer hear Freedom's thoughts. I know he's truly dead. And the diamond is now free for the taking.

Deus Ex shouts, "What's going on? What is that?" She points to the bloody, muscle covered diamond on the floor. She begins walking toward it with a mesmerized expression.

I yell out to her, "Don't touch it!"

"Guards," General Harding orders, "seize the heart!"

Brand points to Freedom's heart on the floor. "Get it, Calli. Save Jonas!"

I can tell the guards are Unaltereds now that I no longer have obsidian blocking my powers. Their minds are similar to my mother's. Whoever picks up the diamond-filled heart will gain ownership. I reach out, pick up the heart, and claim the diamond. Unhampered by obsidian or the protective leather pouch, the immense powers rush through my body, taking my breath in the process. I haven't felt this powerful since I had the whole diamond on my chest on the stone altar.

"Young lady, give that to my guards," General Harding commands, his voice shaking.

I turn to face the observation window with the still quivering heart in my hand. In the window I see Rolf standing behind Chris and General Harding with a petrified expression. I read his mind to find he's afraid, afraid they'll try to shoot his heart out too. He hadn't thought it would be possible to kill a Diamond Bearer until now. He turns and runs from the room.

I speak to General Harding, "No. I won't give it over. Whoever touches it will die."

Chris confirms what I am saying is true, that he's seen what happens with his own eyes.

General Harding refuses to listen. "That's the property

of the U.S. government, and you will hand it over, Ms. Courtnae."

I glance over at Jonas, pale and non-responsive. I know I can heal him, but as long as I hold Freedom's diamond in my hand General Harding and his lackeys will try to take it from me. There's one thing I can do to prevent that. I look at Chris and project my thoughts to his mind. *I have to help Jonas. I'm the only one who can.*

I raise my hand high above my head and say, "Brand, repeat me if this doesn't go well." I take a deep breath to prepare for the pain I am about to experience.

Chapter 14 - The Newest Diamond Bearer

"Wait!" Brand yells. "It doesn't go well enough. You won't be healed in two minutes."

"Will I be healing at all?"

"You're not dead in two minutes, but I don't know if you'll make it. I can't let you go past the two-minute mark or else I can't undo what could be your final act."

Deus Ex stares obsessively at the bloody mass in my hand. She speaks to Brand without taking her eyes off the heart, "What are you talking about, Brand? You can only repeat thirty seconds."

I ignore her and ask him, "Well, am I still standing, at least?"

"No, you're on your knees, doubled over at two minutes in."

"What about Jonas? Is he still alive?"

"I'm not sure. I was focused on you."

"Don't repeat me this time. I think it will be fine."

"What? You *think?* If you die, I won't be able to save you!"

"I don't think I'll die. Take me back again."

Instantly the world around me spins as Brand repeats us back to where I'm holding the diamond high above my head and asking Brand to repeat if it doesn't go well.

For brief a moment, I recall Maetha telling Freedom

that possessing two of the Sanguine Diamonds won't give additional powers to the Bearer. I assume adding Freedom's diamond to the shard I already have in my heart won't be a bad thing. I shouldn't get a "diamond overdose" or anything. At least I hope not.

I bring my hand down and slam Freedom's bloody, heart-muscle covered diamond into my chest as hard as I can. The ensuing explosion breaks my ribs and sternum. The pain is so intense no words could ever describe what I feel. It's beyond pain. I can't breathe. I half expect to have the ground spin as Brand repeats me back, but it doesn't happen. Instead, I fall to my knees with my vision dimming and darkening. I will my body to heal with every ounce of thought and energy flowing through me.

I can only liken the experience of pushing myself all the way to this side of death and back to bungee jumping. The giant elastic band stretches as far as it can go with the weight of the body attached to the end, slowing down as the stretch reaches the maximum extension, and then it recoils with a snap. My diamond shard snaps into action and gives me the power to heal my heart around the whole diamond that I'd introduced into it. Next comes the repairing of bone and skin. The hole closes rapidly while my breasts rebuild. I notice my bra is still intact over my lower sternum, but my shirt has been blasted open.

Before I have healed completely, I move over to Jonas through the massive blood puddle on the floor and place my hand on his open wound. He's unconscious, but not dead. His heart struggles to pump blood and is trying to heal over the diamond, which is truly amazing. However, I wonder if I should remove the diamond from his body, and then heal him.

I look for his future and find blackness. Nothing. The same type of non-future I saw for him at Cave Falls. I change direction in my mind and plan on healing his body with the diamond inside. He's an Unaltered human now. It might work. I look for his future and find he now has one. I see him training with Maetha and Mary on a white sand beach with palm trees and mountains covered with tropical plants in the background.

I project my thoughts to his mind. *Think about good health, Jonas. Fill your mind with what it feels like once you recover from a bad case of the flu. You know, when you appreciate how wonderful it feels to feel good again.* I complete the healing of his heart around the diamond in his chest.

While Jonas's bones knit together, and he starts to regain consciousness, I become aware of my surroundings. This awareness is so intense I can sense the fear, awe, and selfish desires of everyone in the room. I feel the inhaling of breath, the sweat rolling down skin, the hearts of each person as they race inside healthy chests, even full bladders. It's at this point that I begin to wonder exactly how we will be able to escape the compound.

I know as long as I maintain the same pose of healing Jonas, the guards won't try to seize me. I seek out Chris's mind with mine. I locate him, but he's no longer in the room behind the window. He's worried that I'm unaware he and his father are about to enter the room and capture us. Without looking at Brand, I speak to his mind. *Brand, General Harding and Chris are about to come in. It's our only chance for escape. We have to take advantage of the open door. Don't let the door close. I'll tell Deus Ex the same thing.* I wait for him to respond, but hear nothing. *Brand, you hear me? Answer with your mind. Jonas's skin has almost finished healing. We are out of time.*

I attempt to read Brand's mind. Normally I can't get very far, but I have to try. I don't encounter the jumbled mess that I normally do. He keeps thinking the same thought over and over: *Freedom was my dad.*

I interject my thoughts again. *They're coming, Brand! Get your mind in the game!*

I direct my thoughts to Deus's mind. *General Harding and Chris are about to enter the room. Make sure the door doesn't close. It's our only way to escape.*

"What's going on?" she says out loud.

The guards are probably thinking the same thing. They appear to be just as blown away by the miraculous, yet terrifying events that just happened as Deus Ex.

I speak to her mind again. *They're coming. Please work with Brand to help us escape, Deus.*

Chris and his father enter the room.

Brand jumps forward and attacks Chris, punching and pounding on him, yelling with a cracked voice, "You knew he was my dad and you let me kill him! You're just like your father!"

Brand's attack lacks the finesse of the other fights I've witnessed, which leads me to conclude he isn't repeating. He's really upset! He continues to yell obscenities at Chris and swing at him until the nearest guard pulls him off and drags him away. Brand has tears streaming down his cheeks.

General Harding points at me and Jonas. "Seize them."

Our future fills my mind—locked up.

"Deus, repeat!" I order, but the fact that I can still remember what happened proves she has not repeated. I look over to find a guard has snapped a silver cuff around her wrist.

Her eyes widen in shock as she looks at the cuff. Then she yells at Chris, "You were supposed to prevent this!"

General Harding glares at Chris. "What is she talking about?"

A sly smile creeps over Chris's face. "I have no idea."

Jonas croaks out, "Chris?"

I yell at Brand. "Get us out of this, Brand!"

"What do you think I'm trying to do? You keep screwing it up by using your powers. Knock it off! They have to lead us out of the room."

I was about to use the Healing power to "take down" the guard who shot Freedom, but I hold off.

The room spins quickly as Brand repeats us back a couple seconds. I'm holding onto Jonas. He's a little wobbly but regaining strength rapidly.

General Harding points to Brand and says, "Get a cuff on him, then take him and Deus Ex to the cell." Then he points to Jonas and me. "Take them to the medical lab. I want those diamonds!"

Brand shouts, "No!" I see he has just been immobilized with an obsidian cuff like Deus Ex.

Both Repeaters cuffed and halted.

Yet . . . we still have optimistic futures. I can see our successful escape, but how?

We are led into the hallway where Brand and Deus are directed in one direction and Jonas and I in the other.

Brand yells, "Now, Deus."

The two of them begin an assault that seems choreographed to the last detail, leaving me wondering if Brand's cuff actually has Yellowstone obsidian. Deus uses her extensive knowledge of effective fighting skills to break free from her guard and disable him effortlessly. Between her ninja-like skills and Brand's fighting tactics, Jonas and I seem to be in good hands. Soon, every guard is on the ground, either unconscious, or holding their groins . . . including Chris.

General Harding backs up against the wall, fearful of being attacked. Brand grabs his arm and drags him toward the exit. We follow.

Brand says, "Agent Alpha tried to tell you we had figured out how to use the obsidian as a weapon. You should have listened. Here's how this is going to work. You are going to walk with us to the gate, wish us luck, and see us on our merry way. If you try to prevent us from leaving, I'll have Deus Ex snap your neck faster than you can say your mommy's name."

We walk through the door and out into the bright afternoon sunlight. The immediate drain of my powers because of the obsidian-pocked exterior isn't surprising to me, but I can see that to Jonas, who was powerless when he arrived, but who now possesses an all-powerful diamond, the drain is disturbing. This is his first experience with the power-canceling effects of obsidian. I'm just happy his healing is complete and he's whole again.

As we walk carefully across the yard to the security fence, I pull out the vial containing the two topazes that were charged with super-speed and hold them in my hand at the ready. We are quite fortunate to be walking away from this government fortress after the gruesome events that have just played out. It must look sickening to the guards, considering Jonas and I are covered in blood and our clothing is in shreds. I wonder if Mary and Amenemhet are watching on the monitor.

We reach the gate, and General Harding's presence surprises the magazine-reading guard right out of his chair. He jumps to attention, saluting.

General Harding orders the guard to open the gate, after which he escorts us outside the perimeter and stops. My powers rush back into my body as we are now beyond the effects of the obsidian on the building. I take advantage of the situation and enter General Harding's mind for a second.

Freedom never told him about Brand's extraordinary fighting abilities. He also doesn't know much at all about Repeaters, and nothing about Diamond Bearers other than what he's just witnessed with his own eyes concerning the diamond's powers. But the most revealing, shocking information I find in his brain has to do with the research concerning red spinel and the woman named Crimson.

What I wouldn't give to be able to extract his memories right at that moment, but all things considered, I decide taking the time would be a stupid choice. As it is, we haven't escaped entirely yet.

Using my telepathy, I instruct Jonas: *Get ready to catch the topaz I'm about to throw. Then take Deus's hand to lend her running ability and run back the way we came.*

"Well, you have a safe journey then," General Harding says with a tightly controlled voice while waving. "I'll be seeing you sooner than you think."

I hear vehicles approaching. I also sense the ominous black-fog future that can only mean one thing: obsidian. I speak to Brand's mind, *Take my hand now.* He does. With my other hand, I toss the topaz to Jonas. Deus eyes the flying topaz and takes Jonas's hand, obviously understanding what needs to happen. He catches it just as several vehicles approach from behind, skidding to a stop.

Through my peripheral vision, which is aided by sensing air displacement and hearing the slight rustle of clothing, General Harding produces a large piece of obsidian from inside a metal container. Our diamond powers are instantly canceled, but the power of the topaz is still there.

"Run," I yell.

We shoot between the military trucks and SUVs, evading their bullets and capture. The four of us are able to flee the obsidian's effects, which has to be confusing to

General Harding. Maybe he will abandon the idea of obsidian weapons, believing they will be ineffective on a Diamond Bearer.

One can only hope.

Amenemhet, Mary, Beth, and Anika are shocked to see the four of us enter the motel room.

Mary says, "We thought you were Maetha and Neema. They're due back any moment." She pauses, staring at the blood-covered, torn clothing. "What happened? Here, lie down." She takes Jonas by the arm and helps him to a bed.

Anika rushes to his side and takes his hand into hers.

I read Jonas's thoughts and find he was happy to be able to let go of Deus Ex's hand once we arrived back at the hotel. He didn't like how her obsidian canceled his new diamond powers. Yet as soon as his powers returned, they drained once again when Mary touched him because she's still wearing a small obsidian for protection from Freedom.

However, he is quite happy to have Anika responding in such a caring manner.

I say, "He's fine, Mary. We're all fine."

Amenemhet says, "When we saw Rolf run from the building, we figured something was up. But when we saw you leave with General Harding, we knew something significant went down."

"Freedom went down," Brand states without emotion as he walks over to the table and sits down. He grabs a bottled water and drinks half of it.

Amenemhet asks, "Down where?"

Brand wipes his mouth and says, "Wherever it is Diamond Bearers go when they die."

I realize that because Amenemhet and Mary are still

using small obsidians to hide their location from Freedom, they can't tell Freedom's stone lost its owner—and gained a new one.

"You don't need your obsidian protection anymore," I say. "Freedom is dead."

"Dead? But, the diamond. Where's his diamond?" Mary asks, eyes wide and obviously afraid.

Amenemhet has already put his obsidian away in a small metal tin. "Calli has it," he says, then he looks at Jonas, "and Jonas has a diamond as well."

"What?" Mary asks as she puts her obsidian away. She doesn't have to ask any additional questions because she's able to access Jonas's mind and view the events like a movie. I can see within my mind what Mary is witnessing. The events are playing out from both Jonas's perspective and mine.

Anika tightens her hold on his hand.

Beth brings me a Runner's jacket to cover my exposed chest. A commotion outside the door draws our attention and puts us on guard.

Brand speaks from his seat. "It's just Maetha and Neema."

Beth opens the door.

Maetha and Neema enter with several bags and packages and set them on the table by Brand before turning around to look at everyone.

Neema picks up on the strange tension in the room. "What's going on? What happened to Jonas?"

Maetha takes one look at me and rushes to my side. "Are you hurt? What happened?" Her hands search my body wherever blood is present, which is pretty much everywhere. She whirls on Amenemhet and barks out, "How did this happen?"

"Put your obsidians away," Mary says. "You don't

need them anymore."

Maetha coughs. "Excuse me?"

"Jonas's mind holds the information. Come and learn for yourselves." Maetha, Neema, and Jonas sit on the adjacent beds and meditate.

Deus Ex walks over to Brand and sits down across the table. The large pile of boxes and bags partially obstructs their view of each other. "Freedom was not our father," she says. "It's Dr. Awali. He's named in the file."

"I don't care what the file said. Did you ever stop to think that maybe he used a different name? He did with you. He did with Beth." Brand's voice increases and his words are filled with anger. "I saw for myself, Deus. I saw *me* when he smiled. And Chris knew all along, didn't he?" Brand directs his last comment in my direction.

I don't know if that is true or not, so I say nothing.

"Man, Brand, you were awesome!" Jonas says. "Throwing that fake fit made it possible for us to get out."

"It wasn't an act. I had just been tricked into helping kill my own dad."

"Yeah, well," Jonas said coolly. "I'd love to trade shoes with you. If I could help end my father's life, I'd do it."

"At least you grew up with fathers," Deus Ex says to both of them.

Neema interrupts. "Listen, we can sit here and mourn over things we never had, or we can talk about the positive. Freedom is dead! You executed the impossible as a team without the help of the other Diamond Bearers. Even if—"

Deus Ex cuts Neema off with a harsh tone that is downright scary. "No! Let's talk about the fact that no one told me you guys were walking around with freakin' diamonds in your hearts! I detest people who withhold information." She points to Neema. "You especially."

I try to read Deus's mind, but because of the cuff she's still wearing, I can't.

Maetha speaks gingerly. "Deus, only a small handful of people in the whole world know about the diamonds, and now you are one of those people. Freedom was on a path of destruction that would have included killing you eventually. The fact that you worked for him is why I didn't tell you about the diamonds. I couldn't risk you going back to him with even more sensitive info. What if General Harding overheard?"

"Yeah, well, now Harding knows. He saw everything firsthand, just like me. He now knows these diamonds exist and that they are one of the most powerful things on earth . . . right up there with red spinel. You should have told me, instead of making me look like a fool for knowing nothing and staring with my jaw on the floor."

"I told you that if you stayed with us long enough you'd find out why Calli was protected the way she was."

"Yeah, well, I've stayed as long as I'm going to." Deus Ex reaches into Amenemhet's case and pulls out a tool that she uses as a pick for the lock on her cuff. She struggles a bit and then pops the cuff open, depositing it among the bottles of water. "I have to say," she says to Neema as she walks by on her way to the door, "I won't miss *you* one bit."

"Don't let the door hit you on the butt," Neema says.

Deus Ex glares at Neema and then leaves the room.

After a couple moments of silence, Maetha says, "I worry that we haven't even begun to see what she's capable of. Pack up. We'll leave in ten minutes."

Chapter 15 - Chris's Arrival

We check out of the motel shortly after Deus Ex leaves. Beth and Anika are set to head west to go meet up with Clara Winter and the other clan leaders. Jonas and Anika share a tender moment saying goodbye to each other. Their budding relationship is a shame, according to Neema, one that is "doomed and certain to cause heartache." I feel bad for the two of them. They really connected prior to Jonas becoming a Diamond Bearer. I hope for the best between them, but don't look for their futures.

We board Maetha's plane, bound for Indiana. Most of the Diamond Bearers are heading there to celebrate. I just want to relax. I long for Chris. Now that I am an official Diamond Bearer and Freedom is no longer a threat, Chris and I will be able to do anything we want. No more heart pain because of excitement. I wonder what he's thinking right now. I also wonder how long he'll have to remain with his father before he can come back to me.

Brand nudges my shoulder to get my attention. I open my eyes and look at him. He looks exhausted. "Calli, do you realize I'm the only one on this plane besides the pilot who isn't a Diamond Bearer?"

"Does that bother you?"

"Nah, not really."

"But somewhat, right?"

"I guess I just feel like I'm not part of the little club or something."

"Brand, no Diamond Bearer could have done what you did today. Your power is superior in many ways."

He exhales a heavy breath, "I knew, going into the compound, Freedom would die somehow, and the 'somehow' would probably involve me. Maetha and I had a conversation about it in the hotel room."

"I wondered about that."

Brand pushes his body back into his seat and lays his head on the headrest. "I guess I didn't think about how actually doing it would make me feel."

"I'm sorry, Brand."

"For what? This isn't your fault. Well, maybe it is. He wanted your diamond shard." He scrubs his hands over his face. "Sorry. I don't mean it's your fault. I don't know what I mean. I don't know what I feel."

"It's completely normal for you to be upset right now." I pause. "Brand, I read Freedom's mind before he died. Do you want to know what I saw?"

He turns his head and with sadness in his eyes says, "Yeah."

"I saw what his life was like before he became a Diamond Bearer. He had a wife and two kids: a son and a daughter. When the plague hit his village, his wife and daughter died. His son also became ill, but recovered. Neema became part of his life at that time and helped him through his grief and depression. She introduced him to Maetha who invited him to help eradicate a clan of Healers who were not following nature's will. He agreed and became a Diamond Bearer.

"After many years, his son died of old age. I felt his feelings of betrayal toward Maetha for not making his son a Bearer and saving his life. As each of his grandchildren died, he became more and more angry. He became determined to find a way to overthrow Maetha and the other Diamond Bearers. He figured the way to do that was to acquire more of the Sanguine Diamonds.

"He began training another group of Healers how to extract the life essence from regular humans. He knew by doing so, the Bearers would harvest a diamond to be used to re-balance nature."

Brand sits forward and turns in his seat. "He created a reason to expose a diamond?"

"Yes. The person chosen to carry the diamond to the evil 'Vampire' Healer clan was Duncan. Freedom had intended to intercept Duncan and the diamond on its way to delivery, but his plan wasn't able to materialize. Maetha intervened. He didn't know she'd been following him."

Brand says, "She stopped him."

"Yes. But many people had already died because of his efforts to get the diamond. He didn't care. He started working with another group of Healers—who were not misusing their powers at the time—teaching them how to feel healthy tissue and damage it. He personally trained the Death Clan to be able to kill with their thoughts in an attempt to establish his own army. He knew they would rise up and follow the standard course of events that would eventually lead them to their destruction with the use of another Sanguine Diamond. Many more innocent people died before the Bearers stepped in.

"However, before that happened, sometime in the late 1800s, Freedom discovered the Yellowstone obsidian and used it to hide from Maetha and the Bearers. He disappeared for decades at a time and began working with the government. He wasn't aware that Gustave had harvested his diamond for the purpose of eliminating the Death Clan or that I had the diamond. Because of his use of obsidian, he missed his opportunity, again.

"The day he and I met for the first time, he was outside my mother's office. He had been waiting for *you* to leave the building."

"What? Me?"

"Freedom was keeping tabs on you, Brand, watching to see if your DNA exhibited the same change as the other subjects in the program. Freedom was stunned to discover I had a diamond shard in my heart, which meant the diamond rebirth process had already been completed. But he didn't fret over it for long because he knew he had bigger better things in the works. He was working with the government—working with General Harding."

Brand says, "Why didn't he ever talk to me, tell me who he was?"

"He was trying to breed warriors—an army—in an effort to wipe out the Diamond Bearers. When you didn't exhibit a power he thought useful, he didn't pursue you. If you did, he would have manipulated you and your powers.

"So he never cared for me at all." Brand closed his eyes for a moment, his face pinched.

"No."

"Doesn't matter anyway. He would have used me. Instead, I was used by the Diamond Bearers to kill *him*. I'm Mr. Manipulatable." I try to interrupt him but he continues, "Wait, I was like the death row executioner. You know, the guy who flips the switch on the electric chair. Except, I didn't sign up for the position. It was kind of dumped on me."

Brand's thought process sounds a little too familiar to me. "Brand, you understood the severity of Freedom's abilities and reach. You knew what he was capable of and that he needed to be stopped."

"No doubt about that. It's just messing with my mind.

I usually repeat to save lives, not end them."

"You know helping end Freedom's life saved many others. He wouldn't have stopped."

"Still feels like a lousy trade-off somehow." Brand gives a weak smile, then his expression turns down. "I'm not going to stick around for the party. I'm heading home."

"Are you going to find Suz?"

"Eventually. I just need to get my mind around everything that's happened lately. I need to decompress a bit."

"You and me both."

We land in Fort Wayne, Indiana. Brand leaves our group at that point. Maetha gives him a few phone numbers and email addresses to use for communication, and then she hugs him. I'm pretty sure Brand hasn't used his charms on her . . . I mean, why would he? I figure Maetha is trying to help him heal.

We continue to a private air strip near Patoka Lake, where Maetha's resort is located, and we're met by two Diamond Bearers, Duncan and Merlin. Merlin greets me as I step off the plane.

"Calli, congratulations on becoming a Bearer," Merlin says over his shoulder as he loads luggage into the trunk of the car.

"Thank you. Oh, and thank you for the clothing you bought for me in D.C."

"No problem. It's my lesser-known cosmic ability— fashionista extraordinaire."

Maetha waves to us and says, "We'll meet you there, Merlin." Then she runs off with Mary and Amenemhet, leaving Jonas and me to ride with Merlin and Duncan.

Duncan says to Jonas, "Son, you're the first person to possess a diamond who was not born an Unaltered. How are you adapting?"

"Except for running, I can't control the powers, so Maetha told me not to try yet. She's going to take me to her home in Bermuda to teach me."

"Ah . . . the island." Duncan is evidently recalling fond memories of the island paradise. "Every one of us has spent many years there. It's the perfect place to go when you need to be forgotten."

Without warning, I enter Jonas's mind. I feel his present thoughts, emotions, desires, and wishes as if they are my own, as if I'm thinking them too. Right now, he's anxious as he thinks about Anika. He doesn't want her to forget about him, and he wishes she could go with him.

I shake my head to try to control my thoughts. I remember the day the Death Clan died, the day Jonas declined healing from Maetha, and how much respect I felt for him at that moment. I look over at him to see if he can tell I am sensing him.

"Calli, what was that?"

"What do you mean?"

"I felt you inside of me. It was like you resided in my thoughts, watching and observing everything."

"Can you do the same to me?"

He closes his eyes and meditates on the idea that he might be able to enter my thoughts. After a few seconds, he opens his eyes and shakes his head. "I can't focus enough. I wish I could handle the powers of the diamond as well as you did when you carried it to the Death Clan."

Duncan says, "When Calli carried the diamond, it was in the pouch, which minimized its overwhelming effects. She never had full possession of the diamond, only a small piece containing the amount of powers the diamond had when it was in the pouch. Son, you're the first Bearer to have no prior contact with the diamond and then have one blasted into your heart. I'm surprised you lived."

Merlin corrects him. "Duncan, he doesn't have a complete diamond yet."

I glance over at Jonas. His thoughts reveal he's worried about how the remaining shard will be removed from my heart and inserted into his. He doesn't want to hurt me or be responsible for causing me more pain.

I don't want him to suffer either. Yet, I know removing the shard from my heart will be more difficult than inserting it into his.

His voice sounds in my mind. *Whoa, Calli! Can you hear me?*

Yes.

I just read your mind.

This isn't mind reading, Jonas. We share some kind of connection through our shared diamond. The same thing happened when Freedom held the diamond at the compound.

We spend the remainder of the drive to the resort inside each other's minds, learning all about each other. He learns about how much of my time during the delivery journey was spent dwelling on him, hoping I could heal him. He had no idea.

He's modestly embarrassed to have me discover that he has carried a torch for me for the last few years. Even though his heart now only beats for Anika, he had been smitten with me. This intimate connection between our minds leaves no secrets.

In the last three days, Diamond Bearers have arrived from all over the world to take part in the celebration of the return of control, and to decide what to do about Rolf. Maetha gave me a very special Imperial topaz charged with the Grecian Blue power of invisibility. I was instructed to use it sparingly and carefully.

I haven't used it at all. There's been no need.

I have absolutely loved learning the history of several different Bearers and the circumstances in which they were used by Maetha to carry a diamond. These conversations have helped pass the time while I wait to hear from Chris.

Presently, our group is assembled in a large tent by the lake. As we enjoy good food and entertaining stories, my attention is drawn to the parking lot. A vehicle has just arrived. I instantly recognize Chris's profile. I didn't foresee him arriving at all . . . and believe me, I tried to look for his future. I figure that because he was residing in the obsidian-covered building, I couldn't access his future . . . or mine in connection with his.

What a surprise! I am completely caught off guard. My feet are running to him before my butt leaves my seat. As soon as he closes the car door and turns around, I attack him with hugs and kisses, pushing him back up against the car. He takes a moment to catch up, but once he does, he takes over the kissing and twists us around so my back is up against the car. I can't be happier or in a higher state of bliss. I finally have my Chris, and he has me.

I never want to let him go.

Several seconds pass before we exhaust ourselves and bring our public display under control. I lay my head down on his shoulder with my mouth nuzzled against his neck near his ear. His head rests against mine, and he holds me tightly.

He says, "Watching you shove that diamond in your heart was the most horrifying thing I've ever seen, Calli. I was so scared I almost slipped up and blew my cover."

I lift my head and meet his eyes. "I can't believe we actually killed Freedom. If it wasn't for the conversations you had with your father, I don't think we would have succeeded."

"Yeah, but when the diamond entered your heart, I thought I might pass out. But then you healed yourself, and Jonas, too."

I say, "You know, I just want to go find someplace private, and relax with you."

"Me too, but first I need to talk to Maetha."

"Okay. She's in the tent." I lead Chris, walking hand-in-hand to the tent.

After Chris has been congratulated over and over by many people, he sits me in a chair at a table with Jonas and Neema and walks over to talk to Maetha. She's talking to Duncan, Alena, Hasan, and Fabian. When she sees him, she tells them to wait a moment while she speaks with Chris.

They are turned away from me, so I can't read their lips. *But hey, I'm a Diamond Bearer now! I can read minds.* So, I read his. He asks Maetha if she can step outside with him because he needs advice on how to propose to me. Wow! I pull out of his mind and decide I don't want to spoil the surprise by snooping. Maetha says something back to him, at which point Chris leaves Maetha and walks back over to our table.

Just watching him makes my heart race with excitement—the same type of reaction that would render me near death not too many days ago. Chris stands behind my chair and rubs my shoulders. "She's busy for a moment," he says. "I'll have to wait for her."

"What did you need her for?" Neema asks.

"Um, it's kind of personal."

Neema stands and says, "Listen, I've been a Diamond

241

Bearer almost as long as Maetha. If you have a question, I can probably answer it for you. Come on, let's go out and talk."

Chris kisses me on the forehead and winks, sending my heart all aflutter, then leaves with Neema.

Amenemhet enters the tent carrying a large box of supplies and food and sets it down on the table next to me. As he empties the box, a shiny glimmer at the bottom catches my attention: it's the two silver cuffs that Deus Ex and Brand took off in the motel after Freedom died. I reach over to pick one up, expecting to feel the obsidian drain my powers. The cuff I pick up was apparently Brand's because it doesn't have the power-sucking properties. I drop it inside the box and pick up the other cuff—and drop it immediately. It's powerless too!

"What's wrong?" Jonas says.

"Neither cuff has obsidian," I say. "Deus Ex faked her loss of power at the end."

Jonas adds, "Well, it's a good thing she's a great fighter or we might not have been able to escape."

"Yeah, but she made a big deal about how Chris failed. Why would she do that?"

"I don't know. Now that you mention it, something else about the whole fiasco that bothered me was the devious grin Chris gave her when she yelled at him about the laced cuff. Maybe you can ask him why he looked at her that way when he knew the cuff was harmless."

"This is too confusing."

Our minds are thinking as one. I'm hoping Chris acted that way to keep up his appearance in front of his father. Then again, his actions didn't seem fake at all to me. Jonas's mind considers how Deus might have other motivations. My mind remembers not being able to read Deus's mind in the hotel room. I assumed it was because she was wearing the cuff, but now I know the cuff wasn't the reason. Then I remember she has obsidian on the necklace she wears. Jonas voices his concern that something isn't right about the way everything played out.

I stand and say, "I've got to go find Chris and get some answers." I pull out the new topaz that Maetha charged with invisibility. I clutch it firmly, at the ready, and then run out the door in search of Chris and Neema.

Chris's unique scent isn't hard to track, and it leads me directly to the two of them in a thick wooded area. Chris is facing my direction, while Neema stands to his right. He pulls a small velvet box out of his pocket and hands it to her.

I quickly drop to the ground behind a bush, feeling guilty for intruding. I shouldn't be seeing the ring before he gives it to me. I'll just wait here until he finishes talking with Neema, then I'll go ask him about the obsidian cuffs. To my horror, the future suddenly closes in with the unmistakable black fog of impending obsidian.

I tighten my hold on the topaz in my hand and wish I knew how to activate the invisibility power, all the while fumbling in my pocket for the Runners topaz in case I need to flee.

I hear Chris say to Neema, "Don't be alarmed by the obsidian. I don't want her peeking. I figure by placing a small piece of obsidian inside, she'll be genuinely surprised. How should I propose to her?"

Neema pops the box open and I instantly feel her diamond go dark because of the obsidian. I'm a little relieved the situation is innocent. However, I'm unsure of how I feel about Chris using obsidian because he thinks I'd try to sneak a peek.

I move a little to allow a better view of the two.

Chris takes one small step away from Neema while she

holds the box, a smile stretching wide across her face. I wonder if she's remembering happier times in her own life when love was alive and well—quite a deviation from her negative remarks concerning Jonas and Anika. She looks like she's about to speak, but then the air splits open with the sound of a gunshot. A bullet blasts into Neema's chest, tearing her wide open, blowing her heart out the other side of her. It all happens so fast, yet the feeling is one of slow motion because I can't do anything about it. Her lifeless body slowly crumples to the ground, the velvet box landing in a pile of dry leaves.

Confusion and terror takes over my body. I have to get Chris to a safe place. I know if he gets shot the same way Neema did, I won't be able to heal him. I need Maetha's help. I need anyone's help. If only Brand was here, he could repeat this horrible moment into oblivion.

The diamond within me begins to vibrate with awareness, almost speaking to me, letting me know one of the twenty-one diamonds no longer has an owner—the same sensation I experienced when Freedom's diamond no longer had an owner. Tears well up in my eyes, nearly preventing me from detecting the movement to my right. I can't believe what I'm seeing. Deus Ex heads in my direction with a large rifle slung over her shoulder. I want to shout "run" to Chris, but my throat is constricted.

I want to rush forward and tackle her to the ground to protect Chris. I need her to hurt the same way I hurt right now, but I know she's untouchable, being a Repeater. All I can do is hold completely still and hope I'm invisible so she doesn't do the same thing to me.

"This is why I call myself Deus Ex. No one ever expects me to show up," she says as she bends over to pick up the velvet box. "I come out of nowhere and accomplish what no one else can do." She snaps the box shut to hide the obsidian, then tosses it to Chris, who catches it with one hand. He shoves the small velvet box of deception into his pocket.

He responds coolly, "I told you killing a Bearer would be easy."

What? Chris was part of the plan?

His voice holds no remorse, no sorrow, nothing but cold words. The bottom drops out of my stomach, and the air flees from my lungs.

"Why didn't you bring Maetha? You know what, never mind, this kill was much more satisfying. Meet me at the rendezvous point. Go!" She points off into the distance.

Chris disappears in a flash.

Deus Ex stands over Neema's head and says, "I told you I'd kill you someday." She bends down and looks closely at Neema's heart and the sparkly edges of the diamond that are uncovered by the bullet. She reaches out to pick it up. Her hand freezes in place above the heart as if she's contemplating whether or not to pick it up. But it's different than that. I can tell she can't pick up the diamond. She stands and drops a folded piece of paper on Neema's body, then jogs into the forest. A few seconds later I hear the approaching crowd.

I put my invisibility stone back inside the vial as Maetha appears through the trees. "Calli, what's going on?"

"Get down, she's got a gun!" I am still crouched on the ground.

The group obeys without delay, and Maetha begins communicating with her mind. *Where's Neema?*

She's dead! Deus Ex shot her!

Several different Diamond Bearers' voices fill my head at once. *What? How? When?*

Maetha asks, *Where's Deus now?*

She ran to the west a few seconds ago.

Maetha stands and begins yelling out orders for three Diamond Bearers to track Deus's trail. I don't even pay attention to who she sends or which direction she sends them. A few other Bearers run to Neema's body. I stay seated on the ground, too distraught to do anything as the reality sets in of what I'd just witnessed. Chris just knowingly led Neema out to her death with the tempting lure of discussing his plan to propose and give me an engagement ring.

Maetha walks carefully to Neema's body. I know the two of them have been friends for thousands of years, a length of time I can't even comprehend. *What must Maetha be feeling right now?* They'd just gotten back from a long trip together to retrieve more Imperial topaz—stones that are no longer needed to end Freedom's life. Maetha took Neema with her in an effort to separate her from Deus Ex because of the sparks that constantly crackled between the two.

Maetha kneels down beside Neema and reaches up and pulls her lids over her eyes. She takes Neema's right hand in hers and rests it in her lap, her head hanging low. Everyone stills to a silence. The only sounds are from the geese flying overhead, the croaking of nearby frogs, and a few chirping birds in the trees around us. It's a subtle reminder that nature lives on. Neema is dead, but the world around her continues as usual.

Amenemhet bends down and removes the folded piece of paper from Neema's body before covering her body with his jacket. He hands the paper to Mary.

"How did this happen?" Alena cries out. "Why couldn't Neema foresee it?"

"Why couldn't any of us foresee it?" Duncan asks.

Mary unfolds the paper and stares at it.

"I saw Neema leave with Chris," Fabian says. "Where

is he now?"

Mary looks up from the note and says, "Deus Ex took him. She's kidnapped him. She's demanding that all the Diamond Bearers surrender in exchange for his release." Mary sends her thoughts to my mind. *I'm so sorry, Calli.*

"Neema must have died trying to save Chris," Duncan says. "She sacrificed herself fighting a Repeater."

I say nothing. What can I say? I still can't believe what I just witnessed. Is Chris a double agent working for his father *and* for the Diamond Bearers? Why on earth would he help Deus Ex kill Neema? How could he act so nonchalant around Neema mere minutes, no seconds, before her death if he was truly on our side? Freedom had said, "Once a spy, always a spy." Maybe that was the one truthful thing he said.

I guess blood is thicker than water.

And yet he winked at me before he left with Neema.

Was it all an act? How long has Chris been working against us? Was it before he volunteered to go back to work for his father? Has he been gathering information all this time? I have to stop thinking this way! But he had the ring to show Neema, and he kept it in a box with obsidian. Not to mention, Deus Ex pulled a previously composed note out of her pocket. No. This was planned, premeditated. Chris and Deus Ex are working together for a common goal, but what is it?

Maetha softly places Neema's hand on top of Amenemhet's jacket, stands, and says, "We may never know the circumstances that led to her death. What is evident is that Deus Ex knows how to kill Diamond Bearers. None of us are safe now that she knows we all carry a diamond in our hearts."

"She didn't take Neema's, though," Marketa says. "Maybe she was just settling her own vendetta."

A quote my father uses in times like this comes to mind. *Martin Luther said: 'You're not only responsible for what you say, but also for what you don't say.' Always take responsibility, Calli.*

I know what I have to do. Jonas's presence in my mind gives me comfort and reassures me my decision is right. I turn my head and find him standing nearby, offering his hand to help me up. I take his hand and let him pull me upright. Then I walk to Maetha and the others. "Read my mind to see what I saw."

One by one, the Diamond Bearers enter and then pull out of my memories, feeling my pain and loss for both a friend and a soulmate. Some have tears in their eyes. Others are angered by what they see, but Maetha's opinion is what I want to hear most of all.

She says, "Calli, don't be so quick to assume Chris is the enemy here. When he asked me if he could speak with me, I detected a strong self-loathing and self-degradation even though what he wanted to talk to me about was joyful in nature. I needed to finish my conversation before addressing Chris's needs, but by that time I was sensing an unclaimed diamond."

"Calli, they obviously want us to think Chris has been kidnapped," Mary says. "The question is, why and for what purpose?"

Yeok Choo and Chuang walk over to my side. Chuang says, "We believe this kidnapping is Deus's attempt to secure her world. She now views Diamond Bearers as a greater threat than even the vests the government is making."

"Yes, she was astonished to discover the source of our powers," Duncan adds. "Naturally she feels we would try to use our powers against her."

"I think we all need to split up," Alena says. "I view

Neema's death as a failed attempt to secure a diamond. She'll try again."

"Yes, I agree," Amenemhet adds. "We'll need to get bullet-proof vests of our own to wear night and day."

Amalgada reminds us of the gruesome reality. "Let's not forget that another way to end a Diamond Bearer's life is by beheading. Bullet-proof vests are one thing. Protecting our neck is another."

"It would be a good idea for everyone to have topaz charged with future sight," Avani adds. "Then, even up against obsidian, one could see the future."

A wave of agreement filters through the gathered group of near-immortal beings.

Maetha adds, "The supply of topaz we brought back should be enough for everyone to have multiple stones. I don't believe we should separate completely. We should stick together in teams and with no fewer than two."

Hasan shakes his head. "No. Sticking together will only make it easier for Deus to make multiple kills."

A few Bearers agree with Hasan, while others side with Maetha. Jonas's thoughts enter my mind. He's conflicted about what to choose. I send my thoughts to his mind telling him not to worry. He will be going with Maetha to her private island. That doesn't settle his nerves much. I see my own future. I will be going to Maine to join my parents at their cabin. Duncan will be coming with me.

Maetha says, "Jonas will come with me as I take Neema's body to Bermuda. Duncan, will you accompany Calli and take her to her parents?" Duncan nods. "Everyone else will decide for themselves what to do." Maetha steps beyond Neema's body and bends down to pick up Neema's heart. She continues talking as she gently wraps the bloody mass in a shirt Amenemhet gives her. "Rolf will have to decide where his allegiance lies. Soon, we may have two diamonds without Bearers."

Jonas asks, "What happens when a diamond doesn't have a Bearer?"

Mary responds. "The first Unaltered to touch the diamond becomes its owner and the diamond is loyal to him or her. Neema's diamond is now in Maetha's possession until she reassigns it to someone else."

Ruth points out, "If we don't leave this place soon, there will be many diamonds without Bearers." Her words bring the sickening realization that everyone is a target.

Duncan and I arrive at my parents' cabin on the north end of Sebago Lake late the next night. My father lets us in and wakes my mother. I try to reassure them that everything is fine and we should go to sleep and discuss things in the morning, but they won't hear of it. Mom puts a kettle on for tea, and the four of us talk till dawn.

Duncan details the family lineage to my mother and where she fits in, then talks about his journey to becoming a Diamond Bearer.

I try to listen, but I can't focus on his words. I had wanted to hear all about the Healers who the townspeople called Vampires ever since Maetha told me about them, as well as since I'd viewed more about the story through Freedom's memories. Yet, here I sit with the story of a lifetime being laid at my feet, and my mind is a million miles away. There will be time to hear it again, I reason. I don't need to worry about that. I have plenty of other things to worry about.

The conversation slows down, and I use the lull to excuse myself. I take my cup in to the kitchen and refill it with hot water and submerge a new chamomile tea bag.

The sun has not yet topped the hills. I decide to take my tea out to the water's edge to watch the sunrise. Wrapped snuggly in my mother's flannel jacket, I head out through the kitchen door.

The morning birds sing their songs as I walk the short walk down to the lake. I'm in full view of the cabin, so I know if my parents look for me, they won't have to look long. I sit on the large boulder at the edge of the lake facing south, a place where I have been many times before in my childhood. To my left, the sky is painted with pinks and blues from the approaching sun. To my right, heavy storm clouds threaten to put an end to the peaceful morning. And I am sitting right between the two. If I used my running power and ran in either direction long enough, I'd end up bathed in light or drenched in darkness and rain. That's how I view my life right now—caught in the middle, not quite here or there.

Somewhere out to the west, beyond the dark ominous clouds, Deus Ex met up with Chris at a designated rendezvous point. He arrived at the resort unannounced, unplanned, just how it should be in order to successfully trick a Diamond Bearer. The best way to trick someone who can view the future is to make spontaneous decisions. That's why when I carried the diamond with the Runners we didn't reserve hotel rooms. We took whatever was available so we didn't leave a trail to our whereabouts. Chris did the same thing. He didn't alert me to his arrival. In fact, he was careful to prevent me from knowing when he arrived. His first choice, Maetha, wasn't able to accommodate him, so he spontaneously accepted Neema's offer to help. Neema wouldn't have had any reason to look to her future while in the company of someone she trusted, someone who was sharing a beautiful occasion. She was caught off guard, as was I. The little velvet box had removed all precautions, all concerns, and set up the perfect opportunity for a stealth kill due to the obsidian inside. He knew it would work that way. Deus knew it too.

I feel absolute betrayal.

Why didn't he try to warn us? Why didn't he refuse to help Deus? Why did he wink at me before leading Neema to her death?

I think about the kiss we shared when he arrived at the resort, and tears fill my eyes. I sip on my tea to try to clear my head. Drops of rain land on my face as the sun crests the hills. I look to the west and see the rapidly moving storm closing in on me.

I remember Chris's conversation with me on the airplane when he worried that we didn't have a future together. He worried that gaining the full diamond wouldn't repair the void between us, but instead would create new problems. Is it possible he was trying to help me see that he wasn't who I thought he was? When I used the topaz to heal his depression, I felt his despair. When I slipped into Maetha's mind to see what she saw when Chris asked her to step outside, I felt the same self-loathing she'd mentioned feeling. She seems to think he's still on our side, even after he participated in the murder of her longtime friend. And Maetha was the intended victim.

The rain drops fall with purpose now. Tiny droplets of moisture slide to the ends of my hair and drip off. Water streams down my forehead and cheeks. I try to look for the future concerning Chris. All I can see is the familiar black nothingness associated with the use of obsidian.

Why am I so powerless? I finally have a complete diamond and yet I'm no better than before. If I could just see a hint of something positive, a little ray of light, concerning the recent events, perhaps I'd be able to better cope with having my trust ripped from my soul. I should have taken the signs from Chris more seriously. I could have talked to Maetha and possibly prevented Neema's death.

Mary appears in front of me in her bi-located state, her feet hovering above the water. "Calli," she says, "we are all mourning Neema's death, but this is in no way your fault."

Before I can respond, Amenemhet, Hasan, Ruth, Avani, and Merlin bi-locate to my location. Their collective thoughts enter my mind and give me strength. No one blames me.

More Bearers materialize around me. The last to arrive is Maetha. She says, "Obsidian prevents future sight, Calli. You shouldn't be trying to look for your future at this time. Duncan is your protector. Let him do his job to keep you safe. Now, go inside before you catch pneumonia. If we as Diamond Bearer's have learned but one thing, it should be that one never knows when we'll come in contact with obsidian and not be able to use our healing ability. Keep yourself healthy, Calli. You're going to need your strength for the battle ahead."

Thanks!

I hope you enjoyed *The Diamond of Freedom.* Please consider leaving a review on Amazon to help other readers know what the story is about.

The Diamond Bearers' Destiny

In book four of The Unaltered Series, Calli Courtnae learns about Chris Harding's motives behind the recent events, and tries to understand his dilemmas, while at the same time she learns what the big picture actually is, and where she fits as a Diamond Bearer.

General Harding figures out what lies at the heart of Agent Alpha's research project. Harding is determined to complete the studies and become an all-powerful Diamond Bearer—once Chris delivers Calli and her diamond to him. What General Harding fails to understand is Diamond Bearers are not the most powerful individuals on the face of the earth. They are agents of nature, working for Crimson—the creator of the Sanguine Diamond. Upsetting the balance of nature is the last thing General Harding should do.

Follow Calli, Chris, Brand, and Crimson as they battle Deus Ex, undead Healers, and the notorious General Harding, all in an effort to balance nature.

The Diamond Bearers' Destiny
The full book is available at Amazon.

I'd love to hear from you and what you think of my books. Drop me a line and I'll do my best to respond. Visit my website and enter your message on the Contact Me form. I look forward to hearing from you.

Connect with Lorena Angell at:
LorenaAngell.com
Twitter: @LorenaAngell1
Facebook: The Unaltered Diamond Series
Also: LinkedIn, Google+, Pinterest, YouTube, Instagram

48897028R00144

Made in the USA
Lexington, KY
18 August 2019